City of Boys

CITY

of boys

Stories

BETH NUGENT

ALFRED A. KNOPF

1992

New York

THIS IS A BORZOI BOOK PUBLISHED BY

A L F R E D   A .   K N O P F ,

INC.

Some of the stories in this collection have appeared in the following publications:
*The Gettysburg Review, Grand Street, Mademoiselle, The New Yorker, The North American
Review, American Short Story Masterpieces, Best American Short Stories 1985*, and
The Norton Anthology of Contemporary Short Fiction.

Library of Congress Cataloging-in-Publication Data
Nugent, Beth.
    City of boys: stories/by Beth Nugent.—1st ed.
    p.   cm.
    ISBN 0-394-58251-9
    I. Title.
    PS3564.U347C58   1992
    813'.54—dc20   91-32149
                                        CIP

M A N U F A C T U R E D   I N   T H E

U N I T E D   S T A T E S   O F   A M E R I C A

First Edition

FIC

CONTENTS

CITY OF BOYS

C I T Y   O F   B O Y S

—My little sweetheart, she says, bringing her face close enough for me to see the fine net of lines that carves her face into a weathered stone. —You love me, don't you little sweetheart, little lamb?

Whether or not she listens anymore, I am not sure, but I always answer yes; yes, I always say, yes, I love you.

She is my mother, my father, my sister, brother, cousin, lover; she is everything I ever thought any one person needed in the world. She is everything but a boy.

—Boys, she tells me. —Boys will only break you.

I know this. I watch them on the street corners, huddled under their puddles of blue smoke. They are as nervous as insects, always some part of their bodies in useless, agitated motion, a foot tapping, a jaw clenching, a finger drawing circles against a thigh, eyes in restless programmed movement as they watch women pass–they look from breasts to face to legs to breasts. They are never still and they twitch and jump when I walk by, but still I want them. I want them in the back seats of their cars; I want them under the bridge where the river meets the rocks in a slick slide of stone; I want them in the back rows of theaters and under the bushes and benches in the park.

—Boys, she says. —Don't even think about boys. Boys would only make you do things you don't know how to do and things you'd never want to do if you knew what they were. I know, she says, —I know plenty about boys.

She is everything to me. She is not my mother, though I have allowed myself the luxury of sometimes believing myself her child. My mother is in Fairborn, Ohio, where she waits with my father for me to come home and marry a boy and become the woman into whom she still believes it is not too late for me to grow. Fairborn is a city full of boys and parking meters and the Air Force, but most of all it is a city full of my mother, and in my mind she looms over it like a cloud of radioactive dust. If I return, it will be to her. She is not why I left, she is not why I am here; she is just one thing I left, like all the things that trail behind us when we go from place to place, from birth to birth, from becoming to becoming. She is just another bread crumb, just another mother in the long series of mothers that let you go to become the woman you have to become. But you are always coming back to them.

Where I live now is also a city full of boys, and, coming here, I passed through hundreds of cities and they were all full of boys.
—Boys, she tells me, —are uninteresting, and when they grow up, they become men and become even more uninteresting.
I know this too. I see how boys spend their days, either standing around or playing basketball or engaged in some irritating, persistent harangue, and I can draw my own conclusions as to what they talk about and as to the heights of which they are capable, and I see what they do all day, but still I want them.
The one time I pretended she was a boy, she knew it, because I closed my eyes; I never close my eyes, and when I came, she slapped me hard. —I'm not a boy, she said, —just you remember that. You know who I am and just remember that I love you and no boy could ever love you like I do.
Probably she is right. What boy could love with her slipping concentration? Probably no boy could ever achieve what she lets go with every day that comes between us, what she has lost in her long history of love.

What I do sometimes is slip out under her absent gaze.
—Where are you going, what are you going to do? she says, and, wallowing in the luxury of thinking myself a child, I answer: —Nowhere. Nothing.
In their pure undirected, intoxicating meaninglessness, our

conversations carry more significance than either of us is strong enough to bear, together or alone, and I drag it out into the streets today, a long weight trailing behind me, as I look for boys.

Today, I tell myself, is a perfect day for losing things, love and innocence, illusions and expectations; it is a day through which I will wander until I find the perfect boy.

Where we live, on the upper West Side, the streets are full of Puerto Rican men watching women. Carefully they examine each woman who passes; carefully they hold her with their eyes, as if they are somehow responsible for her continued existence on the street. Not a woman goes by untouched by the long leash of their looks.

Ohh, sssss, they say. *Mira, mira,* and when a woman looks, they smile and hiss again through their shiny teeth. In their eyes are all the women they have watched walk by and cook and comb their black hair; all the women they have touched with their hands and all the women they have known live in their eyes and gleam out from within the dark. Their eyes are made only to see women on the streets.

Where we live, on West Eighty-third and Amsterdam, there are roaches and rats, but nothing matters as long as we're together, we say valiantly, longingly. Nothing matters, I say, stomping a roach, and nothing matters, she agrees, her eyes on a low-slung rat sidling by in the long hallway toward the little garbage room across from the door to our apartment. I told the super once that if he kept the garbage out on the street, perhaps the building would be less a home for vermin.

—What's vermin? he wanted to know.

Vermin, I told him, is rats and roaches and huge black

beetles scrabbling at the base of the toilet when you turn on
the light at night. Vermin is all the noises at night, all the
clicking and scratching and scurrying through the darkness.
—No rats, he said. —Maybe a mouse or two, and maybe
every now and then you'll see your roach eggs, but I keep
this place clean.
Together we watched as a big brown-shelled roach tried to
creep past us on the wall. Neither of us moved to kill it, but
when it stopped and waved its antennae, he brought his big
fist down in a hard slam against the wall. He didn't look at
the dead roach, but I could hardly take my eyes off it, perfectly flattened, as though it had been steamrolled against
the side of his hand.
—Maybe a roach here and there, he said, flicking the roach
onto the floor without looking at it, —but I keep this place
clean. Maybe if you had a man around the house, he said,
trying to look past me into our apartment, —you wouldn't
have so much trouble with vermins.
I pretended not to understand what he meant, and backed
into the room. Rent control is not going to last forever in
New York, and when it goes and all the Puerto Ricans have
had to move to the Bronx, we will have to find jobs or hit the
streets, but as long as we're together, as long as we have
each other.
—We'll always have each other, won't we? she says, lighting
a cigarette and checking to see how many are left in her
pack.
—Yes, I always say, wondering if she's listening or just lost
in a cigarette count. You'll always have me, I say. Unless, I
think, unless you leave me, or unless I grow up to become
the woman my mother still thinks is possible.

Today is a day full of boys. They are everywhere, and I
watch each of them, boys on motorcycles, boys in cars, on

bicycles, leaning against walls, walking; I watch them all to see which of them in this city of boys is mine.

I am not so young and she is not so old, but rent control is not going to last forever, and someday I will be a woman. She wants, I tell myself, nothing more than me. Sometimes I think she must have been my mother, the way she loves me, but when I asked her if she were ever my mother, she touched my narrow breasts and said: Would your mother do that? and ran her tongue over my skin and said: Or that? Would your mother know what you want, sweetheart? I'm not your mother, she said, I stole you from a mattress downtown, just around the corner from where all the winos lie around in piss and wine and call for help and nobody listens. I saved you from that, she said. But I remember too clearly the trip out here, in the middle of a car full of people full of drugs, most of them, and I remember how she found me standing just outside the porn theater on Ninety-eighth and Broadway, and she slipped me right from under the gaze of about a hundred curious Puerto Ricans.
—Does your mother know where you are? she asked me.
I laughed and said my mother knew all she needed to know, and she said, Come home with me. I have somebody I want you to meet. When she brought me home, she took me right over to a big man who lay on the couch watching television.
—Tito, this is Princess Grace, she said, and Tito raised his heavy head from the pillow to look me over.
—She don't look like no princess to me, was all he said.
I never thought much of Tito, and she never let him touch me, even though our apartment is only one room, and he was sick with wanting me. At night, after they'd finished with each other, she crept over to me in my corner and whispered in my ear, —Sweetheart, you are my only one.
As Tito snored through the nights, we'd do it at least one

more time than they had, and she would sigh and say,
—Little sweetheart, you are the one I wanted all the time,
even with all those other boys and girls who loved me, it was
always you that I was looking for, you that I wanted.
This is the kind of talk that kills me; this is the kind of talk
that won me, in addition to the fact that she took me in from
the hard streets full of boys and cops and taxicabs, and
everywhere I looked, the hard eyes of innocence turned.

That first time with her, I felt as though my mother was
curled up inside my own body giving birth to me; each time
she let me go, I made my way back inside her.

The long car pulls up to the sidewalk and I bend to see if it
has boys in it. It is full of them, so I say: —Hey, can I have
a ride?
—Hey, they say. —Hey, the lady wants a ride. Where to?
they ask.
—Oh, I say, —wherever. I look to see where they are heading. —Uptown, I say, and the door swings open, so I slide
in. The oldest boy is probably sixteen and just got his driver's license, and he is driving his mother's car, a big Buick
or Chevrolet or Monte Carlo—a mother's car. Each of the
boys is different, but they are all exactly alike in the way
that boys are, and right away I pick the one I want. He's the
one who does not look at me, and he's the oldest, only a
couple of years younger than I, and it is his mother's car we
are in.
—How about a party? the boys say. —We know a good party
uptown.
—Let's just see, I say. —Let's just ride uptown and see.

Sometimes I wake up to see her leaning on her thin knees
against the wall that is stripped down to expose the rough

brick beneath the plaster. I dream that she prays to keep
me, but I am afraid that it is something else she prays for, a
beginning, or an end, or something I don't know about. She
came to bed once and laid her face against my breast, and I
felt the imprint of the brick in the tender skin of her forehead.

She herself is not particularly religious, although the apartment is littered with the scraps of saints—holy relics of one
sort or another: a strand of hair from the Christ child, a bit
of fingernail from Saint Paul, a shred of the Virgin's robe.
They are left over from Tito, who collected holy relics the
way some people collect lucky pennies or matchbooks, as a
kind of hedge against some inarticulated sense of disaster.
They are just clutter here, though, in this small apartment
where we live, and I suggested to her once that we throw
them out. She picked up a piece of dried weed from Geth-
semane and said, —I don't think they're ours to throw out.
Tito found them and if we got rid of them, who knows what
might happen to Tito? Maybe they work is what I mean.
And besides, she went on, —I don't think it's spiritually
economical to be a skeptic about absolutely everything.

When Tito left, his relics abandoned for some new hope,
she was depressed for a day or two, but said finally that it
really was the best for everybody, especially for the two of
us, the single reality to which our lives have been refined.
Tito said he was getting sick of watching two dykes moon
over each other all the time, though I think he was just angry
because she wouldn't let him touch me. I was all for it, I
wanted him to touch me. That's what I came to this city for:
to have someone like Tito touch me, someone to whom
touching is all the reality of being, someone who doesn't do
it in basements and think he has to marry you, someone who
does it and doesn't think about the glory of love. But she
wouldn't have it; she said if he ever touched me, she would

send me back to the Ninety-eighth Street porn theater and
let the Puerto Ricans make refried beans out of me, and as
for Tito, he could go back to Rosa, his wife in Queens, and
go back to work lugging papers for the *Daily News* and ride
the subway every day and go home and listen to Rosa talk
on the phone all night, instead of hanging out on street corners and playing cards with the men outside the schoolyard,
like he did now. Because, she said, because she was paying
the rent, and as long as rent control lasted in New York, she
would continue to pay the rent, and she could live quite
happily and satisfactorily by herself until she found the right
sort of roommate; one, she said, fingering the shiny satin of
Tito's shirt, who paid the rent.

So Tito kept his distance and kept us both sick with his
desire, and when she finally stopped sleeping with him and
joined me on the mattress on the floor, even Tito could see
that it wasn't going to be long before we'd be taking the bed
and he would have to move to the floor. To save himself
from that, he said one day that he guessed he was something
of a fifth wheel around the joint, huh? and he'd found a nice
Puerto Rican family that needed a man around the house
and he supposed he'd just move in with them. I think he
was only trying to save face, though, because one day when
she was out buying cigarettes, he roused himself from the
couch and away from the television, to say to me, —You
know, she was married before, you know.

—I know that, I said. —I know all about that.

How she pays the rent is with alimony that still comes in
from her marriage and I know all about that and Tito wasn't
telling me anything that I didn't know, so I looked back at
the magazine I was reading and waited for him to go back
to the television. He kept looking at me, so I got up to look
out the window to see if I could see her coming back and if
she had anything for me.

—What I'm trying to say, he said, —what I'm trying to tell you is that you're not the only one. You're not. I was the only one, too, the one she was always looking for. I was the one before you, and you're just the one before someone else. I could see her rounding the corner from Ninety-sixth and Broadway, and could see that she had something in a bag for me, doughnuts or cookies. I said nothing, only looked out the window and counted the steps she took toward our building. She was leaning forward and listing slightly toward the wall, so I guessed that she must have had a few drinks in the bar where she always buys her cigarettes. When I could hear her key turning in the lock to the street door, I went to open our door for her and Tito reached out and grabbed me by the arm.

—Listen, he said. —You just listen. Nobody is ever the only one for nobody. Don't kid yourself.

I pulled away and opened the door for her. When she came in, cold skin and wet, I put my face in her hair and breathed in the smell of gin and cigarettes, and all the meaning of my life.

The next day Tito left, but he didn't go far, because I still see him hanging out on street corners. Now all the women he has known are in his eyes, but mostly there is her, and when he looks at me, I cannot bear to see her lost in the dark there. Whenever I pass him, I always smile.

—Hey, Tiiiiiiito, I say. —*Mira, mira,* huh? And all his friends laugh, while Tito tries to look as though this is something he's planned himself, as though he has somehow elicited this remark from me.

I suppose one day Tito will use the key he forgot to leave behind to sneak in and cover me with his flagging desire, his fading regrets, and his disappointments, and she will move

on then, away from me; but rent control will not last forever
in New York, and I cannot think ahead to the beginnings
and the ends for which she prays.

The boys in the car lean against one another and leer and
twitch like tormented insects, exchanging glances that they
think are far too subtle for me to understand, but I have
come too far looking for too much to miss any of it. We drive
too fast up Riverside, so that it's no time at all before the
nice neighborhoods become slums full of women in windows, with colorful clothing slung over fire escapes, and,
like a thick haze hanging over the city, the bright noise of
salsa music. Like the sound of crickets threading through
the Ohio summer nights, it sets the terms for everything.
—So, one of them says, —so where are you going, anyways?
—Well, I say. —Well. I was thinking about going to the
Bronx Botanical Gardens.
The Bronx Botanical Gardens is no place I'd ever really want
to go, but I feel it's important to maintain, at least in their
eyes, some illusion of destination. If I was a bit more sure
of myself, I'd suggest that we take the ferry over to Staten
Island and do it in the park there. Then I could think of her.

When we went to Staten Island, it was cold and gray and
windy; we got there and realized that there was nothing
really that we wanted to see, that being in Staten Island was
really not all that different from being in Manhattan.
—Or anywhere, she said, looking down a street into a cor-
ridor of run-down clothing stores and insurance offices. It
was Sunday, so everything was closed up tight and no one
was on the street. Finally we found a coffee shop near the
ferry station, where we drank Cokes and coffee, and she
smoked cigarettes, while we waited for the boat to leave.

—Lezzes, the counterman said to another man sitting at the
counter eating a doughnut. —What do you want to bet
they're lezzes?
The man eating the doughnut turned and looked us over.
—They're not so hot anyways, he said. —No big waste.
She smiled and held her hand to my face for a second; the
smoke from her cigarette drifted past my eyes into my hair.
—What a moment, she said, —to remember.
On the way back, I watched the wind whip her face all out
of any shape I knew, and when I caught the eyes of some
boys on the ferry, she said, not looking at me, not taking her
eyes from the concrete ripples of the robe at the feet of the
Statue of Liberty just on our left, —What you do is your
own business, but don't expect me to love you forever if you
do things like this. I'm not, she said, turning to look me full
in the face, —your mother, you know. All I am is your lover,
and nothing lasts forever.
When we got off the ferry, I said: —I don't expect you to
love me forever, and she said I was being promiscuous and
quarrelsome, and she lit a cigarette as she walked down into
the subway station. I watched her as she walked, and it
seemed to me to be the first time I had ever seen her back,
walking away from me, trailing a long blue string of smoke.

Something is going on with the boys, something has changed
in the set of their faces, the way they hold their cigarettes,
the way they nudge each other. Something changes when
the light begins to fade, and one of them says to me: —We
have a clubhouse uptown, want to come there with us?
—What kind of club, I ask, —what do you do there?
—We drink whisky, they say, —and take drugs and watch
television.
My boy, the one I have picked out of this whole city of boys,

stares out the window, chewing at a toothpick he's got wedged somewhere in the depths of his jaw, and runs his finger over the slick plastic of the steering wheel. I can tell by his refusal to ask that he wants me to come. This, I suppose, is how to get to the center of boys, to go to their club. Boys are like pack creatures, and they always form clubs; it's as though they cannot help themselves. It's the single law of human nature that I have observed in my limited exposure to the world, that plays and plays and replays itself out with simple mindless consistency: where there are boys, there are clubs, and anywhere there is a club, it is bound to be full of boys, looking for the good times to be had just by being boys.

—Can I join? I ask. This is what I will take back to her, cigarettes and a boy's club. This will keep her for me forever: that I have gone to the center of boys and have come back to her.

—Well, they say, and smirk and grin and scratch at themselves. —Well, there's an initiation.

The oldest of the boys is younger than I, and yet, like boys everywhere, they all think that I don't know nearly so much as they do, as if being a woman somehow short-circuits my capacity for input. They have a language that they think only boys can understand, but understanding their language is the key to my success, so I smile and say: —I will not fuck you all, separately or together.

My boy looks over at me and permits himself a cool half-smile, and I am irritated that he now holds me in higher regard because I can speak a language that any idiot could learn.

Between us there are no small moments; we do not speak at all or we speak everything. Heat bills and toothpaste and dinner and all the dailiness of living are given no language in our time together. I realize that this kind of intensity cannot be sustained over a long period of time and that every small absence in our days signals an end between us. She tells me that I must never leave her, but what I know is that someday she will leave me with a fistful of marriage money to pay the rent as long as rent control lasts in New York, and I will see her wandering down the streets, see her in the arms of another, and I say to her sometimes late at night when she blows smoke rings at my breasts: Don't leave me. Don't ever ever leave me.

—Life, she always says to me, —is one long leave-taking. Don't kid yourself, she says. —Kid, and laughs. —Anyways, you are my little sweetheart, and how could I ever leave you, and how could I leave this—soft touch on my skin —and this, and this.

She knows this kills me every time.

Their clubhouse is dirty and disorganized and everywhere there are mattresses and empty beer bottles and bags from McDonald's, and skittering through all of this mess are more roaches than I thought could exist in a single place, more roaches than there are boys in this city, more roaches than there are moments of love in this world.

The boys walk importantly in. This is their club; they are New York City boys and they take drugs and they have a club, and I watch as they scatter around and sit on mattresses and flip on the television. I hang back in the doorway and reach out to snag the corner of the jacket my boy is wearing. He turns to me without interest.

—How about some air? I say.

—Let me just get high first, he says, and he walks over to a chair and sits down and pulls out his works and cooks up his dope and ties up his arm and spends a good two minutes searching out a vein to pop. All over his hands and arms and probably his legs and feet and stomach are signs of collapse and ruin, as if his body has been created for a single purpose, and he has spent a busy and productive life systematically mining it for good places to fix.

I watch him do this while the other boys do their dope or roll their joints or pop their pills, and he offers me some. I say no, I'd rather keep a clear head, and how about some air?

I don't want him to hit a nod before any of it's even happened, but this is my experience with junkies, that they exit right out of every situation before it's even become a situation.

—Let's take the car, he says.

You are my sweetheart, she says, and if you leave me, you will spend all your life coming back to me. With her tongue and her words and the quiet movement of her hand over my skin, she has drawn for me all the limits of my life, and of my love. It is the one love that has created me and will contain me, and if she left me I'd be lonely, and I'd rather sleep in the streets with her hand between my legs forever than be lonely.

In the car, the boy slides his hand between my legs and then puts it on the steering wheel. A chill in the air, empty streets, and it's late. Every second takes me farther into the night away from her; every second sends me home. We drive to Inwood Park, and climb the fence so that we are only a few feet away from the Hudson.

—This is nothing like Ohio, I say to him, and he lights a cigarette.

—Where's Ohio?

—Don't you go to school? I ask him. —Don't you take geography?

—I know what I need to know, he says, and reaches over to unbutton my blouse. The thing about junkies is that they know they don't have much time, and the thing about boys is that they know how not to waste it.

—This is very romantic, I say, as his fingers hit my nipples like a piece of ice. —Do you come here often?

What I like about this boy is that he just puts it right in. He just puts it in as though he does this all the time, as though he doesn't usually have to slide it through his fingers, or between his friends' rough lips; he just puts it in and comes like wet soap shooting out of a fist, and this is what I wanted. This is what I wanted, I say to myself as I watch the Hudson rolling brownly by over his shoulder. This is what I wanted, but all I think about is the way it is with us; this is what I wanted, but all I see is her face floating down the river, her eyes like pieces of moonlight caught in the water.

What I think is true doesn't matter anymore; what I think is false doesn't matter anymore. What I think at all doesn't matter anymore, because there is only her; like an image laid over my mind, she is superimposed on every thought I have. She sits by the window and looks out onto the street as though she is waiting for something, waiting for rent control to end, or waiting for something else to begin. She sits by the window waiting for something, and pulls a long string through her fingers. In the light from the window, I can see each of the bones in her hand; they make a delicate pattern that fades into the flesh and bone of her wrist.

—Don't ever change, I say to her. —Don't ever ever change. She smiles and lets the string dangle from her hand.

—Nothing ever stays the same, she says. —You're old enough to know that, aren't you, sweetheart? Permanence,

she says, —is nothing more than a desire for things to stay the same.
I know this.

—Life is hard for me, the boy says. —What am I going to do with my life? I just hang around all day or drive my mother's car. Life is so hard. Everything will always be the same for me here in this city. It's going to eat me up and spit me out, and I might as well never have been born.
He looks poetically out over the river.
—I wanted a boy, I say, —not a poet.
—I'm not a poet, he says. —I'm just a junkie, and you're nothing but a slut. You can get yourself home tonight.
I say nothing and watch the Hudson roll by.
—I'm sorry, he says. —So what? So I'm a junkie and you're a slut, so what. Nothing ever changes. Besides, he says, —my teacher wants me to be a track star because I can run faster than anyone else in gym class. That's what he says.
—Well, that sounds like a promising career, I say, although I can imagine the teacher in his baggy sweatpants, his excitement rising as he stares at my boy and suggests after-school workouts. —Why don't you do that?
—I'd have to give up smoking, he says. —And dope.
Together we watch the river, and finally he says, —Well. It's about time I was getting my mother's car home.
—This is it? I ask him.
—What were you expecting? he says. —I'm only a junkie. In two years I probably won't even be able to get it up anymore.

—Look, I say, coming in and walking over to where she sits by the window. —Look. I am a marked woman. There is blood between my legs and it isn't yours.

She looks at me, then looks back at what she was doing before I came in, blowing smoke rings that flatten against the dirty window. —Did you bring me some cigarettes? she asks, putting hers out in the ashtray that rests on the windowsill.

—A marked woman, I say. —Can't you see the blood?

—I can't see anything, she says, —and I won't look until I have a cigarette.

I give her the cigarettes I bought earlier. Even in the midst of becoming a woman, I have remembered the small things that please her. She lights one and inhales the smoke, then lets it slowly out through her nose and her mouth at the same time. She knows this kills me.

—Don't you see it? I ask.

—I don't see anything, she says. —I don't see why you had to do this.

She gets up and says, —I'm going to bed now. I've been up all day and all night, and I'm tired and I want to go to sleep before the sun comes up.

—I am a marked woman, I say, lying beside her. —Don't you feel it?

—I don't feel anything, she says, but she holds me, and together we wait patiently for the light. She is everything to me. In the stiff morning before the full gloom of city light falls on us, I turn to her face full of shadows.

—I am a marked woman, I say. —I am.

—Quiet, she says, and puts her dark hand gently over my mouth, then moves it over my throat onto the rise of my chest. Across town, no one notices when she does this. Nothing is changed anywhere when she does this.

—Quiet, she says again. She presses her hand against my heart, and touches her face to mine and takes me with her into the motherless turning night. All moments stop here;

this is the first and the last, and the only flesh is hers, the only touch her hand. Nothing else is, and together we turn under the stroke of the moon and the hiss of the stars; she is everything I will become, and together we become every memory that has ever been known.

C o c k t a i l   H o u r

My mother pulls the kitchen curtains closed and the room goes from a kind of dull whitish to a dim yellow.
—▬▬, she says, and sits at the table. —▬▬ ▬▬ ▬▬.
I really am going to die this time. She puts her hand to her forehead. —▬▬, she says again.

My father watches her from the stove, where he is scrambling eggs. —You know, he finally says, —if you wouldn't smoke so much, you wouldn't get such bad hangovers. Look at me, he says, —I never get hangovers. And why?

He pauses as if he expects her to answer, though they have this same conversation on the average of twice a week. My mother reaches in the pocket of her robe for her cigarettes.

—Because, my father says triumphantly, —because I don't smoke. He smiles and my mother lights her cigarette.

—Is there any coffee? she says. My father puts his spatula down and pours her a cup of coffee; when he brings it to her, they look at each other for a moment as she takes it from his hand.

—Your eggs are burning, she says, and he turns and looks at the stove. My mother watches him as he pushes the eggs around in the pan.

—I don't know, he says, —these eggs look bad. He holds the pan up to his nose and sniffs. —I think these eggs are bad, he says.

My mother leans back in her chair and pulls the newspaper toward her as my father brings the pan of eggs to her.

—What do you think? he says. —Do you think these eggs are bad?

My mother looks at the eggs, then away. —I don't know, she says. —Don't show me any food.

My father holds the eggs out to me. They look a little odd, separated into shiny yellow clumps and pale liquid, but before I can say anything, he scrapes them into the garbage.

—There, he says. —I think those eggs were bad. You'll have to have cereal, he tells me. —If we have any.

—Honey, my mother says to me. —Be an angel and see if one of the neighbors has a Pepsi for my hangover.

It's a Sunday today, in a world before stores are open all the

time, and my parents know how to depend on neighbors—
especially new ones.

—See if they have some eggs too, my father says.

—████, says my mother, and bends her cigarette into the
ashtray. —Don't worry about the eggs, honey. Just get the
Pepsi.

My father sits down at the table and she lights another cigarette. They both watch her smoke drift through the dusty
light.

I stand outside the kitchen window, to decide which neighbor to try and to hear if they say anything about me when I
am gone. My parents have only a few topics of conversation:
the cocktail party they have most recently hosted or at-
tended; my father's career; my mother's smoking; and, less
frequently, me. I know each conversation by heart.

—You know, my mother says. —You shouldn't have her
asking all over for eggs. She hasn't even made any friends
yet.

—Well, my father says after a while, —I don't see how
that's our fault.

The conversation dies here for a moment, and I imagine my
mother turning her neck to look at the crossword puzzle in
the paper, my father gazing at the table.

—Well, my mother says finally, —she is at that delicate age.
Maybe this move wasn't such a good idea.

My father is silent, considering which of his many counter-
arguments to use here. Whenever they have this particular
conversation, I feel as if I am standing at the edge of a wood,
facing a dark wall of trees, but when I turn to go back, there
are trees behind me as well, and on either side. I am aware
of being at that delicate age, though it seems to me that
there has been no age at which I have not felt delicate, and
no time at which a move did seem like a good idea. It is

possible, perhaps, that when I was a baby, it mattered less. When I go through our boxes of snapshots, I see pictures of myself, an unfamiliar baby held awkwardly in unfamiliar arms, or an older, uneasy-looking child, in front of unfamiliar houses, in the company of children whose names I have forgotten. I try to remember a single place of origin, one place that seems like home, but all I can see are my parents in lawn chairs, smiling into the sun, or at cocktail parties, raising their glasses happily, with shining eyes. These are the images of my history, and they transfer easily from state to state, as do we, with hardly a jarring note.

The neighborhoods we live in are all alike: neat, nearly new houses with driveways; inside they are all the same, too, with pale walls and light, hollow doors. Any bedroom I have had looks like any other bedroom I have had, and sometimes the things I own or wear or love seem to me to be as much a part of the houses we have lived in as things that are actually mine. The companies my father works for always move everything for us, so that on moving day, whole rooms are suddenly disassembled and disappear, reappearing in much the same arrangement in the new house. A doll I have had since childhood precedes me, carefully lifted from, then laid again upon the pillow of my bed, carried by whichever of the movers has a small daughter at home. Whenever I enter a new bedroom, she is already there, staring at the doorway with blank doll eyes, her blond hair stiff and clean.

In my new schools, my teachers sometimes ask me to tell the class interesting things about my travels, and I try to think of some, but in fact the America I have seen is exactly like itself: Franklin, New Jersey, differs, from my perspective, not at all from Arlington, Virginia, or Syracuse, New York. The houses and the neighbors and the streets are all just exactly alike, without difference enough even to help me make something up.

* * *

My father finally counters my mother with his trump, which
is that he moves, after all, for his career, and his career is,
after all, for us. Their conversation ends at last, as most of
them do, in a kind of busy hush, and I look around wondering which neighbor is most likely to have a Pepsi. I have
seen a girl about my age in the house across the street, so I
start there, and it is she who answers the door. She looks
exactly like I want to look: sleek hair, a fine long nose, and
long thin arms and legs. She is clearly on the edge of adult-
hood and, facing each other, we seem to be going in exactly
opposite directions, from roughly the same starting point.
The room behind the girl is in shadows, and she looks at me
but says nothing.

—Do you have any Pepsi? I say, but she just stares blankly. —It's for my mother, I add. —She has a hangover.
The girl's eyes drop from my face to my torso, to my legs
and feet, then travel back up again, along my arms, gauging
my appearance.

—No, she says finally, —we don't have any Pepsi.
I turn to leave, but she opens the door wider and looks out
past me at my house, as if she has heard something about
it; then she stands back. —You can come in if you want,
she says.
This is the smallest house on the block, and the dark room
behind her is a living room that looks hardly used, full of
large stiff furniture and slick clear tables.

—My parents aren't up, she says, —but you can come to
my room.
From somewhere in the house comes the sound of a television, and we walk up the short flight of stairs to an upper
floor with only two doors. The room she takes me into has a
boy in it, lying on one of the twin beds. He holds a comic a
few inches from his face and does not look up as we enter.

—Beat it, Tommy, she says, and he lowers the comic. He seems to be about her age, and his long arms and legs stick out gracelessly from his cotton pajamas.

—You beat it, he says. They stare at each other for a moment and finally the girl turns and walks out. Tommy lifts his comic back up over his face. Comic books are scattered across the bed and on the floor around it, and a few shiny violent covers are tacked to the wall above his pillow. On the other side of the room, everything is drawn into neat little piles, stacked against the wall.

I follow the girl downstairs and into the kitchen; the sound of the television seems to come from the basement, which, in my house, is what they call a family room. The girl opens the icebox and leans on the door, gazing at the food inside.

—You share a room with your brother? I ask.

—So? she says. —Don't you have a brother?

Behind her, in the icebox, I can see a whole six-pack of Pepsi.

—No, I say.

She pulls open the meat drawer and flips through the cheese and bologna.

—A sister? she says.

—No.

She turns and looks at me. —You're an only child, she says, as though she has deduced this information from subtle clues.

—Don't you mind sharing a room with your brother? I ask, and she turns back to the icebox.

—Look, she says, —we do have Pepsi after all. She pulls one from the six-pack and hands it to me. —Here, she says, then hesitates a moment. —Do you want some ice cream? she asks.

*   *   *

I wait at the table while she carries over ice cream, spoons, bowls. She gives me some ice cream, then puts the rest–almost half the container–into her own bowl, and slaps her spoon on top of it.

—Okay, she says. —What do you think would be the worst way to die?

She holds the spoon against her tongue and closes her eyes to think of the possibilities; while her eyes are still closed, a man comes into the room and stands in the doorway. He too wears pajamas, as well as a robe, and slippers that show his flat white heels.

—Annie, he says, and she opens her eyes, but waits a beat before she turns to look at him.

—Who's your friend? he asks, and I realize I have not told her my name. She stares at me for a moment.

—Anne, she says. —This is Anne.

—Well, Anne, the man says, and he leans over the table to hold out his hand. —It's very nice to meet you. His skin is cool and dry, and I let go of his hand quickly.

Annie mashes her ice cream into soup and her father stands back. He watches us for a few moments, looping and un-looping the ties of his robe as Annie brings her spoon to her mouth and sucks in her ice cream.

—That ice cream looks pretty good, he says; he watches her eat a moment longer, then turns and leaves.

Annie glances at my ice cream, takes her bowl to the sink, and pours out what's left. Then she goes to the front door and stands by it, not looking at me, but not looking at anything else. I'm not finished with my ice cream, but I rise with my bowl.

—Oh, she says, —you can leave that. Tommy will eat it.

She closes the screen door behind me, and when I turn to look back from the street, she's still standing there, her face and neck and head outlined by the dark room behind her.

The Pepsi is warm when I get home, but by now my mother's hangover is gone and she is bent over the crossword puzzle. When she rattles the ice in her empty glass, my father rises to take it from her. Tomato juice runs unevenly down the sides.

—Sally, my mother says, —we were worried about you.

—Here's your Pepsi, I say, and hold it out to her.

—You drink it, honey, she says. —I don't need it anymore. She touches the tip of her pen to her lip and leaves a tiny black dot when she takes it away. —What's a five-letter word for horse race? she asks my father, and he stops putting ice in her glass and stands still to think. Smoke from the freezer drifts past him and his face is perfectly blank. Finally he shakes his head and drops the ice into her glass, then pours in tomato juice, which turns pale pink as he adds vodka.

I pop open my mother's Pepsi and sit at the table with my parents. My mother stares at the puzzle, occasionally writing in a word, and my father rattles through the paper, scanning each page for important stories. He sets each section of the paper onto one of two piles: those with important stories he will have to go back and read, and those without. He looks up and down each page with a kind of desperation, hoping that nothing will require a closer look, so that this part of his day will be over. The Pepsi is too warm and too sweet, but I drink it from the can and watch my mother take an ice cube from her glass and hold it to her forehead.

—███████, she says. —They *would* send you someplace hot. My father looks up from his paper and watches ice melt onto my mother's puzzle.

—Damn, she says, and blots up a drop that has fallen onto the paper, blurring the word she's just written in.

—It's got a good paper, though, my father says. —You have to give it that.

She says nothing and runs the ice cube down over her face and throat. My father watches the drops of water slip down the fine bones of her chest into her shirt; then he looks away and rises to make another drink.

—Honey, my mother says, —aren't you bored? Why don't you watch some television?

Like our neighbors and our houses, our streets and our trees, television changes hardly at all from place to place, and the same shows and songs and faces accompany us around the country. I watch a movie I have seen in two other states, and through the window I can see Annie's house. I imagine her going back to the room she shares with her brother and sitting on the edge of the bed, watching him read his comics. I can't think what else she might do in that house, unless she sits on the big stiff couch in the shadows of the living room.

In the kitchen, my father finishes sorting the paper, sighs, and turns to the large pile full of articles he must now read; he stares dully at each story, and whenever my mother asks him for help with her puzzle, he stops reading and gazes straight ahead to think until, unable to help, he goes back to his article and she moves on to another clue. Like this the afternoon creeps slowly away; most of our days pass like this, slowly, the same things happening over and over, and at the rate time passes for us, it seems possible that I may never become an adult.

The movie ends, another begins, and I watch that too, until my parents begin to move, anticipating the beginning of cocktail hour, which is almost upon us. Cocktail hour eases the abrupt decline of the day, transforming it into a gentle slide toward evening, and it changes everything–even the light turns a kind of soft gold, and it shines directly on my parents. I am not in the light, but I am close enough to it to feel its warmth, along with the sting of my mother's martinis

and the odd mellow wave of scotch on my father's breath as
he leans over me to hand my mother her drink.

There is a kind of excitement that comes with cocktail hour,
a feverish awareness that all things are possible; my parents' eyes turn bright, their voices lift, their gestures grow
large and happy. There is a sharp sparking light here, and
when I look outside, all the other houses seem colorless and
unreal, just a part of the fading blue landscape of evening.
The families inside are having dinner and doing homework and watching television together; they will do tonight
what they did last night and what they will do again tomorrow. Even Annie's house is dim, lit only by the dulling
orange blaze of sun reflected off the building behind it.
I turn back to the television and listen as my parents come
alive.

The next day when I open my front door, Annie is there,
leaning against the doorjamb, looking nonchalant. She has
not knocked and may have been standing here all morning,
since anytime after my father left for work.

—Oh, she says, as though it is she who has opened her door
to find me.

—Hi, I say.

—Listen, she says. —I never got your name.

—Sally, I tell her, and she nods.

—Sally, she repeats. —There are already three Sallys at
school.

She picks at a thread hanging from her cuff and pulls at it,
but it is attached, and she smiles as her sleeve begins to
unravel. —I hate all three of them, she says, and looks in
the direction of the school, which is only a short walk away.
My parents try to live close to schools so that I can walk
there, and they try to plan our moves around the school
schedule, so that, as they put it, I won't be starting off on

the wrong foot. I will have, they say, as much chance as anyone to make new friends. And it is true, I always make friends in my new schools, and they are always the same: shy girls with thin hair and glasses and shy boys with pale round heads. They are so much like each other that I hardly remember them from town to town, their names or their personalities. Sometimes we exchange a few short, stuttering letters, but soon they are replaced by new friends who speak like them and walk and look and dress like them, who in fact resemble them so closely that only their ages change, and it is as though they are the same group of friends getting older with me.

I find my new friends at the beginning of each school year, and they are always to be found, like me, scattered along the sides of classrooms, or creeping along the walls of the hallways—out-of-the-way positions we take to watch the rules of school play themselves out. Annie is not at all like my usual friends.

—So anyways, she says now, —what were you doing?

—Nothing, I say, and she gazes at me, waiting. —You know.

She says nothing, so finally I say, —I was just watching TV.

—TV? she says, and looks over my shoulder. Behind me the television runs smoothly from show to commercial to show again, and she listens to try to tell what's on.

—My parents don't let me watch much TV, she says, still looking past me, and soon we are sitting together on the rug in front of the television.

—Oh, she says, —I love this show. She sits only a few feet away from the television, but I can see her eyes traveling all around the room. She leans sideways to look around the corner into the kitchen.

—What's she doing? Annie asks.

—I don't know, I say, —maybe the crossword puzzle.

After a moment my mother comes into the room and when I tell her Annie's name, Annie darts a look at me, surprised and a little suspicious, since she has never exactly told it to me, but she takes my mother's hand and smiles.

—You have a very lovely home, she says, and my mother looks startled, then glances around at the white walls, the plain, sturdy furniture.

—Thank you, she says, and when our show comes back on, she stands politely smoking behind us as we settle back down to watch. Beside me, Annie sits quietly, but I can see her still looking around without moving her head, and behind me my mother breathes smoke in and out; she alone seems to be watching the show, and when a commercial comes on, she goes back into the kitchen, cradling her cigarette ash in her hand.

—Girls, she calls out after a while, —do you know a six-letter word for child's toy?

Annie looks at me.

—So, I say, —what's the school like here? Though I already know what it is like; it is like every other school.

—Oh, Annie says as a new show begins. —Look. She sinks back deeper onto the rug to watch, her elbows propped uncomfortably behind her, and stares at the television, her mouth half open.

When my father comes home from work, Annie stands immediately. She crosses one long leg coyly behind her and smiles up at my father in a way I can tell she cannot help.

—You have a very lovely home, she says, and he smiles, pleased.

—Well, he says, and arranges the pens in his front pocket, pulling them out and putting them back in one by one. My mother watches him and puts another word in her crossword puzzle. When he goes to the icebox and opens the freezer, she folds her newspaper away.

—Honey, she says to me, —would your friend like to stay for dinner?

She says this quite naturally, as though, like all families, we always have dinner when my father comes home from work. He looks around at her, his hand still on an ice tray, and, without waiting for an answer, she takes a pot from the cabinet under the stove and opens a cupboard. Annie doesn't answer, and we all watch my mother as she pulls out cans and looks gaily at the labels. Finally she opens one, and we stare, transfixed, as she empties a can of peas the color of olives into a pot. When the can is empty, Annie takes a step back.

—Thanks, she says, —but my parents will be expecting me. My mother looks up, confused; she has gone through all of this only for Annie.

—See you tomorrow, Annie says to me, and when the door clicks behind her, my mother looks down at the can in her hand, then at the pot on the stove; finally she puts the can down and turns off the stove as my father drops ice in her glass. I watch Annie walk slowly home, zigzagging across the street.

—You're not hungry are you, honey? my mother asks, and I shake my head and go back to the television as my parents settle into cocktail hour. In the neighborhoods all around us, the boys and girls who will be my friends are getting ready for school to start; they eat their dinners quietly and dread the beginning of another year spent hovering on the borders of things.

When we finally have dinner, we are all a little dull. I have watched too much television, and my parents have passed beyond the excited flush of cocktail hour. It is too late to eat, so we just sit, pushing the pale green peas from one side of our plates to the other.

* * *

Annie appears in just the same way the next day, lounging carefully beside the door when I open it.

—Hey, she says, —only one more day till school.

She looks past me and down at my hands and feet and around at my house while she talks. —Do you want to see the school? she says. —You do, don't you? We can walk there together. She looks at me when she says this, then nods.

—Come on, she says and turns, so I follow her, leaving the television running and my mother in the kitchen scribbling down different combinations of words in the margins of her puzzle.

Empty, the school playground looks tiny and flat, even though in only a day it will seem enormous and unmanageable, full of children going through the initial sorting out of every school year. Annie sits on a swing and circles around, twisting the chains tight; her feet trail in the sand, leaving long furrows; then she spins back around and kicks up all the dirt.

—I know, she says, —let's start a fire.

—A fire? I say.

She looks at me and raises an eyebrow. —Don't *you* start fires? she says, and her tone makes me say, —Sure I do, although it has never occurred to me to start a fire.

—Okay, she says, and looks around. She begins collecting things—loose papers, leaves, handfuls of dry grass—and piles it all at the base of each leg of the swingset. I hand her what scraps of things I find, and when there is a little heap at each leg, she smiles at me and lights the first match. She kneels carefully at each corner of the swingset and when all four little fires have caught, she takes my hand and we run to the fence at the edge of the playground. We crouch behind it to watch the swingset burn; flames rise along the slanted metal legs, then, eventually, fall back down. I can feel Annie's excitement as she watches, holding tightly to the chain links of the fence. When the fires have gone out, she turns to me and her face is radiant.

—Wasn't that great? She nods her head. —That was great. She stares back at the swingset for a moment, then abruptly rises and walks away. I follow her home, but all along the way I try to imagine what it must be like to be on the swingset when it's burning, the heat rising through the metal seat and me in the middle, rising and falling back to earth, surrounded by flames.

—Well, Annie says when we reach our street. —My mother said you can come for dinner tonight. If you want. She glances at my house. —If it's all right with your mom. Without waiting for me to answer, or even consider her invitation, she leads the way into my house and stands stiffly in front of my mother while I ask for permission.
My mother smiles brightly at Annie.
—Of course, honey, she says, then turns back to her puzzle. Annie looks around at our kitchen. —We can watch TV until dinner, she says, and goes into the living room to turn on the television.

For dinner, Annie's family has carrots and potatoes and chicken and bread, all piled onto the plate at once. I sit next to Annie, across from Tommy, who eats in a steady, fixed rhythm: each time he takes a bite, he looks around at the food on the table; as he chews, he stares at Annie and me. The faces of Annie's parents are like plastic; their skin is smooth and light and their expressions hardly change at all. Each of us has a tall glass of iced tea sweating by our silverware, but no one seems to drink any of it.

—It's nice that Annie has a new friend, her mother says to me. —Annie doesn't have many friends.

Annie keeps her head down and eats her carrots, putting bite after bite into her mouth until the side of her cheek is swollen.

—Annie, her mother says, —stop that. Slowly, Annie begins to chew; her brother stares at her but says nothing, and by the time she has swallowed all of the carrots in her mouth, I have finished most of the food on my plate.

—You have a very good appetite, her mother says to me.

—I wish Annie had as good an appetite as you.

At this moment all activity stops, and everyone looks at my plate. I try to think of something to say but nothing comes to mind, so I take a drink of my tea and the others return to their food. Next to me, Annie crams her mouth with food until her cheeks are full, then brings her napkin to her mouth. Like this she clears her plate, and it is amazing to me that no one notices. When she is finished, she takes her napkin with her to the bathroom.

—Don't you get hungry? I ask her when dinner is over and we are in her bedroom.

—No, she says, and opens a drawer, from which she takes a bag of caramels. —I don't like that food, she says. —I only like candy.

She unwraps a caramel and eats it quickly, hardly chewing it before she swallows, already unwrapping another as her jaws pop in and out; then she eats that, then another, all with a kind of desperate look, as though this is something she must accomplish in a certain amount of time. I hardly know what to do while she eats, so I collect the wrappers and smooth them out, flattening one on top of another.

I have a perfect little pile when Tommy comes in and sits on the corner of his bed. He stares at Annie while she eats. A glaze of sweat shines across his forehead, and when he pulls his shirt up to wipe it, his stomach is white and thin. I look away when he drops his shirt.

—Why don't you eat like normal people? he says, and she swallows the candy in her mouth and closes the bag.

—Shut up, Tommy, she says and turns her back on him. He watches us for a moment longer, then throws himself back on his bed and reaches for a comic.

Annie closes her candy drawer and leans back against the headboard of her bed. —You can spend the night if you want, she says. —My mother says it's okay.

I can feel Tommy shift on his bed to listen, and I try to imagine what it is like in this room at night, Annie's thin body pressed against the wall while Tommy pulls the sheets up and down over his aching flesh, turning over and over on his comic books.

—I can't, I say. —Not on a school night.

—Okay, she says, and leaves the room. I follow her, and Tommy watches us as we go.

Downstairs in the family room, Annie's parents sit side by side on the couch, watching television. All the lights are out, the room is full of shadows, and the cold light of the TV plays against the walls like something moving under the paint. We sit in front of the television and Annie stares at the screen. I can hardly hear her parents move or breathe behind us, so intently do they watch. At the commercial, Annie gets up, and again I follow; her parents smile mildly at us as we leave, then look back at the television to watch the rest of the commercial.

Annie opens the icebox.

—Do you want some ice cream? she asks. She swings the door open and closed. —Cookies? she says. —Pepsi?

—No, I say. —My parents will be worrying about me pretty soon.

—She moves some bottles around on the top shelf. —Well, she says, —I'll come get you for school tomorrow.

When I leave, she is still in front of the icebox, and does not turn to watch me go. Outside, it has grown dark. My parents will still be having cocktail hour, and from Annie's driveway I can see my father move around the kitchen, cracking ice, pouring drinks. Although my mother is out of sight, I know she is sitting at the table smoking and watching him.

Here in the dark, the houses look the same as they always do, but inside, nothing—dinner and homework and television —seems familiar. I am the only person not tucked behind a safe, lighted window, and for a moment I am frozen here, surrounded by a strange world, unable to go back to Annie's, unwilling to go home. Finally I cross the street to my house, and at my door I make a noise and wait, to give my parents a chance to assume their usual polite expressions. When I come in, they smile and have another cocktail, but when I am in bed, I listen carefully, and over the rattle of ice in their glasses I am sure I can hear the sound of skin peeling away from their faces.

Annie and I walk past the swingset on our way to school, and she pokes me with her elbow. A boy and girl are kissing, pressed back against one of the slanted metal legs, but Annie pays no attention to them, only to the burnt-out grass at their feet.

—We did that, she says and laughs, an odd brittle giggle, as she pulls me away. The boy and girl look up as I glance back at them; it is hard for me to believe we are responsible for the big patches of black grass under the swingset. Annie dawdles as we approach the doors, waiting until the last minute to go in.

It is new for me to start school with a friend. Usually I move quickly to the outskirts of a crowd and form my friendships with those who are already there; then we watch the others and try to comfort ourselves with the knowledge that we are smart and do well in school.

Annie has mentioned no school friends, though I feel sure she must have some. Her brother goes to our school, too, a grade ahead of us, but when we pass him, part of a pack of boys outside the doors, he does not look at us. All of the boys wear dark T-shirts with pictures on them. Annie and I walk down the hall together and she speaks to no one. Every now and then she takes my elbow and whispers hotly in my ear what she knows about the people we pass.

—That's one of the other Sallys, she says, or, —See that boy? He tried to kill himself.

When we separate to go to our different classrooms, she digs her nails into my palm. —Meet me right here, she says. —For lunch.

As my new teacher lists the major exports of Brazil, which I learned at my last school, I watch the other students and pick out my new friends. The classroom configurations are the usual ones: smart, anxious students sit attentively in front; bored angry boys stare out the windows from the back row; the girls who, it is already clear, are going to be pretty and popular sit in a knot of energy near the door. The ones who will be my friends are scattered around where there are available seats, considering themselves lucky if they can sit on the side rows or in the back, near no one in particular. They seldom raise their hands, but take notes earnestly. Outside, cars pass on the street beyond the schoolyard fence. After a while I too begin to take notes. *Coffee*, I write, *Brazil nuts*.

Annie is standing in the middle of the hallway staring at the door to my classroom when I come out. Two girls with

glasses and thin brown hair glance at me, but when they see
that I have a friend waiting, they go on ahead down the hall.
Their light blue sweaters fade into the crowd.

Annie and I walk with our trays through the lunchroom,
toward the empty end of a table; no one speaks to us and we
speak to no one. Tommy sits at a table full of boys. He eats
steadily and looks up at us as we pass. For a moment there
is silence; then Annie smiles at the boys and their faces grow
cold; nothing moves above their necks, even as they continue to unwrap food and wad up the paper. When we walk
on, they turn their eyes to follow us, but Annie does not look
back.

We take the two seats at the end of a table, and no one looks
up at us as we sit down. All Annie's bought for lunch is
chocolate pudding, and as she removes the plastic wrap
from the bowl, she points at a girl sitting at a table full of
people whom I would feel comfortable with. The girl's hair
is cut unevenly across her forehead, and she has a long,
reddish birthmark running down her cheek.

—Look, Annie says. —That's one of the other Sallys. She's
adopted.

Annie points directly at the girl, who glances at us nervously
and looks away, but Annie gazes at her a moment longer,
then goes back to her pudding, which collects in dark
creases at the corners of her mouth.

After school, as children gather in groups, Annie pulls me
to the playground.

—Let's get out of here, she says. —I hate this place.

She throws a rock at the swingset when we pass it.

—Let's go to your house, she says. When we get there, my
mother looks up from her puzzle and smiles as we go up the
stairs to my room.

—Is that all your mother does? Annie asks.

—No, I say. —She does a lot of things.
I try to think of other things my mother does, but the only
way I can see her in my mind right now is bent over a puzzle,
her head lifting to stare into a world of half-completed
words, some needing only a letter or two to make sense.
Annie looks around at my room, carefully arranged by men
whose faces I will never see. —What a boring room, she
says.
She bounces on my bed and leans sideways, staring into the
eyes of the doll that rests against the pillow.
—You still have a doll? she says, and picks it up by its leg.
She rubs the doll's stiff hair between her fingers. —This
would go up like hay, she says. —This may even *be* hay.
She smiles and takes a pack of matches from her pocket.
—Let's see.
—We can't, I say. —My mother would notice.
—Right, she says, and laughs. She lights a match, and all I
can do is watch as she holds it to the very tip of the doll's
hair. There is no flame, only a crackle, as each hair sort of
fizzles crisply down to the plastic head and goes out.
—Well, Annie says, —that was disappointing.
The doll's head looks cooked, and smells worse. I run my
hand over the warm bumpy plastic, and Annie looks at me.
—Well, she says, —I better go.
She turns at the door. —See you tomorrow.
My mother looks up when I join her at the table. —It must
be nice to start school with a friend, she says, and looks
down to fill in a word. The scratch of the pen across the
newsprint is like something sharp moving over the surface
of my own skin.

It takes almost no time for life here to assume the shape of
lives we have led elsewhere, except that here Annie is my

friend. We go to school together and we leave school together and all around me new alliances are forming, while
Annie and I move above them or past them or through them.
The boys who are Tommy's friends watch Annie with an odd
kind of attention. They seem to know something about her—
and, because I am her friend, about me—and even when I
am away from her, leaning over the water fountain to get a
drink, or standing in front of my locker, they look at me with
something in their eyes; what it is they know they don't
understand, but it is enough to make them stare.

I watch the students who would normally be my friends;
already they have found each other in the back rows and in
the corners of the lunchroom, and I watch them with a kind
of longing. I know what we would be talking about, the plans
we would make, the television shows we would discuss.
When Annie comes down the hall, she cuts through them
like a flame and they pull away, but I long to be with them,
fading into the green tiles lining the walls. Annie watches
me as I follow their progress, and she points out their flaws.

The only empty table is near Tommy and his friends, and
when we sit down they laugh and slap at each other. Just as
Annie unwraps her pie, a piece of bread lands on her tray,
splattering mustard and little shreds of lettuce. Annie stares
at it as she eats her pie, and finally she stands and takes it
to the table of boys.

—Tommy, she says, —I'm going to tell Dad.

She drops the bread in front of him and his friends all smirk
and watch him, waiting. He looks around nervously, at his
friends and at me and at Annie; as I watch his face I can tell
a thousand words go through his head, but when he finally
chooses one, it surprises even him.

—Cunt, he says, and I can see by the shock on his face that

this is the first time he has said it. It takes him a moment to adjust, and then he says it again: —Cunt. He smiles and his friends smile and they look at her, then over at me.

We are surrounded on all sides by innocence, except for this tiny knot of confusion here in the center of the lunchroom. Annie comes back to our table and everything goes on just as it did before, except that the boys have grown bolder and more sure of what it is they think they know. They jerk their shoulders up high and smile, but they are frightened and angry, and in their excitement they smash cans and toss potato chips at each other. In the middle of it all, Annie finishes her pie, staring straight ahead at nothing.

It is cocktail hour and my parents sit happily at the table, planning the first cocktail party they will give in this new town. When I consider how quickly my parents make new friends, and compare it with my own slow, predictable progress, I think I may be adopted. But, like mine, their friends in each new city resemble exactly those from the last: nervous, bony women with black dresses and long fingernails, and faceless men under thinning hair, in white shirts and dark jackets and ties. It is almost as though they accompany us, a crowd of cocktail guests creeping in a black cloud that follows us down the highway. Within weeks of a move, my parents are attending and hosting cocktail parties, and tonight they smile in the golden light as the world slows to the even motions of my father rising and sitting again, and to the quiet excited hum of their voices as they go through all the names of their new friends.

On the way to school, I tell Annie I am sick and will be going home early today, so she should not wait for me for lunch, and at lunchtime I stay in my classroom until the halls are clear. From the cafeteria door, I watch Annie move with her tray alone to the end of a table and eat her food quietly. Her head is down and she doesn't look at anything. I take my lunch to the other side of the room, to a table full of the kind of people who would ordinarily be my friends by now. There is space at the end, which I take, and though they ignore me, we are like an island here, surrounded by an ocean of boys and girls who know more than we do. I watch Tommy and his friends walk by Annie's table. They stand over her, but she doesn't look up; she slowly fills her mouth with potato chips, slowly chews them. When the boys go on, she looks up, around the room, and sees me at my new table. The bell rings and she blinks; then we rise together.

—Sally, she calls, —hey, Sally, and all the other Sallys turn their heads to the sound of their name, but I move out of the room and into the hallway, where I can't hear her over the noise of boys and girls talking to each other.

At the end of the day, she is waiting outside my room.

—Hey, she says, —didn't you hear me?

—What? I say. —No.

—I called your name, she says. —Didn't you see me?

—No, I say, and watch as people gather into their groups. Any one of the groups would be fine, and I look back at Annie, at her long thin arms and legs. She looks down at herself to see what I am looking at, and watches me watch the others leave. They are already drawn together in tight arrangements that won't open very easily to admit me.

—Well, she says. —Let's go.

—I guess I'm going to stay late, I say. —To help out, is all I can think of to explain it, but she nods and moves away. I hold my books to my chest and watch the boys she passes, to see if they turn.

On Friday I stand near a group of quiet girls who are planning something, but they take no notice of my presence and

finally they break off into smaller groups and say goodbye
and wander off with their mild happiness, leaving me to go
home for my parents' party. I stand at the school door until
Annie is almost all the way across the playground; then I
follow her to our street.

My mother empties and fills ice trays for the party and from
my window I can see Annie in her front yard. She stares at
our house and finally she heads across the street. I wait
several minutes for her knock, but when it doesn't come, I
open the door and find her sitting in our yard, pulling up
blades of grass one by one.
—Oh, she says. —Hi. You know, your dad should mow your
yard one more time before it gets cold. She brushes her
hand lightly over the top of the grass.
—So, she says. —You can come over tonight if you want.
My parents are coming to your party.
—I guess I'd better stay home, I say. —You know, to help
out.
—We have ice cream, she says. —And cookies. We can
watch anything we want.
—I have to help my mother right now, I say. —She's making
ice.
—Oh, Annie says, —okay.
I go back in my house, but she stays in the yard looking
down at the grass all around her.

My parents are getting dressed for their party. My father
carries my mother her drink and looks at her in the mirror
as she holds an earring to her ear. Their eyes meet and
quickly separate. Downstairs the living room is set with
bowls of food no one ever touches at these parties: peanuts
and potato chips and olives. From my mother's window, I
see Annie's parents emerge from their house and cross the

street side by side, like two dogs on a leash. They are right
on time, but at least half an hour earlier than anyone is
expected; aside from that, I can tell by the way they're
dressed that this is their first cocktail party. Annie's mother
is wearing a skirt and sweater, and her father wears a jacket
but no tie; their clothes are the same color as their skin, a
kind of light beige, and they will stand out like little sandy
spots in a sea of dark suits and dresses. Annie's mother has
had her hair done into a stiff blond bubble around her head,
and she pats at it mechanically as they come up the walk.
Behind them, their house looks dark; somewhere inside
Annie and Tommy have the evening to themselves. When
Annie's parents knock, my mother looks toward her bedroom door and my father goes to answer.

—███████ my mother says. —Who would come so early? She
clips her earrings on, and with a long, pink fingernail traces
the line of lipstick around her mouth.

—Won't this be fun, honey? she says to me.

By the time I follow her downstairs, more guests have arrived. Annie's parents stand quietly by the coffee table; they
hold their drinks uncomfortably and only taste at them with
their tongues as they look around our house.

—You have a very lovely home, they both say, separately,
to each of my parents as my mother smiles and my father
gently removes their drinks from their hands to make fresh
ones. I help carry them back and Annie's father beams at
me.

—Anne is a very good girl, he says to my father, who looks
at him blankly, until he remembers that this is Annie's father.

—Yes, he says, —she certainly seems to be.

—You must be very proud of her, Annie's mother says, and
my father looks around, confused, then realizes that they
are talking about me.

—Yes, he says and looks at me oddly, as if it is possible that my name actually could be Anne and he has been getting it wrong all these years.

—Yes, he says again, —I suppose we are.

They smile uneasily at me and at each other, and my father cannot stop himself from reaching for the drinks he has just given them, to freshen them up. I wander around the party holding out little plates of crackers and cheese to the party guests, who look down at me and smile briefly, then go back to their conversations. When I return to the coffee table, Annie's parents have moved to the couch, where they sit side by side, eating the peanuts and potato chips from the bowls on the table. Annie's mother bends to look at the olives, and touches one warily with the tip of her finger, then pulls her hand back. They hold their drinks carefully, still hardly touched, and as they eat, they look up and around them at the other guests, all of whom are standing, laughing and talking to each other as though they have all been friends for years. Annie's parents must wonder where all these people live, and why they've never seen them at the grocery store, or the gas station. Under the clatter of ice and glass and talk, there is music playing, something quiet and easy to listen to. A few women sway to it gently. Although there is never any real dancing to speak of, occasionally, as the party wears on, one or two couples will lean close together and move around in little circles in the corners, while their husbands and wives watch from the couch, making loud, bitter comments as my father freshens their drinks. These are usually among the last guests to leave. My mother passes Annie's parents and smiles graciously down at them.

—It's so nice to have you here, she says to them. —I hope you're having a good time.

Annie's mother opens her mouth to answer, but my mother

has turned away before she's gotten a word out. She turns
to her husband, but he has filled his fist with peanuts, which
he pops into his mouth one by one. She takes a sip of her
drink and watches my mother talk to a man in a black suit.
He takes her hand and his thumb catches on her ring.
—It's very nice to have you in town, he says, and my mother
smiles and begins to look away, but he keeps hold of her
hand.
—Really, he says. —I mean it.
This gets her attention and she slowly turns her head and
looks directly at him. My father is in the kitchen making
drinks, and when I go in to watch him, he smiles happily at
me.
—Isn't this great? he says. —Aren't these people great?
He brings the bottle he is pouring from to his lips and closes
his eyes as he drinks. He winks at me when he puts the
bottle down, then leaves with a tray full of fresh drinks.
—Sally, my mother says when I walk by her. She takes my
shoulder and turns me to face the man in the black suit.
—This is Mr. Wheeler.
I hold a plate of crackers out to him and he smiles nervously
at me.
—Well, he says. —You fit right in, don't you?
My mother smiles proudly. —When Sally was little, she
says, —she loved our parties. She used to kiss all the guests
good night.
Mr. Wheeler nods politely, but it is true: I remember shuffling from one guest to the next like a little pet, the brush of
their cheeks across my lips, the smell of smoke and perfume, and the warm scent of bourbon on their breath.
My mother looks down at me with the fondness of a
stranger, running her hand over my hair. —She couldn't go
to sleep without kissing them all, she says.

—Like mother like daughter, says someone behind us, and my mother's face freezes for a moment; then she turns her smile in the direction of the voice.

My father laughs loudly at whatever jokes he overhears as he moves efficiently in and out of the kitchen, and the party glitters around me like a light I can't quite catch as it passes on the edge of my vision. My friends who are not my friends are all together at someone's house, making popcorn and watching movies on television. Later, perhaps, they will gather their courage and wander in a small crowd to the pizza shop where the other children all meet. The bravest among them will insist on going, and the others will follow reluctantly; perhaps, on the way there, they will be attracted by an ice-cream store, or a movie, and stop, relieved to find this distraction; or perhaps they will go and sit in a corner booth, glancing around over their pizza, wondering what is happening. And across the street, Annie sits in a little circle of darkness in front of the television, listening to the hum of Tommy's nerves as he turns the pages of his comic books.

When the phone rings, my mother turns from her conversation with Mr. Wheeler and my father looks up from his tray of drinks. I answer it for them.

—Oh, Annie says, —I was just wondering if you changed your mind.

She waits. —You know. About coming over.

Her voice is high and strained.

—I can't, I say. —I have to help.

—Oh, she says, but she does not hang up. I think I can hear, from the basement below her, the mean laughter of boys as they watch television.

When I hang up and my mother asks me who it was, I say it was no one.

Before I am grown, I will live in a dozen more houses, and attend a dozen more schools; soon Annie will be just another face without a name, and I will forget whatever it is that is happening to her right now, behind the dark windows of her house.

I leave the party without kissing the guests good night. From the top of the stairs I turn to watch them. My mother smiles directly into the eyes of a man she has just met, while my father entertains the man's wife in the kitchen. Around them move people without faces, speaking in high, excited voices, and in the middle of the room Annie's parents sit together, staring around them with big haunted eyes. I try to guess what my mother is thinking as she smiles at the man, if in her mind she is groping for a five-letter word for frying pan or mousetrap.

From my bedroom window, I watch Annie's house, dark except for the kitchen and the flickering glow of the television downstairs. I turn out my light just as Annie comes out of her house. She sees me and waves me over, but I pull back out of sight. I cannot cross the street to meet her; downstairs is a room full of people I don't know, and ahead of me there are rooms full of people I don't know. Under my skin the nerves are moving like tiny people trying to get out. I watch Annie walk around her yard, collecting papers, twigs, early leaves, which she piles in ragged mounds against the brick wall of her house. She turns to me again, and in the darkness her face is a pale little moon, lit by the bleak shining faith that she can somehow cause the dry bricks to burn and save herself in the flames of a fire that can never catch.

L O C U S T S

The car is long and black, with fake wooden sides that are peeling away from the body in thin metallic strips. It honks even before it stops in front of our house, but my parents pay no attention.

The car continues to honk, and finally my mother lifts her head from her book.

—██████, she says, then walks to the bathroom and locks the door behind her. My father rises from his chair, dragging his eyes away from the baseball game on the television.

—Helen, he says sharply to her, then notices me by the window. He smiles grimly and wipes his hands across the front of his shirt.

Francine launches herself from the car first; she is splendid in hot pink, blue designer jeans, and breasts, which are clearly distinguishable from the soft bulk of her back and shoulders and stomach. They are a new addition since her last visit here two summers ago when she and I lay on the hot pavement at the pool spreading our hands flat across our chests, searching for even the slightest swelling in the flat bony shapes of our bodies.

This summer we will not go to the pool, since I am still recovering from an unusually severe and inexplicably contracted bout of hepatitis that kept me out of school for the first half of the year. I know that Francine will be uneasy about my hepatitis; she will wonder where I got it and how, but she will decide immediately, looking me over, that its origin could not have been in anything sexual. For the first few nights, I know she will lie awake in the bed across from mine and listen to my breathing, trying to detect germs issuing from my mouth in a thin stream, heading relentlessly toward her. There will be some satisfaction for me in Francine's first few sleepless nights.

Aunt Louise and Uncle Woody follow Francine up the walk, Aunt Louise looking vaguely displeased with the sky and the street and the air, Uncle Woody rubbing his thick palms together as he comes up the path to the door.

Francine drops her little square night case on the floor and

looks me over, then looks outside. —What's that noise? she
asks.
—Locusts, I tell her. —Seventeen-year locusts.
The locusts have been here since the beginning of summer;
quietly breathing underground for seventeen years, they
have emerged to their few months of life, and they are everywhere, eating. It is only the first of August and already the
bare branches of trees are beginning to show through; so
far, because of my father's constant spraying, only the grape
arbor in the back yard has withstood them, but that will go
too, eventually. Every tree and bush is covered with the
abandoned shells shed by the locusts; transparent brown
and intricately limbed, they are far more frightening than
the insects themselves, which are slow and pathetically
graceless. They seem capable of little other than eating, and
don't even bother to fly away when approached, as though
survival is not a concern for them; they simply continue to
eat until caught or killed.
At lunch one day, I sat at a table across from a boy who ate
his entire meal with a brown paper bag quietly buzzing and
shifting at his elbow. Every now and then the boy looked at
it with a kind of grim satisfaction, but it was only after he'd
wadded the remains of his sandwich and its wrapping into a
tight little ball that he opened the bag to show me about
twenty locusts, their wings torn off, stumbling over and over
each other in helpless dumb confusion.
—These bastards won't be eating any more trees, the boy
said. —That's for ███damn sure.
They'll be gone by the end of summer, and by next spring
the leaves will come back, the bushes will bloom again, and
everything will be as it was before. We'll forget they were
ever here, my father says, but I think I will never forget the
sound they make. It is an incessant humming, a whirr that
goes all the time, day and night, and won't stop until the

locusts have eaten all the leaves on all the trees and at last laid their eggs and died.

One night my father put his tape recorder on the windowsill and let it record the locusts until the tape ran out.

—That's crazy, my mother said. —Isn't it bad enough we have to listen to them all the time without having them on tape, too?

My father paid no attention to her; he rewound the tape and played it back. Even though it was only a cheap tinny echo of the sound outside, there was something terrible about hearing it like that. For the first time I realized what it was that we were listening to every minute of every day, with no change in pitch or intensity, and for a few hours I could hear nothing else—not the voices of my parents, not the television or the shouts of children outside, only the fevered drone of the locusts inside my head.

I point out a bush covered with locust shells to Francine; she thinks they are ugly and is afraid of them. I tell her not to be, that when one of them flies into her hair, all she has to do is shake it out gently. She quivers delicately. She is disgusted.

—Helen's in the bathroom, my father is saying to Aunt Louise and Uncle Woody. —A bug.

He ignores Aunt Louise's meaningful look, and begins to manage the luggage with Uncle Woody. They make great show of carrying the suitcases inside and upstairs. Women, they are saying, can't go anywhere without a closetful of clothes. Aunt Louise examines me carefully.

—Well, she says, —you've certainly gotten thin.

—Yes, I answer, —I guess so.

—Are you all over that trouble?

I look at the bathroom door and wonder how long my mother can stay in there. I admire her determination; surely she knows there will be consequences.

I nod to my aunt. —All over it, I tell her.

—Still, she says, —it's a shame you had to miss so much of your first year of school. I suppose you didn't get much chance to meet many boys.

She is right, I didn't, but I don't want to talk about it, and I am trying to think of a lie about a handsome tutor, or a hospital intern, when a little bubble of cruelty rises to her surface.

—Francine has lots of boyfriends, she says. —All the boys at Cross want to take her out.

All the boys at Cross fuck her, I would like to say, although I am sure this is not true. But I can see them, crowded around her, darting quick looks at her breasts, while she sends out gracious, smug smiles to the other girls passing by unnoticed. —Where is Francine? I ask.

—In the kitchen. She's hungry. Aunt Louise looks fondly toward the kitchen door. —It was a long drive.

My uncle and my father come downstairs, dusting off their hands. My uncle looks me over while my father stands tentatively in front of the bathroom door, smiling weakly.

—Well, my uncle says, —aren't *you* becoming a little lady here. How old are you now, Susie?

—Almost sixteen.

—Sixteen, he says. —Sweet sixteen. I bet you have a lot of boyfriends.

—No, Uncle Woody, I say, —not yet.

—Oh, he says. —Not yet. Well. He leans forward, with a little smile. —I bet you'd like one, he says. —Wouldn't you? A nice little boyfriend to bring you candy? And take you out in his car?

—Woody, my aunt says.

—Well, he says, —I brought you some candy.

He holds out a bag of candy corns, already opened. He has brought them ever since I snuck into the Halloween candy when I was six or seven; I ate two bags of candy corns and was too sick to go out trick-or-treating the next night. Uncle Woody thinks it is a very funny story. He always brings the candy, but each time he presents it to me as though it is the first time.

I take the candy from him and put it on the table. When I turn back, he is looking at my legs, my knees.

—Woody, my father says, —I want to show you the grape arbor. Maybe you can figure out some way to stop these damn locusts. They're eating everything in sight.

Francine emerges from the kitchen with a strawberry yogurt in one hand and several cookies in the other. A spoon sticks up out of her back pocket.

—Let's go up, she says to me.

As we walk up the stairs, I hear the bathroom door open and my aunt's voice. —Well, Helen, she says, —how are you feeling?

I stop to listen for the answer, but Francine bumps softly into me from behind. —Come *on*, she says, and we walk slowly up to my room, where she sits on the bed cross-legged and lays her cookies out in a neat row in front of her before she opens her yogurt. She is going to tell me about her boyfriends, about the football games and pep rallies, about cruising McDonald's with her friends, about the parties. I cannot hear this, and concentrate instead on the tight painful folds of flesh and denim that blossom when she crosses her legs. So where does everybody hang out? she will want to know. What does everyone *do* around here? she is going to ask me. We will spend a long afternoon, at the end of which she will say, So what are we going to do tonight? There is a carnival just outside town, in the parking lot of the mall; I have driven past it with my father once or twice, and I offer it to Francine.

She looks around my room, which has not changed much

since her last visit here, then picks a crumb from her shirt and places it carefully on the tip of her tongue. Boys, her eyes are saying, don't you know any boys? She will want to hang out and find some. She slides her spoon back and forth across her lips and assumes a look of boredom. This is going to be a long summer, she is thinking already.

Like the locusts, they will be here until nearly the end of summer, almost three weeks. When I asked my mother why they were staying so long, she looked up from her book and gazed at me.

—Ask your father, she finally said. —They're his family.

He looked away briefly from the television, just long enough to say, —Helen, then turned back in time to watch the next play.

—Go ahead, she said to me. —Ask him.

My father got up and walked into the kitchen; the icebox door banged open, ice clattered into a glass, and in a few moments my mother put down her book and followed him in. Their voices were just an angry murmur over the ball game, but after a while the back door slammed and the car started. When my mother came back into the living room, she seemed surprised to see me there.

—Susan, she said, —it's late. Why don't you go to bed?

I woke up later to hear voices outside, from the back yard. When I went to the window, I saw my mother and her best friend, Carol, sitting close together in a pool of light on the patio below me. My mother leaned against Carol, and Carol ran her hands smoothly over my mother's hair. It's all right, she was saying over and over; in the half-light of the moon, all the blue suburban lawns stretched out quietly until they blended into the darker blue of whatever lay beyond us.

I went back to bed, and in the morning we were all pleasant at breakfast; there was no sign of the night before, nothing but a neat circle of cigarette butts pressed onto the white concrete of the patio. Later in the afternoon, I watched my father pick them up and scrub at the dark stains they'd left until there were only a few faint smudges, which would wash away in the next rain.

Francine opens her suitcase and stacks her clothes neatly in the space I have left for her in my dresser; her clothes make a bright square of color next to mine in the drawer. Then she opens her little night case and begins pulling out jars of makeup, lipsticks, combs, all of which she lays out on the top of the dresser, humming to herself as she unpacks, as if I am not here.

For dinner there is corn, mashed potatoes, chicken. Usually we do not eat so formally; my mother serves us from pots on the stove and we carry our plates to the table or into the living room to eat, but tonight all the food is piled in dishes and bowls around the table. My mother's third martini sweats by her hand, a cool spot in the middle of the steaming dishes. My uncle looks at me.

—Susie, he says, —I'll take a breast.

I'm not sitting near the chicken, so I pass him an ear of corn instead.

My mother stares at the chicken thigh on her plate and fingers the stem of her glass; when she asks my father to make her another drink, he rises silently, avoiding the look my aunt shoots him across the table.

Uncle Woody is telling us all about the trash masher he just bought, the convenience, the ecology, the sheer beauty of the thing. Bits of corn cling to his lips, and his chin gleams with grease from the butter. I wonder why no one mentions it, but then realize that only my father and I are listening to him. My mother stares at her plate, or at her glass, or out the window; Francine examines her food carefully as she eats, turning it around and around, searching out the perfect marriage of teeth and bite, while Aunt Louise watches my mother with a kind of narrow-eyed curiosity; every move my mother makes provokes my aunt to turn her head sharply and gaze at her for a few long, obvious moments. Only my father and I pay any attention at all to Uncle Woody, and we are too polite to mention the butter. On this, our first night together, someone–perhaps Uncle Woody, perhaps my mother–has lit candles, and we sit here in the hot flickering dusk, knitted together by light and the sound of Uncle Woody's voice. Over all of us is the hum of the locusts, hanging in the air, resting on us like a benediction.

After dinner, my father finds a ball game on TV, and Uncle Woody stays at the table to smoke and watch Francine and me carry the dishes into the kitchen. Though we have plenty of ashtrays, he taps his ashes onto his plate, dropping them into the little puddles of melted butter. Aunt Louise seems to be herding my mother around the kitchen; each time we come in, they are in a different corner, until finally my mother is trapped by the stove. When I bring in the bowl with the mashed potatoes, Aunt Louise takes it from me and sets it in the sink.

—You girls go on now, she says. —Ask your Uncle Woody to drive you to the carnival.

I stand just outside the kitchen door, waiting for Francine to change her clothes and Uncle Woody to finish his cigarette.

—Well, my aunt says, inside the kitchen. —You *look* all right.

A match strikes, then a deep breath. —I'm fine, Louise, my mother says. —We're all fine.

Before Aunt Louise replies, my uncle is standing in front of me.

—Ready for the carnival? he asks. He has wiped the butter from his chin, but his skin still glimmers as he smiles down at me. —You can ride up front with me.

* * *

At the carnival, my uncle takes my arm and steers me toward the Ferris wheel. He points up at the top car, swinging crazily as the two boys inside pump it back and forth.

—Now that's a ride, he says. —That's the first one we'll go on.

Francine's eyes shine as she gazes around at the bright thumping neon. —Look, she says, pointing to a group of girls at a concession stand. —Do you know them?

The girls are about my age and probably go to my school, but I shake my head.

—How about them? she says, gesturing toward several boys tossing baseballs at stuffed cats, and I shake my head again.

—Don't you know anyone? she asks. She looks disappointed, but perks up when she spots a display of giant pink stuffed panda bears, and sets off in their direction. My uncle winks at me, then follows behind her, leaving me alone in the middle of this explosion of light and sound, surrounded by roving clumps of boys and girls I don't know.

We fall quickly, after the first few days, into a sort of routine: Francine's eyes open on a day without love and settle hopelessly on mine. Boys, they say, where are all the boys? Then breakfast, then the day, which we all pass separately. Francine covers herself with a glistening coat of tanning oil and sits on the patio, playing solitaire or reading fashion magazines that are too old for her, full of tips on how to meet more men at work, and what kinds of cosmetic surgery can best improve a problem figure. My father, who is taking his vacation from work now, lies on the couch in front of the television, and Aunt Louise sits beside him, knitting, her needles clicking steadily over the noise of the game; I turn the pages of my books without sound, and my mother wanders in and out of the house, trailing smoke and Uncle

Woody, who stops every now and then to offer me a handful
of candy corns. After dinner, someone takes Francine and
me to the carnival, and at night, although it seems we have
hardly done anything during the day, we all fall exhausted
into bed. Francine plummets immediately into a heavy, re-
sentful sleep, and I lie awake, listening to her gentle snore.
Some time before morning, I wake to hear my uncle creeping along the hall. He stops outside my door and listens. Or
he does not. His foam soles do not give him away; his bones,
his breathing do not give him away. He pauses and listens,
then creeps to another door, listening.

As I watch a squirrel run up a tree, my uncle's big laugh
comes right in my ear.
—What is that damn squirrel up to anyway? he asks, and
suddenly his huge hand comes down on my shoulder. It is
like a cement glove, pressing me into the ground and already
I have begun to sweat, which Mother warned me against.
While this is not something I remember my doctor mentioning, and I'm not entirely sure it's not something my mother
made up, since she herself doesn't care for the heat, all the
same, I try to stay out of the sun, and the thin trickle of
sweat running down my ribs feels alarming and cold.
—Candy, Susie?
When I look up at him, he smiles. I come only to his chest,
and I can hear a slight wheeze as he breathes. He holds out
his fist and opens it to show me several candy corns, pressed
together into a waxy little lump.
—No thank you, Uncle Woody.
—Oh, he says. —You take them. You're a skinny little
thing.
He dislodges a few candy corns from the lump in his hand
and drops them into mine, then presses my fingers closed
over them; the candies are warm and slick and I drop them

on the grass. Uncle Woody laughs, then opens his mouth wide and pops his hand over it, throwing the lump of candy in. He winks at me as he chews, and wanders back to the house, shaking his head. I can see him through the windows, moving from the kitchen to the living room, where my father is already watching the doubleheader between Cincinnati and Chicago.

I am in the bathroom taking inventory. Cheekbones: flat; chin: receding; hair: thin; breasts: the same; appearance: problematic.

I have borrowed a few of Francine's cosmetics, and they are spread out on the sink in front of me when she comes in without knocking, wearing a fluffy pink robe. She looks at the makeup on the sink and I begin to offer some explanation, but she moves past me and turns on the water in the bathtub. From the pocket of her robe she takes a little bottle, which she opens and smells; then she pours some of the liquid under the running water. Bright bubbles burst up immediately in the tub, and she smiles as she turns to me.

—Bath oil, she says. —It makes your skin silky and smooth to the touch.

Who is going to touch you, Francine? I think. She lowers herself into the tub and sighs.

Who? I think, and then I say it: —Who?

—What? she says. She lifts a palmful of bubbles to her face and blows them into the air. —I've got a date tonight, she says.

I am mystified. How could she have a date? There are no boys. I look casually into the mirror.

—Oh? I say. —Who with?

—A boy, she says. —A boy I met at the carnival last night.

Last night, I think, and run over the evening in my mind. She must have met the boy when my uncle and I were on the Ferris wheel, or when my uncle was throwing rubber balls at the clown, or when my uncle was buying me candy.

—Where are you going? I ask.

—We're meeting at the carnival, she says, waving her hand over the tops of the hills of bubbles that surround her breasts. I imagine them high up over the lights of the mall parking lot, swaying in the Ferris wheel's artificial ecstasy, an enormous pink fluff of cotton candy in Francine's arms, the boy's hand under her sweater, holding the soft candy of her breast.

We all stand around the front door as Uncle Woody prepares to drive Francine to the carnival. My aunt reaches out with a Kleenex to blot away a little smear of lipstick from Francine's chin.

—Don't you want to go, too, Susie? my uncle asks. —You don't want to stay in all night with us old folks.

—I don't feel well, I tell him. —I'll just read.

—If you want, he says, —we can go to a movie. Just you and me. Like a regular date. I'll buy you popcorn and we can sit in the back row and watch the smoochers.

—Woody, my aunt says, —Francine's going to be late.

Francine turns at the door and tosses me a smile. —I'll see if he has any friends, she says.

Aunt Louise watches them walk out to the car and my father goes back to the living room. I realize that my mother has not been standing with us; she is in the basement, perhaps, or on the patio. When the car pulls out, Aunt Louise turns happily to me.

—Francine is very popular, she says. —Wherever she goes, she seems to make new friends.

I nod, and try to think of something to say, but she turns her head sharply at the suck of the freezer door opening, and heads off toward the sound of an ice tray cracking.

* * *

My father stands by the television, tapping absently against
the screen. He is torn: either he can watch the game
between L.A. and Cincinnati or he can watch the game between Cleveland and Detroit. He looks out the window at
the final stretch of evening sun over the grape arbor and
wipes his fingers delicately against the front of his shirt,
then selects a few candy corns from the bowl on top of the
television, put there by my uncle to lure me to the flickering
screen while he waits alertly in the shadows. My father finally chooses his game and sits unhappily to watch it, thinking only of the game he is missing, though before long he
will be asleep.

Traveling through the house and into my bedroom, the baseball announcer's voice is reassuring: summer, father, home,
it says, and its insistent rise and fall blends with the murmur
of the locusts. My father lies on the couch, dozing or dreaming, his drink propped on his chest, while beside him Aunt
Louise runs her hand over some model in *Vogue* or *Cosmo-
politan*, thinking: I want this, I want this. My mother and
my uncle are gone, pursued or pursuing under the dark
trees, and somewhere some boy's narrow palm strolls over
Francine, charmed by the give of her skin, the resistance of
her nipple. Surprised and delighted, he strokes her in the
moonlight somewhere. There is no light here but the blue
light of the TV and no sound but the sound my uncle does
not make, creeping from door to door, the sound not made
by the squeaking of his shoes, the protest of his bones.

I go to bed before Francine returns, and when I wake up
later, I don't know if she's back yet, but my uncle's shape
is dim in the moonlight that comes through my window, and
his heavy bulk causes my bed to creak dangerously. The
wooden slats underneath are mismatched, and sometimes

they slip from the frame, the mattress collapsing right through to the floor.

—Susie, he says. —Susie. He shakes my shoulder. —Susie, wake up.

I feign drowsy confusion and turn away, but he puts his hand on my forehead, turning my face back to him.

—Susie, he says. —I want to tell you a bedtime story. Which one's your favorite?

He brings his face close to mine and shakes my shoulder again. —Which one? he says. —Which one?

He smells of gin, which is what they all drink, and cigarettes, and something else–a sweet, dark, excited smell. I keep my eyes closed. I cannot remember any story except this one.

—Suuusie, he says, his voice rising and falling as if he is calling me from a long distance, and I open my eyes. He smiles. —I knew you were awake, he says.

—I'm tired, Uncle Woody. I want to go to sleep.

—Let me tell you a story first. Look. I brought you some candy.

He opens his hand above me and scatters candy corns on the sheet over my stomach, my breasts.

—I'm sick, I say. —I have to go to the bathroom.

He lies down beside me, pressing himself into the narrow space between my body and the edge of the bed.

—Once upon a time, he begins, —there was a little girl. He moves the hair gently from my face and sighs happily, his breath wet and heavy.

—I'm sick, I say again, and struggle against the sheets to sit.

—Wait, he whispers, and reaches out. —Wait, and then the bed breaks and I am out of it.

* * *

Under the bright lights, against the white tile of the bathroom, this is all a dream. The face that stares back at me in
the mirror is dreaming. When I come back to my room,
everything is as it was before: the bed is neatly on its frame,
the candy gone. This is a dream, and I will forget it by
morning. In the moment before I fall back asleep, I realize
that I have forgotten to check for Francine, but then I remember that this is a dream.

In the morning, all is as usual, and when my English muffin
pops up, my aunt hands me the butter.
—Woody says he scared you last night, she says, turning to
put another muffin in the toaster.
I carry the butter to the table with my muffin. —Scared me?
—He said he had too much to drink and came into your
room by mistake.
She watches me carefully as I spread butter on my muffin.
—Oh, I say. —I wasn't scared.
I sit at the table, by the window; outside, my uncle and my
father are walking around the yard, examining the bushes
carefully. When he sees me watching them, my Uncle
Woody waves cheerily and my father looks around to see
what he is waving at. A locust hums suddenly past the window, like a tiny dense bird. Somewhere, I've heard, they eat
them, fry them up and eat them, a delicacy, like caviar or
oysters. My father and Uncle Woody continue their walk
around the yard, occasionally plucking locust shells from
the leaves.

—Disgusting, my aunt hisses, —disgusting. Her voice cuts
through the night like a line of fire burning all that is in its
path, straight to my ears. —You're a disgusting fool, she
says, —and don't you think everyone can't see it.

Francine sleeps, or pretends to, though I can hear my aunt's voice clearly, and does not stir when I get up to go to the bathroom. I walk without sound, counting my breaths with each step.

—Listen to me, she says. —You ▆damn fool.

I imagine my uncle, next to her in the bed, his jaw working.

—Listen, she says again, and then there is the slap of her palm against his skin, a hideous hurting sound in the night.

—You listen to me.

He must be awake, his skin stinging, staring into the night, surrounded by nothing but her voice. Someday he will kill her. He will come upon her in the laundry room when she thinks he is watching television, and he will creep up on her in his foam soles and bury her face in the soft sweet-smelling sheets she piles up against tomorrow. He will bury her face in the sheets and he will bury her body in the garden and then he will come upon me like rain. Candy, Susie, candy, he'll say, and I'll come running.

I put my hands over my ears, but Aunt Louise's voice filters through my fingers like smoke, like light through the leaves.

—Disgusting, she says, —disgusting.

My mother is thirty-six years old today. I was born when she was twenty; she has had me all those years. Since she was twenty, there has been me. In four years I will be twenty. For her birthday today, there will be a small dinner with the family and a few of my parents' friends. Uncle Woody has got several bottles of champagne and a big net to play volleyball, or badminton. Carol comes first, early in the day, to help with the dinner. She brings a small present, wrapped in bright blue paper, and a bouquet of flowers, blazing orange and white, like an armful of fire. As Aunt Louise runs for a vase, Carol gives a small flower to me, and the largest

and most beautiful flower she puts behind my mother's ear,
a flame in her hair.

—There, she says, —now you look like a birthday girl.

My mother almost smiles as she touches the flower, and
Carol looks away to where my father and Francine are struggling to put up the net in the back yard. Aunt Louise returns
with the flowers in a vase and looks at the flower in my
mother's hair.

—Don't you think you'd better put that one in the water,
too? she says, and my mother removes the flower and gives
it to her. I tuck mine into my top buttonhole.

—Susan, Carol calls from the window. —Come here. Look.
She points to the leaves of a bush that rests against the glass
and shows me a large locust, stuck to the leaf with a gummy
liquid that comes from its body. It struggles to free itself,
but each time one leg comes loose, the locust must put it
back down to work loose the other, and so imprisons itself
again.

—That means they're going to die soon, Carol says. She
smiles. —I'll sort of miss them. I've gotten used to the
racket. Imagine how quiet it will be with them gone. We'll
be able to hear ourselves think again.

—Well, Aunt Louise says, —that will be a nice change for
all of you. She smiles pleasantly as she carries the vase of
flowers into the dining room.

I am standing in front of the kitchen window, chopping for
the birthday dinner, cutting up carrots and onions and pep-
pers, which will go into the sauce for the lamb, my mother's
favorite. Late-afternoon sun glitters from the knife, and I
concentrate on the play of my fingers and the blade, my
hand moving steadily back along the spine of a carrot, the
knife relentlessly pursuing. Everyone has left the house.

Francine and Aunt Louise are picking up the birthday cake; Uncle Woody and my father have gone to buy the portable trash masher that will be the family's gift to my mother; my mother and Carol are in the back yard picking grapes, perhaps the last of the season that the locusts will not eat.

I am wondering if, right now, picking up the cake at the bakery, Francine is making new friends, meeting boys who want to date her, and I look up out of the window to see my mother and Carol standing together under the grape arbor; the leaves are still damp from an early shower and they shine in the bright sun as Carol gropes through them looking for grapes. She plucks one out and holds it up, then drops it into the blue-and-white bowl my mother holds. Something she says makes my mother smile—just for a moment, but before the smile is gone, Carol takes my mother's face in her hands and holds it to her own. My mother's face disappears as I watch them kiss under the damp leaves, the grapes hanging above them like ripe flies. The bowl falls from my mother's arms and lands on its side; grapes tumble out over the grass, and as Carol and my mother move together, a shower of rain from the leaves comes down over their heads. Rings are growing around this moment, this sky, this sun, racing over the damp leaves like tiny bullets of light, dazzling my eyes. Uncle Woody will come upon me now like a storm. The sun fades suddenly, blotted out by a cloud, and I look away, back to the counter. Around my hands vegetables lie like piled-up dead. I am amazed I have not cut myself. When I look back at the grape arbor, Carol and my mother are gone; the bowl is no longer on the ground.

At dinner, a little mound of black grapes sits in the middle of the table; they are like cocoons, breathing inarticulately against the blue-and-white pattern of the bowl. I pass rolls

to Uncle Woody, next to me; I hand him the salt, the pepper,
and I lift my own glass when he raises his in a toast to my
mother, who gazes at the trash masher on the floor by her
chair. I smile at whatever it is my uncle is saying in his
toast, but I saw them kiss, I think, I saw them kiss under
the damp leaves, where the grapes stirred above them like
sluggish flies. My uncle's words trail over the grapes and
around each curve, warming them; my eyes travel the
grapes as if on unknown territory, and I follow the trail of
my uncle's sentences as if on a map.
—You're going to love this trash masher, Helen, he is saying.
I try to imagine my mother dropping things into the trash
masher, cans, napkins, paper plates, but her face disappears into the wide blue sky, the damp leaves, the fat black
grapes.
—Ours has saved me plenty–time, effort, money–and let
me tell you, that adds up.
Carol cuts her meat up carefully, and my aunt is watching,
wondering: What now? What now?
After we have all finished doing whatever we are going to do
with our food, my aunt and Francine bring in the birthday
cake, a big white thing with my mother's name spelled art-
lessly across the top and at least three or four too many
candles. Carol and my father struggle to light all the candles
before the lit ones drip on the frosting, but they are clumsy
and too slow, and little blue puddles of wax spread out over
my mother's name.
—Make a wish, someone says, and she closes her eyes, then
blows out the two or three candles closest to her. Francine
stands up and blows out the rest, her eyes closed dreamily,
thinking already of the boy she met in the bakery, or in the
parking lot of the store. My uncle's hand hovers over the
grapes. Do not touch them, I think; do not disturb this. He

stops at the grape where I have let my eyes rest, and touches it, catching my eyes on his hand. When he plucks it from the bowl, he smiles.

—Cat got *your* tongue, Susie? he says.

Like hot ash descending, he will come upon me now. My aunt watches him with cat eyes.

Waking, I hear my uncle creep along the hall. He comes to a stop at my door, or he does not, then creeps on.

In my dream, I am sitting in a ring of chairs in a circle of sunlight in the exact center of a long sloping green lawn. In the middle of the circle of chairs is an orange-and-yellow flower, like a flame in the heart; it matches the smaller flower I wear at my breast, in the folds of my dress. Over everything is the sound of the locusts, the soft beat of wings, and in the distance I can hear the voices of men. Behind me is a dark wood, where my mother and Carol stand under the heavy wet leaves. As they kiss, the leaves move and stir and fly away, leaving the branches bare and empty. I run away from them, and behind me my uncle follows, when suddenly the sky is dark with locusts, flying in a huge cloud. My uncle falls back, calling, Candy, Susie, candy, but his voice is obscured by the hum and whirr of the sky.

When I open my eyes, I hear Francine's even breathing coating the night, sliding across the air. I can hear all the different sounds of the house. Disgusting, it breathes; candy, it breathes; carnival, love. I put my hands over my ears, but I can still hear, as if underwater, Francine's slight moan as she dreams a pair of hands worming up out of the sheets to move over her, to push the hair back from her face softly, to touch her lips.

—Francine, I whisper, —Francine. I cannot listen to her.

* * *

In the hall at the top of the stairs, it is too dark to see my own hand. My mother sits down beside me before I know she is there, as if the darkness has muffled all my senses. She lights a cigarette and I watch the smoke rise from her face. She smooths back my hair and wipes away my tears with the corner of her robe. Her arm around me, we rock back and forth on the top step; my face is against her neck and she rocks me as if I have awakened from a bad dream, as if we are all alone in the world.

—Susie, she whispers, —Susie, and her voice is like the locusts, a whisper of sound that lies over everything, that lies over the breathing of the house and quiets it. This is all I ever wanted.

She looks at me and her eyes shine in the light cast by her cigarette. There are so many things she could say.

—I'm thirty-six, she finally says, and shakes her head. —Who ever thought everything would be so awful?

I put my face in her hair; the brown is soft and the gray is wiry, and I can hardly hear my own voice. —You'll always have me, I say.

She pulls away and looks at me a moment, then out into the dark room at the bottom of the stairs. They'll be gone soon, I want to tell her; they'll be gone soon and we will be back among ourselves, and everything will be as it was before. Nothing will have happened. There are so many things I could say. Her cigarette is burning down close to the end and I can see the fine white bones of her hands and fingers. There are so many things I could say, but the hum of my heart swallows every word, and when she finally turns her eyes on mine, they are like locusts, moving helplessly against the white of her skin.

As Alice's mother walks down the aisle toward them, she puts her hand firmly on the top of each seat to steady herself against the jerking of the train, and her purse bumps the backs of the seats behind her. People look up, annoyed, and Alice goes back to her book, but she can feel her father watching each slow step, until her mother finally lurches into the seat across from them.

—For Christ's sake, Adele, he says. —You practically hit all those people in the head.

Alice's mother looks down along the row of seats, then back to him.

—I think if they were bothered, she says, —they could have said something.

He looks down at the map spread over his lap, and she gazes out the dirty window at the passing fields.

—Don't you think? she finally asks. —Don't you think they would have said something?

Alice's father rattles the map, then looks up. —Of course, he says. —That's exactly what they would have done. Exactly.

—Well, she says, —that's what I'd do.

She looks back and forth between him and Alice, but he is bent again over his map, and Alice leans out to look up the aisle. People have gone back to their books or their card games or their conversations; already they have forgotten that they were disturbed.

—Honey, her mother says, and leans forward. —Are you having a good time? She smells of fresh air and cigarettes, from standing in the breezeway between cars to smoke, rather than going all the way to the smoker.

Alice nods and her mother pats her on the knee, then settles back into her seat. Outside, the landscape changes from gray to brown to gray again, as they pass fields, then farms, then fields. They are traveling through the southern Midwest, from their home in Ohio to the wedding of a cousin of Alice's father, in Arizona. Alice has never met the cousin before, cannot even remember her ever being mentioned, but, her father said, they were invited, and she is family, and they would go. It is less clear to her why they are taking the time to travel by train, though at some point it seemed like a good idea, a nice way to break things up. This is how her father had put it: a nice way to break things up; and God knows, he had said, they could all use a change. They had also thought it would be a good experience for Alice, a chance to see different parts of the country, but so far everything they pass looks like everything else they have already passed.

As they rush toward the Southwest, she has seen little that has surprised her; occasionally a dog or a child runs across a spotted field, but mostly what she will remember is a frozen ground of dirt and snow, and the herds of stiff cold cows grazing hopelessly against trembling fences. And everything seems to be the same color; even the cities they pass through are featureless and brown, like little towns built of sand.

They have been traveling since early morning, and will not arrive in Arizona for another two days. Because the trip is so long, they have rented a little cabin, with a set of bunk beds and a bathroom. When they boarded the train, they went straight there, where they stacked their luggage carefully against the wall, then looked around the tiny room.

—This isn't how I remembered it from when I was a child, Alice's mother said. —The cabins seemed so big then.

For several minutes all three perched gingerly on the edges of furniture that was bolted to the wall or the floor; then they moved quickly to their seats in the coach car, where they have so far spent most of the ride.

Before they left home, Alice's father roughly charted out their route on a map, and for the first few hours of the trip he pointed things out to her—landmarks, universities, historic sites—but since then, they have all sunk into a gloom, watching without interest as the towns and the fields and

the late-winter sky spin by. They are in Indiana now–they
have been here for days, it seems–and although her father
has stopped pointing things out to Alice, he still keeps careful track of their journey. He holds his map out to Alice now
and points to a tiny dot at the border of Missouri.
—See this? he says. —This is where we'll stop next.
Alice looks down at the map; they are still at least four large
boxy states away from Arizona.
—Let's see, her father says. —The nearest big city is Poplar
Bluff, and the population is–he stops and looks along the
side of the map—three thousand.
—You know, Alice's mother says, —that map is at least five
years old. It's probably not very current.
He puts his finger over the little dot and looks up at her.
—I don't think, he says, —that the configuration of the
states will have changed much over the past five years. Do
you? he asks Alice, and she looks down at the map.
—Maybe the populations have changed, she says. —Maybe
that's what she meant.
—I'm not talking about the populations, her father says.
—The *states* are the same. And that's what we're looking at
here. The states.
He smooths the map out over his legs and looks down, then
lifts his head. —Unless, of course, he says to Alice's
mother. —Unless you know something I don't. He gazes at
her until she turns her head toward the window.
—Oh, she says, —look. And they all look out at a gray field
dusted with frost; in the center of it a girl skates a halting
figure over a frozen pond. She stops and goes back over the
figure.
—That could be me, Alice's mother says. —You know, she
says to Alice, —I might have had a career as a figure skater.
I was very good.
Alice has heard this before, and as her mother leans forward

to watch the girl, Alice tries to imagine her skating. The girl passes out of sight and Alice's mother leans back.

—I could skate a perfect figure eight in college, she says. —Perfect. Couldn't I? she asks Alice's father.

—Yes, he says, still staring out the window, although all there is left to see is a long stretch of high cold grass, hardly bending under the weight of the winter afternoon. —Perfect.

—But things were different then, she says to Alice. —I didn't have your opportunities.

She opens her purse and fumbles around inside it, then looks up at Alice. —You, she says, —you can do anything. She nods. —Anything you want. You can be anything.

—Jesus, Alice's father says, —she's only twelve.

—I know, Alice's mother says. —I know how old she is. I was just explaining how things have changed, that's all. Things are different now. She *can* be anything.

He looks down at his map.

—You don't know, she says to him. —You got to do everything you wanted.

He does not look up, but his mouth tightens as he runs his finger along the blue line he has drawn from Ohio to Arizona.

—It was different for girls then, Alice's mother tells her. She pulls out her cigarettes, then remembers that she cannot smoke in the coach, and puts them back. —I'd give anything to have that chance again, she says. —Anything.

Alice looks out the window just in time to see the shadow of a cloud pass over the field, and she thinks of the girl on the pond, her hair glazed with frost, bending to try to read some meaning in the shape she's just cut on the surface of the ice.

*   *   *

The train pulls slowly to a stop, and Alice's father rises, as he has done at every stop, and says, as he has said at every stop, —Well, I think I'll stretch my legs. He walks carefully down the aisle and waits at the door for the train to come to a complete stop. He gets off at every stop to pick up, he says, a little of the local culture, always bringing back with him a local newspaper, which he adds to a pile on the seat across from him, next to Alice's mother.

—We'll want these when we get home, he says each time he adds a new paper. —To see what's been going on everywhere we've been.

When he steps off the train, Alice's mother folds her magazine in her lap. —Are you really having a good time, honey? she asks, and Alice nods. Her mother smiles. —Well, that's good, she says. —At least there's that.

The stop is brief, and Alice's father comes back with a Kansas City *Star*, which he shakes open as he sits down.

—Okay, he says heartily, —let's see what's happening in Kansas.

—This is Missouri, Alice's mother says without looking up from her magazine. —Kansas City is in Missouri.

He looks at her over the paper. —Oh, he says. —Well, Kansas, Missouri, what's the difference?

He raises the paper. —Now, he says, —what's happening here? He murmurs as he reads, then stops abruptly.

—What? Alice's mother says, but he is quiet while he reads.

—Listen to this, he says finally. —A man checked into the Holiday Inn last night and jumped from the seventh floor. Killed himself. He shakes his head as he goes back to the article. —They don't even know who he is yet. Or where he's from.

Alice's mother shakes her head. —Imagine that, she says.

—Imagine going to all that trouble just to kill yourself. Why not stay home and do it?

—Oh, Alice's father says, —I can see it. He nods and reads the rest of the story, then looks up at Alice's mother. —I can see it just perfectly.

Alice looks over at the paper, but there is only a grainy picture of a hotel, with a little white circle around one of the windows. Alice turns her head and looks at the outskirts of the city, a few squat colorless buildings that give way to wide empty fields.

—I guess I can, too, her mother says. —He was probably depressed by the scenery. He probably couldn't stand to look at one more cornfield.

She puts her magazine down next to her, on top of the stack of newspapers. —I don't think I can either, she says and stands. —I'm going to smoke.

She walks down the aisle with her purse held in front of her, balancing herself gently, with only one hand against the seats, but even so, people look up as she passes. Alice's father waits until she is gone, then says, —Well, that shows you something right there. Those are wheat fields, not corn.

He folds the paper and lays it over Alice's mother's magazine, then opens his map. —Okay, he says, —if we're in Missouri, then Arkansas is next.

He traces his finger along the route. —And after that, Oklahoma. He smiles. —Now Oklahoma. There's a state. You're going to love Oklahoma. Let's see how far it is.

Alice bends over the map with him as he inches his knuckle along the blue line. Each small interval is approximately sixty miles, and there are just short of seven of them from the border of Missouri to Oklahoma.

—Six times seven, he says, and stops. —Thirty-six, he says after a moment, —so that means three hundred and sixty miles. That's not so far.

Alice leans back; just beyond the fields outside she can see

a little suburb, a flat, treeless patch of houses that seems to grow right up out of the land, hardly distinguishable from it, as though it is all—land, houses, bushes, cars—made of the same gray substance. It is so different from their orderly white neighborhood in Ohio, with its bright green lawns and fresh white sidewalks, the grass carefully clipped every Sunday by men just like Alice's father.
—Wait a minute, he says. —Six times seven. Six times seven.
He pulls a pen from his pocket and writes it down, 6 × 7, in the margin of the map. —Six times seven, he says again, and she wants to tell him the answer, but instead she closes her eyes and waits for it to be time for dinner. In Ohio, she thinks, under the snow, the stiff green grass is growing. In the summer, her father will cut it, and it will grow back again, and again, stiff and frozen. She half sleeps, half listens, and over the rattle of the train, she can hear her father quietly going through the multiplication tables.

The dining car is only half full when they have their dinner, and as the waiter puts down their plates, Alice watches the ice in her parents' drinks shake with the motion of the train.
—Well, her father says cheerfully, —only five hundred miles to Oklahoma. He picks up his knife and fork, and looks down at his roast beef sandwich. —You're really going to like Oklahoma, he says to Alice. —I've always loved it there.
Alice's mother looks around for an ashtray, then finally leans her cigarette on the lip of her butter plate. —You've never been to Oklahoma, she says.
Alice's father puts down his silverware and places his hands on either side of his plate. Then he leans forward until his tie is almost touching his gravy.

—I've been to Oklahoma, he says quietly. —I was there when I was fifteen. At a basketball camp.

—Oh, she says. —Well, I didn't know that. You never told me that. I can't see why you would expect me to know that.

—I've told you, he says. —I've probably told you ten times. Twenty.

Alice watches a family across the aisle from them, and wonders what they're talking about. There is a girl about her age, and a boy, younger, and she wonders how life would have been different if she'd had a brother, but she cannot imagine another presence in their house; though it is large, it seems barely able to contain each of them as it is.

Alice's father picks up his fork. —Oklahoma, he says, —is a wonderful place. I think I had the best time of my life there. The best.

He cuts his sandwich in half and watches gravy spread across the plate. —I could probably do very well for myself there. I could probably make a very satisfactory life for myself there. Maybe, he says, —maybe I'll look into it.

—Fine, Alice's mother says. —And we can all eat dust. She smiles at Alice. —Oklahoma is a state full of dust, she says. —Nothing but dust. And dirt.

Alice's father looks up. —I didn't say we would all go, he says, and he stares at Alice's mother a moment as Alice watches her peas tremble in their small bowl. She looks up as the waiter approaches and stands quietly by their table.

—Excuse me, he says apologetically to Alice's mother. He hands her an ashtray. —I'm afraid we don't allow smoking in here. He puts the ashtray down, then leaves, and Alice's father watches as she puts her cigarette out.

—Probably everyone was complaining, he says. —Probably everyone in the whole car. He smiles as he stabs his fork into his sandwich.

* * *

After dinner, they retreat to their cabin and sit nervously on
the bolted furniture. All they can see of the world outside is
a square of darkness in the window: no moon, no stars, not
even the reflections of houses, or city lights, just a square of
black, and in it their own reflections, trapped like ghosts in
the glass. Finally, Alice's mother stands.
—I think I'll go to the smoker, she says. —At least I can
find some conversation.
When she is gone, Alice's father smiles. —Isn't this fun? he
says.
—I guess so, Alice says. She pats at the hard bottom bed of
the bunk and sits, then leans back against the wall with her
book.
—Hey, her father says, —you don't have to stay in here
with me. There's lots to do on a train. You just have to know
how to find it.
He gazes at her until she puts down her book and leaves the
cabin.
She walks down the center of the aisle, not touching the
seats as she passes them, maintaining her balance by shifting her weight with the movement of the train. She stops in
the cold breezeway between the cars; when the train comes
to a jerk in the tracks, the hooks that hold the cars together
rattle but hold fast, and she wonders what would happen if
the train came apart right here, right underneath her; she
would have to think quickly, and leap for either car, but she
has a crazy vision of herself straddling the empty air between them, stretching wide as they separate.

Just outside the door to the smoker, Alice can see her
mother, sitting, with her back to Alice, at a little white table,
across from a man in a dark sweater. As Alice approaches,

she watches the man watch her mother; he smiles every now
and then, lifts his eyebrows, nods. His eyes move across her
face, down to her hands, back up again.

—I could do a perfect figure eight, Alice hears as she approaches. Her mother takes a drag of her cigarette and
smoke rises, a delicate frame around her head. —I was, in
my way, she goes on, —a kind of prodigy.

The man nods and looks around the room. When Alice stops
at the table, he smiles vacantly, and Alice's mother turns.

—Oh, she says. —Alice. Alice, this is Mr. Gregg. He's traveling to Albuquerque. On business.

—Alice, he says. —What a pretty name.

—Yes, says Alice's mother. —Isn't it?

She puts her cigarette out and smiles at Alice. —It's a family name, she says, but Alice cannot remember anyone in
her family named Alice. The man looks out through the
window at the dark screen of the world passing by, and
when he looks back, he seems surprised to see Alice still
there.

He smiles grimly. —Well, Alice, he says, —what do you
want to be when you grow up?

Alice looks at her mother and tries to imagine what she
herself will be, what she will do when she is that age; probably by then she will smoke, and she will be married to a
man much like her father, and in the summers she will
probably take vacations with him and their little quiet children. She closes her eyes a moment and tries again: instead
of all that, she will have a different life, one in which she
will doze after she has had her breakfast, and in the evening
she will lie down after supper. She will have a cat that sits
quietly in her lap, and when it dies, she will get another.

—I don't know, she says finally. —A nurse.

—Ah, the man says. —The medical profession.

Her mother smiles at her. —That's what I wanted to be, too,

she says. —A nurse. She looks at the man. —And I could
have been. I would have made a good nurse.

She stops and taps a cigarette from her pack. The man picks
up his lighter, but she looks down at the cigarette and does
not bring it to her lips.

—I'd still like to be a nurse, she says. —But it's too late for
that.

—Oh now, he says. —It's never too late. Not for a woman
like yourself. You're still quite a young woman.

Alice's mother looks at him and smiles. —Really? she says.

—Oh yes, he says. —Oh yes. He flicks his lighter and Alice
watches the flame pass across her mother's dark eyes.

Her father is in the chair by the window when she returns to
the cabin; the map and newspapers are spread open around
him on the floor and in his lap is the Kansas City paper.
From the door Alice can see the photo of the hotel with the
white circle around the window. He looks around at her and
drops the paper on the floor.

—Where's your mother? he asks.

—Smoking, Alice says. —She's still in the smoking car.

—I suppose she's making friends, he says, and Alice nods.

—Your mother is a very friendly woman, he says, gazing at
her, and she can tell he is waiting for a response, but she
sits on her bed and picks up her book. Finally he reaches
for one of the newspapers on the floor, and over the top of
her book Alice watches him read: his eyes run quickly
across the paper and all the way down it, but when he finishes, he comes back to the top, without turning the page.
He is waiting for Alice's mother to come back; he is waiting
for something to happen, Alice can tell, and she wants to be
far away when it does, but already she knows that it will not
happen without her; if she is gone, it will wait for her to
return–to come out of the bathroom, or to arrive home from

school, or to wake up–and while it may not be something too terribly awful–a word, a look, a small mean flick of the hand–she will be there for it; she is a part of it by now. There was a time when her parents, having quarreled, would turn to her with sad shocked looks for all that they asked her to witness, but now it goes on as though she is not even there. Her father abandons the paper and looks out the window; the only light is that of the train, cutting through the black country. She wonders if he is thinking of the life he might have had in Oklahoma, or of her mother, or if he thinks nothing at all, his mind an empty field, crossed only from time to time by a few thoughts rattling over a rusty track.

By the time her mother comes back, Alice has finished her book, and her father is cheerful again, back to plotting out their trip. He looks up and smiles briefly at Alice's mother as she sits on the chair by the bed. She picks up a magazine and stares at it for a while, then closes it.

—Do you remember, she says to him, —that I wanted to be a nurse?

He looks up from the map and makes great show of closing it up carefully, along its original folds; when he is done, he smiles. —No, he says. —I don't remember that.

—Well, she says, —I do.

He looks out the window, and she nods. —You know, she says, —I am still relatively young. I am still a relatively young woman.

He does not answer, but his lips are moving and as he gazes at the passing scenery Alice tries to tell what he is saying. After a moment she realizes he is going through the multiplication tables.

She puts her book down and goes into the tiny bathroom to brush her teeth for bed, and one by one they all go into the bathroom, then emerge in their nightclothes. Alice's father climbs onto the top bunk first, and her mother follows. Just before her mother pulls her leg up, Alice sees at her ankle a fine spray of blond hairs that she has missed with her razor. She wonders what her mother was thinking that day, leaning over her long white legs; if perhaps she was thinking of all the things she might be doing instead of that. Alice turns her face to the wall, wondering who has slept in these beds before them, what family took this room before tonight. She concentrates on not listening, but it's an unnecessary effort: her parents make no noise at all; they lie above her like stones, and she cannot even hear them breathe.

She wakes to darkness, not knowing if it's the jerking of the train that woke her, or her mother, who is in the chair near the bed, watching her. Her hair is outlined in the feeble light from the window, and her eyes are dark smudges in the dark circle that is her face. She leans forward and touches Alice's arm gently.

—You know, she says softly, —I really did want to be a nurse. I wanted to work in a hospital. I really did. It's not just something I made up out there like you did. I really wanted that.

Alice closes her eyes and feels the train move underneath her. She wonders what state they're in now, what city it is that casts the dirty light over the fields outside. She wonders how long it will take them to reach Oklahoma, and she hears and does not hear her mother move from the chair; she feels and does not feel her mother's cold lips on her forehead, her hand smoothing her hair back; she sleeps and does not sleep, so that when her mother leaves the room, she knows it but does not hear her go. Above her, her father finally moves, turning over on the thin mattress, and Alice can feel

that he is awake. When she falls asleep again, she dreams
she is in a tall empty room without windows, her feet buried
in sand and her face in flames.

She wakes with a sudden jolt of the train and she is startled
by her first sight: the world rushing by in a cluttered blur
of objects. Then she remembers where she is and closes
her eyes to try to recall that moment of opening her
eyes and not knowing where she was, but it is too late. All
around her on the train, people are waking to a world
that is not their own, and for just a moment they forget
everything: husbands, lovers, children, wives, even the
destinations toward which they rush with such determination; then they look around; their eyes fall on their clothing, the faces of their children, their familiar suitcases
and books, all of the things they carry with them. The mattress shifts above her and she wonders what it must be like
for her parents to wake to each other every day–if, for only
a moment, it is a surprise. She opens her eyes again and
sees her mother's face dangling over the mattress, smiling upside down at her, and she can hear her father brushing his teeth in the bathroom. He comes out dressed,
smiling tightly.
—Okay, he says. —Another day. He walks to the window,
then to the door, and paces alertly around the room, tapping
his hands against his thighs as he walks, waiting for Alice
and her mother, but when they are finally dressed and ready
for breakfast, he is in the chair, watching them dully.

The family that sat across from them at dinner is gone,
replaced by an old couple who eat steadily and do not
talk. They take bites of food almost simultaneously, and
chew as they look around the room, then wearily bring
their forks to their mouths again. Alice is torn between

French toast and poached eggs, but when her mother chooses French toast, she decides on eggs, curious to see the effect of the motion of the train on the trembling skin of the egg. When the eggs come, they are overcooked, and when she breaks the center of one with her fork, only a disappointing dribble of yolk bleeds out over her toast. Mr. Gregg enters the car and sits at a table across the room from them. He watches them eat, and when Alice meets his gaze, he nods at her in a businesslike way. She smiles, then looks away, and her father turns to see whom she is smiling at. He watches Mr. Gregg open his newspaper and prop it up in front of his face, then turns back to Alice.

—Looks like you have a friend, he says. Alice mashes her egg down into her toast.

—Alice, her mother says, —don't play with your food. You'll be hungry later if you don't eat now.

—It's overcooked, her father says. —Can't you see it's overcooked? He smiles at Alice. —Who's your friend? he asks.

—Will you leave her alone? her mother says. —Will you just leave her alone and let her eat her eggs?

They are all quiet a moment and Alice's mother scrapes her fork across the top of her French toast, then pushes her plate away.

—I'm already sick of the food on this train, she says. —I'm sick of the food and I'm sick of the room and I'm sick of the goddamn scenery. I'm going to smoke.

Mr. Gregg does not turn as she passes him on her way out of the car, but when she is gone, he looks around to see the door close behind her.

Alice's father pulls her plate of French toast toward him.

—I'm afraid, he says, —that your mother is not a very happy woman. He pours syrup over the French toast. —No, he says. —Not a very happy woman at all.

He cuts the French toast into quarters, then into smaller pieces, and does not once look behind him as he begins to eat.

Back in the cabin Alice's father kneels over the paper he has most recently bought, looking for stories about the suicide, but, he tells Alice, they must be too far from Kansas City to get any coverage.

—Wait, he says. —Here's something. It says here that he was a family man. Everyone was very surprised. They didn't even know where he was going. He gazes out at the floor over the newspaper.

—I can understand that, he says. —I really can. When he looks up, he seems startled to see her.

—Hey, he says, —you should be having fun. You should be *doing* something. What would you be doing at home right now?

—I don't know. Reading. Watching TV, Alice says, but what she would in fact do after breakfast is go to her room and sit on her bed and run her hands up and down her legs from her ankles to her knees, pushing the nerves one way, then the other, until her parents called her for lunch or dinner.

—Well, he says, —you can do a lot more than that here, and he sits back on his heels and waits for her to leave.

Through the window of the smoker, Alice watches her mother, who is sitting at a table by herself. She lights her cigarette and smokes it without looking around, but her shoulders stiffen each time the door opens at either end of the car. She is waiting, but not for Alice, so Alice goes to her seat by the window in the coach car. Outside, dogs and cows and pigs are clumped against the gray dirt, or sit under dry trees. As the train slows through a crossing, Alice looks out at a blue car waiting for them to pass; a woman is at the wheel, and a boy beside her; in the flash of passing, Alice is sure the boy has looked up and met her eyes. She imagines herself in the car. The boy and his mother might be going to swimming practice, or skating, perhaps, or to a store to pick out a new outfit, but sooner or later they will drive past these same trees and go home again. They know nothing of what it is to be on this train.

Soon the train pulls into another stop, and Alice watches the platform outside for her father; he appears just outside her window, but does not see her inside. He stretches, and stands still for a moment, looking out away from the train, then bends and pushes coins into a newspaper box.

When Alice wakes, it is late afternoon. The sun hangs at the edge of a field, and she watches for signs to see where they are. After several slow miles, she sees a sign for an Oklahoma bank, and she stands to go to the cabin. She is dizzy from her nap, and her brain buzzes nervously as she walks to the room, where her father is kneeling over a newspaper and her mother sits in a chair, reading Alice's book.

—Well, her mother says, —you were certainly out cold when I came to get you for lunch. Did you have a good nap?

—Yes, Alice says, —I guess so.

—Well, her mother says, —you didn't miss much. I think we're taking the long route. She snaps the book closed.

—You might have missed a pig or two.

Alice's father looks up. —Are you trying to say something? he says.

—No, she says. —I was just commenting on the scenery.

—Oh, he says. —I see. He lays the newspaper down on his lap. —I think it's time for dinner.

Alice's mother nods, but does not rise from her chair. —It's just, she says. —It's just that this is an awfully long trip for Alice.

Alice's father looks at Alice. —Don't you worry about Alice, he says. —Alice can take care of herself.

—I know that, her mother says. —But you know, it's just that there are lots of other things we might have done on this vacation besides go to the wedding of someone we don't know.

He looks down at the paper a moment, as if he might be reading.

—Okay, he says. —Next year you can decide what we do. And the year after that. And the year after that, too, and every year after that until we die. His voice is even and contained, but Alice can see that his hands are trembling a bit as he presses his palms into his knees.

—I'm just saying, says Alice's mother, —that this is a long trip.

He folds the paper and runs his fingers carefully along each sharp crease, then stands. —Jesus Christ, he says. —Jesus Christ Almighty.

Alice looks down at her sneakers. They are new, bought just for this trip. She tries to think of someplace on the train she might go, someplace she hasn't been yet, but she knows already that it's just car after car of the same. Her mother sighs heavily and stands.

—I'm going to smoke, she says. —If anyone wants me.

After she is gone, Alice's father lays his newspaper down gently and goes to the window. —I could get out right here, he says. —I could just get out right here in Arkansas.

—It's Oklahoma, Alice says. —We're in Oklahoma now. I saw a sign.

He does not turn from the window. —Arkansas, he says.

—Oklahoma. What's the difference? It's all the same. And
it goes on forever and ever.

Outside, evening is creeping across the fields. Already, behind them in the east, night has fallen, but ahead it is still
light, and it seems to Alice that if they continue to follow the
sun west they will keep riding into day, and night will never
come, but even as they rush ahead, the cabin grows dim and
they travel in the chilly half-glow of evening until the train
comes into a station.

—Well, Alice's father says, —I guess I'll stretch my legs.

He closes the cabin door softly behind him, and Alice picks
up his map. Little blue circles are drawn around all the
cities in Oklahoma that fall along the blue line her father
has drawn to trace the train's route south. She looks at each
city and tries to remember which is the capital of Oklahoma
as she waits for the train to pull out. When they have built
back up to speed and her father has not returned, she goes
to her bed and opens her book, willing herself not to look
out the window until they are completely out of the town,
but she looks too soon, and in one quick glance she sees a
bank, a hotel, a grocery store; out of each building walk tall,
gray, unhappy-looking men who look just like her father.

My father now lives in Oklahoma, she thinks, and she practices saying it out loud. —My father lives in Oklahoma, she
will say to her friends at school, to her teachers, to the
boyfriends she will have before too long. —He does very
well for himself there.

When they have left the town behind, she puts her book
down and leaves the cabin, closing the door quietly. As she
walks up the aisle, she lets her hands drift across the tops
of seats, hardly touching them at all. At this moment, her
father is sitting down to coffee in a restaurant, being served
by a middle-aged waitress with frosted hair, and when she

smiles at him, he will explain to her that he is not a happy man, that he has never been a happy man, despite his many opportunities. It's his wife, he will tell the waitress, and his daughter, and she will nod; she has an unhappy man at home just like Alice's father. Alice imagines him taking bites of his sandwich and smiling, wondering which hotel to stay in, what kind of car to buy, if he will have dessert. In her mind he is just about to pay the bill when she sees him, swaying in the breezeway just ahead of her. She is close enough to see the muscles in his jaw work as he looks out and watches his new life pass before him, and she turns and walks the other way. In the next car, or the car after that, her mother sits and smokes, waiting for someone to talk to, but before Alice can reach her, she feels a hand on her shoulder and turns to face Mr. Gregg.

—Well, he says, —imagine finding you here. I was just on my way to meet your mother.

He waits politely for a response, but Alice says nothing. Behind her is the door to a bathroom and she leans against it.

—You know, Mr. Gregg says, —your mother is a very re-markable woman. He smiles in a way that has nothing to do with Alice.

—She's not my mother, Alice says, and turns to enter the tiny bathroom, smaller even than the one in their cabin. It has a stainless-steel sink and toilet, both clogged with soggy lumps of paper, and a thin stream of water leaks from the faucet.

Alice looks at herself in the mirror. It is too soon, really, to tell what she will look like as an adult, whom she will most resemble, and if she will be beautiful, and although she knows she will care about that later, right now it does not matter. Right now she longs only to be done with all of it, to be old at last, and to creep about with a cane and sit in the sun, caring for nothing, all that she once loved tucked safely away from the sorrows of life. It is before her like a dream —to be an old woman, her skin gone dry and spotted, her hair a fragile cloud about her skull, just a frail relic in the middle of a field with nothing to do but let her eyes fill with sand. Right now it is all she wants to be, that old woman, but between them crouches the enormous responsibility of her own life. The train shudders over a warp in the track and Alice steadies herself against the sink and looks into the mirror, but there is no one there; she is already gone, disappeared into the bright frozen world that waits ahead.

```
┌─────────────────────────────┐
│                             │
│      A N O T H E R          │
│                             │
│      C O U N T R Y          │
│                             │
└─────────────────────────────┘
```

—Honey, my mother calls, and her voice echoes over the wooden floor into the kitchen, where I am spreading peanut butter on my toast. I lift my head and wait for her to call again.

—Honey, she says, louder. —Come in and meet your Uncle, and she pauses a moment, then says, —Carl.

I come into the room, where she is standing next to a tall, bored-looking man who fingers the change in his pockets and glances at me without interest.

—Hi, I say.

—Hi, he says in my general direction. —Are you ready? he asks my mother. —The show starts soon.

—We're going to the movies, my mother says to me as she wraps a long blue scarf around her neck. —You'll be okay alone?

She turns to the man with a radiant smile. —Let's go, baby, she says.

When she bends to pick up her purse, his eyes travel slowly down her body; then he glances quickly at me, then at the floor and around the room, but he does not look at my mother again. As he turns away, jingling, my mother holds her coat out to him, but he is already at the door and she puts it on herself.

—Don't wait up, baby, she says, blowing me a kiss, her eyes already on the man's back as he walks out of our apartment.

I lock the door behind them and listen to my mother's heels tap down the hallway.

—Cute kid, the man says, his voice slightly muffled as they walk away.

—She's not a kid, my mother says. —She's sixteen. She pauses a moment. —Seventeen, she says.

The heavy glass outer door bites off the rest of their conversation, and I go to the window to watch them pass. Our apartment is at street level, and I can see them only from the knees down–my mother's long thin legs and ankles, and behind them the man's beige slacks and flat brown shoes. They kick up leaves as they go by, and I can tell by the tilt

of my mother's heels that she is leaning against the man.
Above me I hear Mr. Rosenberg wheel to his window. Because he is higher up, he has a better view—he can see if
they talk or kiss as they walk. I can only imagine them at
the street corner, my mother's arm draped loosely around
the man's shoulder as he looks up and down the street,
lights a cigarette, pulls his coat tightly about him. Mr. Rosenberg can watch them for two or three blocks, but all
I can see is the street, the wheels of cars, and the featureless walls of the buildings across from me. There is really
nothing else to see from this window, but my mother
spends most of her time here, looking out through the
iron bars. —You can tell a lot from people's shoes, she
tells me, —and the way they walk, but when I ask her to
tell me then what a pair of red sneakers says to her, or
some penny loafers, she looks off through the dusty glass.
—Well, she says, —they're really going by too fast to tell
much.
Even though we have lived here for years, I still find myself
expecting the view to change, but as every season passes, it
is always the same: in the winter, feet kick dirty snow
against our window, and the rest of the time they scuffle
through stiff leaves or trash. Sometimes a scrap of paper
catches in the window bars and flaps in the wind until someone pulls it out or it blows away.
When my mother is out of his sight, Mr. Rosenberg pounds
on the floor, but I stay at the window. Across the street small
children in tiny white uniforms enter the building that
houses a karate studio upstairs. Mr. Rosenberg pounds
again, and I walk into the kitchen and turn on the radio.
Above, he follows me, a rubbery running squeak along the
ceiling. He listens as I switch stations. I leave the radio on
as I go out and I close our door as quietly as I can, turn the
key in the lock slowly until I hear a faint click, and climb

the stairs on tiptoe, but when I knock on his door, he is already waiting at the other side.

—Who is it? he asks, and when I tell him, he begins undoing his locks, then pulls the door open against the chain and looks at me.

—Oh, he says. —You.

In the dreary sliver of world protected by the weak chain, a burglar would see nothing of value: an old television set, a splintery piano covered with photographs in cheap frames, Mr. Rosenberg's thin dry face. He closes the door and un- hooks the chain.

—So, he says, wheeling toward the television. —Your moth- er's gone out.

The television is already on, humming quietly in the corner, throwing a shifting pattern of light out across the floor and walls. My mother never let us have a television. —It's the one thing I ever did right with you kids, she sometimes says. And, as children, we sat through long evenings while televi- sions flicked on in the houses all around us, changing the shadows, changing the color of the night outside the win- dows; every day at recess, when the other children came together to talk about their favorite shows, we stood loosely by, feigning disinterest, but hungering for news of people we had never even seen. I don't think Mr. Rosenberg ever turns his television off, just lowers the sound when there is nothing on that he wants to watch. Sometimes, early in the morning, before anyone is awake, I'm sure I can hear it hum through our ceiling, and I wonder what might be on, as Mr. Rosenberg sits dozing in front of it, waking occasionally to watch, then sliding back to sleep. He spends the rest of his time rolling restlessly around his apartment; if he ever really sleeps, it is in his chair, sitting up like a cat or a horse, and only for short periods of time.

He turns the sound up now, and as a show comes on, he

rolls back to the shadows in the corner, and I sit in the straight wooden chair he leaves for me in the middle of the floor, close to the television. He chooses what we watch, which is generally whatever channel the TV happens to be on, and we never speak, not even during the commercials. Occasionally he makes a noise, a sigh, a small exclamation, but I never turn around. The only other sound comes from the TV and the steady rhythm of his breath as he lights and smokes cigarettes. He has a large plastic ashtray taped to the arm of his wheelchair, but only rarely does he use it; usually when he has smoked a cigarette down to the filter, he drops it on the floor beside him and lights another. His floor is covered with the small dark scars of burnt-out cigarettes. In good weather, he rides the rickety elevator downstairs, then parks himself outside in front of the doorway to our building where he sits and smokes all day, all by himself, unless someone stops and talks to him. —Step on that, he'll say, dropping a burning butt on the ground, and he's got another one lit before you've lifted your foot.

—One of these days, my mother says, —he'll burn the place down. He'll kill us all, she says with satisfaction, but she smokes the same way, constantly, and our apartment is gray and grimy with smoke.

—Oh, your father hated it, she says. —That's why our marriage broke up. He said I was trying to give him cancer.

At other times, though, she says it was money, another man, another woman that broke up their marriage. Once, she turned sadly to me from the window and said, as if she'd been thinking about it for a long time, —You know, before you kids were born—and her voice trailed off. —I don't know, she went on. —Things just seemed to be different then.

She lit a cigarette and looked right through me, while outside on the street a woman walked by wheeling a broken grocery cart full of plastic bags.

Mr. Rosenberg lights a cigarette behind me and I get comfortable in my hard chair. In front of us, flickering image gives way to flickering image, family succeeds family, plot follows plot, and Mr. Rosenberg lights and drops cigarettes, the sharp hiss of a match followed by the sharper inhalation of breath. When the news comes on at eleven, Mr. Rosenberg stirs.

—So, he says. —So. Found your brother yet?

I turn the sound on the television down low, but I keep my eyes on the screen. Mr. Rosenberg has been asking this question regularly since my brother left more than a year ago.

—He's not lost, I say. —He just moved out.

In truth, though, we have not seen him for several months, and I don't know where to find him, so I suppose he could be called lost, and I do spend part of most days looking for him.

—Well, Mr. Rosenberg says, —he's going to be lost if you don't find him pretty soon.

I say nothing and watch a young man being carried out of a burning building on the lower East Side.

—I don't know, Mr. Rosenberg says. —It's a wonder you haven't disappeared too, the way things go.

—He hasn't disappeared, I say. —He's around.

—Listen, he says. —You just listen. My Kathy. She was around, too, and then, all of a sudden, just like that, she wasn't. She was lost. Just like that.

He gestures at his array of photographs, all of them but one pictures of girls and women–his wife and five daughters. In the odd one, he is standing next to his wife, watching her smile as she brings a cigarette to her lips. All the girls look

pretty much alike to me, thin and dark, with the routine
false smiles and startled eyes of photographs. Mr. Rosenberg shakes his head.

—I don't know, he says. —I should have seen it then, in the
picture. I don't know, he says again. —Maybe not. There
were so many of them.

On the news a man is being pushed through a crowd, several
grinning policemen at his back. Downstairs the front door
opens and snaps closed, and footsteps follow in the hallway.
I rise.

—I guess I'd better go, I say. —That might be my mother.

Mr. Rosenberg looks at his watch. —Hah, he says. —Too
early. He nods, but I stay standing as someone clicks down
the hall and climbs the stairs slowly past us and up to the
floors above.

—See? he says, but I say I'd better go anyways.

—What are you in such a hurry for? he asks. —You got no
TV. Your mother's not home.

On the news someone charts a pattern of snow from North
Dakota through the Midwest, on its way to New York. I
cannot imagine what North Dakota could be like.

—What do you do down there anyways? Mr. Rosenberg
asks.

—I read, I say. —Or do crossword puzzles. I listen to the
radio.

I don't tell him how sometimes when I am alone I follow the
rubbery trail of his chair as the floor creaks above me, tracing his passage from room to room, imagining his face, the
smoke in his lungs, the things he thinks about. Every now
and then I can feel him poised directly above me, listening,
and we wait together, breathless, until one of us finally
steals away, leaving the other hovering uncertainly. These
are some of the things I do, but mostly what I do is wait,
with my mother or without her, for something to happen.

Mr. Rosenberg drops his cigarette on the floor and wheels over to me.

—What else?

Sometimes, I tell him, I feed the pigeons in the alley. The roofs here are covered with pigeons that flutter down to eat from the Dumpsters in the alley. Because we are on the first floor, our side windows are too thick to see through–the glass is greenish and dimpled–so I used to throw bread on the walk out front and watch the pigeons from our window, but my mother said it depressed her to watch all those birds scrabbling after a few crusts of bread, so now I feed them in the alley. No matter how regularly I come with food, they still scatter at my approach, then gently descend as I toss the bread, but they won't come near me, and wait until I back out of the alley to eat any bread that's dropped near my feet. They cover the ground efficiently, crowding so close together that when I watch them from the sidewalk, if I almost close my eyes, they look like one big bobbing gray and white shape, like something from a dream.

Before my brother left, he sometimes came with me to feed the pigeons, but now that he is gone, I go out alone. Their feathers are getting thicker as winter approaches.

Mr. Rosenberg wheels around and looks at the wall that faces the alley. His windows are clear glass, but he keeps his shades pulled most of the time, since the building next door is only a few feet away.

—Pigeons, he says. —Rats with wings. He lights a cigarette and tosses the match on the floor. —Get a cat.

—I want a cat, I say, —but my mother says it's too expensive.

—Expensive? he says. —What's to buy? I had cats. Five of them. Beautiful. Pigeons. Hah.

He stares at the television for a while. —What else?

—What?

—What else? What else do you do?

My only other activity is walking up and down streets, looking for my brother. I don't even know anymore why I do
this, except that somehow I feel it is expected of me; also,
things were different before he left, and I suppose I think if
he was back, things would be different again, but this is not
something I want to tell Mr. Rosenberg, so I finally say,
—Nothing.

—I thought so, he says, dropping his cigarette. —You ought
to do something, he says, and wheels over to the wall. He
stops under the photograph of his daughter Brenda. She is
smiling and her body is split by a wide red sash that reads
"Miss Florida."

—Be like Brenda, he says. —Do something.

In the lighted windows of the karate studio across the street,
neat rows of children jump up in the air with their legs
extended. When they land, their mouths open and close
silently. Mr. Rosenberg lights another cigarette.

—Maybe your mother won't come home tonight, he says.

—Who knows? It happens to everybody sooner or later.

He holds his cigarette to his lips and gazes at me. When I
leave, he is still sitting under Brenda's picture, but I wait on
the steps, and after a moment I hear him roll across the
floor, then, as I walk downstairs, each lock snapping home.

I try to turn my locks as quietly as possible, try to move from
room to room to room, and get in bed, and turn out the light,
all without making a sound, but even so, I'm sure I can hear
him follow me; he gives himself away with the tiny whisper
of a match, and the slow hiss of wood as the floor burns
above my head. I have lived here for a long time, though,
and sometimes I'm not sure exactly what I imagine and what
is really happening. There is so much that seems real, yet
can't be. Underneath us, the subway passes and the whole

building shakes. Mr. Rosenberg wheels away and turns up the volume on his television.

I lie in bed listening to the blowing leaves rattle against the windows, watching the light change against the smokey glass on the alley, and I plan my dream about New Jersey. For months now, I have been dreaming of New Jersey, where we lived once; it is where my father lives now, with his new family. In my mind, it is all beautiful lawns, trees, grass, and children, but when I told my mother this, she just laughed.

—New Jersey, she said. —Everybody wants to get *out* of New Jersey. Why do you think they have so many bridges and tunnels? Just be glad you're here already and don't have to make the trip.

—But we were happy there, I said, and at the moment I believed that we were, although I don't really remember it.

She laughed. —Nobody's happy in New Jersey, she said.

—Don't you remember? But all I remember is a green lawn, a black dog, and my brother's bony brown legs as he played in the yard.

—That part about the dog, my mother said. —You're making that up. We never had a dog. Your father's allergic.

But I could swear I remember it waiting for me in our yard, and I could swear I remember waking up to feel its rough fur, as it slept at the end of my bed. I could swear I remember this.

In my dream, Mr. Rosenberg sits in a circle of smoldering cigarettes; the building is burning, and my mother is inside, but when the wall crumbles and falls, our window is left standing, and my mother's image is seared against it, striped with shadows of the iron bars. Behind her, men rise from the ashes and walk toward me. —Honey, my mother whispers, —baby.

* * *

The train cuts through my dream and the world trembles
every time it passes. When my mother comes home, Mr.
Rosenberg rolls restlessly across the floor above us. My door
opens a crack and through my closed eyes, I can see my
mother in the strip of light. From the bathroom comes the
sound of water, a toilet flushing. She closes my door gently,
and Mr. Rosenberg follows her trail to bed. —Honey,
she whispers, —baby, and Mr. Rosenberg listens for a
while until the radiator comes on and the hiss and clatter
drown out all other sound. He wheels slowly back across
to the windows over my room. I can hear each cigarette
butt hit the floor. He sits, staring out the window, smoke
rising around him, and when I finally fall asleep, the city
is beginning to stir: the horses in the Park stables snort
and lift their heads, pigeons flutter around men in doorways, and cabs come out to cruise aimlessly as dawn splits
the city open.

At breakfast the man is gone and my mother's face is tired
and pale. She picks up the newspaper and glances at the
headlines.
—More bad news, she says. —I don't know why you get this
thing.
—For the puzzle, I say. —It's got the best one.
—That's a lot of bad news for one puzzle, she says, and
pokes in her pockets, looks around the table for her cigarettes, then goes into the living room.
—Damn, she says. —Listen, honey, she calls, and comes
back into the kitchen. —Would you go get me some cigarettes? Carl smoked all of mine. There's money in my purse.
She sits down and picks up the paper. —Unless he took that
too, she says to herself.
Just before the door closes behind me, she calls my name

and I catch the door with my foot. —Baby, she says. —Get
me a bottle of gin, too, would you?
I don't ask her about the man. He will come back or he will
not come back, and either way, sooner or later, he will be
replaced by another. At first, right after my brother left,
they stayed awhile, days sometimes, even a week or two. A
couple of them even moved in, in a haphazard kind of way.
I would come home to see a pair of shoes under the couch
and my mother would call me in to meet a man who nodded
at me, then looked quickly back at my mother, hardly believing his good fortune at finding a woman so beautiful.
Like this they came and went, but each of them had a life
somewhere else that waited impatiently for his return, and
sooner or later they were routed out by a wife or a girlfriend,
or driven home by the sight of a fatherless child on the
corner. Now they stay only briefly and never move in, but
they still come and go, and they all pay pretty much the
same attention to me. I wonder if they remember me when
they think back on their time with my mother. Sometimes I
see them on the street, and they look away so quickly I can't
tell what they are thinking. My mother sits by the window
and waits for them to come back to her; she watches feet
pass by and wonders which of them belong to a man she has
loved. Every now and then she turns to me where I sit reading a book or working a puzzle, and she looks at me as if she
is trying to place me exactly. —I've been a good mother to
you kids, she says. —Haven't I? I always nod and she turns
back to the window to count the cars, the men, the moments. She is sitting there now, waiting for me to return
with her gin and her cigarettes.

—Well, well, says the boy at the liquor store, and he slicks
his hair back before leaning forward into the thick glass
partition between us. —It's my sweetheart. Hi, beautiful,

he whispers, then stands up straight. —You busy tonight? he asks. —Me and my friends, we're having a party. He winks when he says the word "party."
—Jimmy, his uncle says from behind him. —Just get the lady her merchandise. We have other customers.
I look around, but aside from a few drunks scattered across the sidewalk, I am the only person here.
—So, the boy says, —what will it be today? Champagne? Perhaps a bottle of our finest Chablis?
—Gin, I say, and he laughs.
—Your mama sure does get thirsty a lot these days.
I slide a fifty through the slot, and he picks it up, examines it carefully, holds it to the light. —You don't got nothing smaller?
He bags a bottle of gin and slides it partway through the slot, but when I take it, he pulls it back, holding on to the neck.
—Oh, baby, he says. —What you do to me.
He turns and raises his eyebrows to his uncle, who laughs.
—Jimmy, he says, —I think the lady don't like you.
—Oh, Jimmy says, —she likes me okay. He turns back to me and presses his damp forehead against the glass.
—You're gonna love me, he says. He shrugs. —Who else you gonna love?
I can hear him laughing as I walk down the block with the gin.

My mother turns from the window and smiles when I hand her the bottle. —Well, she says, —I guess it must be cocktail hour.
Above, Mr. Rosenberg follows her into the kitchen, listens to the rattle of the paper bag and the clink of ice. My mother looks up at the ceiling.
—That crazy bastard, she says. —Doesn't he have anything better to do?

*   *   *

When I go out to look for my brother, she is back at the window. The world trembles as a train passes and I say goodbye, but she doesn't notice me leave.

My searches for my brother are halfhearted and fruitless, but they give me something to do. When he first left, he moved in with a boy named Tony, whom my mother called his "friend." After he'd been gone a few months, he brought Tony to meet us.

—Your brother and his . . . friend are coming for dinner, my mother said, and we cooked macaroni, peas, chocolate pudding, all of his favorite foods. I expected Tony to be reserved and uninterested in us, but he was friendly and tried to help my mother with the food. My brother's eyelids were smeared with blue, his cheeks painted a fainter shade of red, perhaps, but otherwise he'd hardly changed in the few months he'd been gone. At dinner he said almost nothing, ate even less.

—Honey, my mother said, —aren't you hungry?

He looked straight at her for a moment, beating his long lashes as he blinked, then shook his head.

—No, he said, and held out his hand. —Look at this. He circled one thin wrist with his fingers. —I've gained weight since I moved in with Tony.

Tony shifted uncomfortably. —You should have seen him when I met him, he said. —Skin and bones. He shrugged. —I'm Italian. I tell him to eat. He doesn't eat.

When my brother finally left him, Tony called us. He had gone back to Buffalo, where he was from, and wondered if my brother had come back home.

—He probably found a nice girl, my mother said when she hung up. —He'll bring her home to meet us and everything will be fine. Like before, she said. —Remember?

But all I remembered of him before he left were the glances exchanged between the liquor-store boy and his friends behind my brother's back as he walked bravely down the street, his eyes and cheeks painted impossible colors.
—Faggot, one of them would call out sooner or later.
—Little faggot, and a strange small smile would cross my brother's face as they threw names at his back.
For a while after he left, I used to see him around, standing on some street corner talking to a boy as beautiful as himself, or I'd catch sight of him through the window of a coffee shop, always talking, always moving his thin hands, opening and closing his black eyes. The last time I saw him—in the spring, I think—he took me to his apartment. On the way there I imagined a thousand different, tastefully decorated rooms, but his place was a tiny box at the top of five curving flights of stairs. I could hear his breath shorten as we rose, and I concentrated on the wallpaper as I climbed behind him, running my hand over the bumpy yellow pattern.
His apartment was the shade of twilight. He had hung blankets and towels over all the windows, and only bright bits of light poked through holes here and there.
—The sun keeps me up, he said, reaching for the light switch. —Close your eyes. But I kept them open, and when the light came on, cockroaches scattered across all the surfaces, scrabbling into holes, ledges, dark spaces. My brother smiled sadly as one rushed across the sink. —When I lived with Tony, we didn't have any cockroaches. I don't know why. Maybe he did something special.
He turned the water on, but the roach darted safely up over the side of the sink. —I wish now I'd paid attention, he said. The light in his apartment wasn't good to him; it turned his skin a kind of flat orange, and he looked weary and bored,

but when the phone rang, a sharp little light came into his
eyes, and his smile, as he talked, seemed genuine.

—Darling, he said. —Of course I'm free.

When I left, he was leaning into the bathroom mirror, paint-
ing blue lines around his eyes, one eye at a time. —Keep in
touch, he said, turning to look at me with one dark eye, the
other as light as the sky, surrounded by pale, blind skin.

After I hadn't seen him for a while, I went back to the
building, and climbed up to his apartment, but the door
opened with a harsh bright glare, and the ratty-looking man
who peered out at me was no one my brother would ever live
with. I asked about him anyways, and the man shook his
head.

—How the hell should I know who lived here before me? he
asked. He came out on the landing and watched me walk
down the curving stairs. —How the hell should I know? he
shouted down at me; he was still standing up there when I
left the building.

Every so often I come back to this neighborhood, and make
wide circles around the building, just in case; my brother
looks out at me from the face of every young man who walks
along, eyes darting as he searches out, yet turns away from
his own desperation. They are all made old with that rav-
aged, too soon sense of their own ends, and as they walk on,
they drag their gazes behind them, laying them like a net
across the city. I watch them turn and stroll with a fevered
weariness, exhausted by each stroke of time, each beat of
the heart that moves them, until, tired of watching, I leave
for home.

—Darling, I hear behind me, but it's not meant for me and
I don't even bother to look back. A scarf flicks through the
air across the street, a blue-and-orange splash, but it's
caught in the hand of another man, and I walk on.

* * *

—Honey, my mother says, —say hello to your Uncle Nicky, and the man she is with turns to me, a shady smile on his broad face.

—Hiya, kid, he says, and his eyes pass from my face to my feet and right back up again. —Cute little thing, arntcha?

—You have food on your tie, I say, which is true.

He looks down at his tie and glances nervously at my mother, his face reddening. —Shouldn't you be in school? he asks me. —How old are you anyways?

My mother smiles cautiously at him, her eyes darting to the greenish stain on his tie, then back to his yellow eyes.

—Back so soon, says the boy at the liquor store. —I knew you couldn't stay away from me.

I pass the money through, take the bottle, and turn away.

—Hey, he says. —No kiss from my sweetheart?

—I'm not your sweetheart, I say.

—What? he says. —You don't like me? Maybe I'm not pretty enough? Like your brother? You like your boys pretty?

—You're pretty enough, I say, and he is, dark skin and dark eyes over a gleaming white T-shirt. He's pretty like all his friends, who stand on the corner, waiting for him to get off work. In the winter they wear black leather over their white shirts, but they always look the same, and they are never in a group of less than three. The years will pass quickly for them, but now they are young, and they have big plans; today they gaze at a bundle of rags dozing on the sidewalk across the street. As Christmas comes closer, the winos and junkies get bigger handouts, and the boys have had their eyes on this one for a while. They lean against the wall and wait for the man's hand to slip, and his green bottle to go

rolling across the pavement. Sooner or later, one of the boys
will cross the street, take what's in the man's pockets, and
spend it on a new pair of bright white sneakers.

It's not even Thanksgiving yet, but big red bows are tacked
onto the telephone poles, and nearly every tree that struggles up out of the sidewalk is draped with a string of lights.
If Christmas comes and goes, it will be the first we have had
without even a visit from my brother. Although we do not
really celebrate holidays, they seem a convenient way to
keep track of time. Things are always happening here, but
they are always the same things: children scuttle in and out
of alleyways until they finally settle, tired and confused,
against a wall; boys become men, who drift along until
something catches their attention; women put their hands to
their mouths and call their children home. Something is
always happening here, but it's never exactly what we were
waiting for, so we just go on with our lives, and what occu-
pies us right now is waiting for my brother. My mother grows
nervous as the days cool and the nights turn cold.

—He's going to get the flu, she says. —He's going to freeze
to death in those awful apartments down there.

She shakes her head and looks out at the chilly street.
—What could I do? she says, turning to me. —I've tried.
I've tried to be a good mother to you kids.

The sun is going down, and behind her the building across
the street glows pink in the dying light. Above her, Mr.
Rosenberg wheels back and forth over a little worn square
of floor, thinking of his daughter Brenda.

—Honey, my mother says. —Kiss your Uncle Nicky hello.
He stares at her with no expression at all on his face.
—Nick, she says abruptly. —Your Uncle Nick. His thin
blond hair is combed straight back; the skin on his head is

the same pinkish yellow color as his hair, and his eyes are
like stains in the middle of his face.
—Well, he says. —That's right. He smiles down at me.
—That's right, he says again. —Kiss your Uncle Nick. You
can call me Nicky, he says, and my mother watches him,
twisting her scarf around and around in her hands.
When they come home, I bury my head under my pillow. I
don't hear them, but Mr. Rosenberg creeps quietly across
the floor and listens as I sleep.

In the middle of the night, I open my eyes and Nick is
standing in my doorway. He does not move, does not
breathe; he simply stands and watches me. I can't see his
eyes. He could be anyone. Above us, in his excitement, Mr.
Rosenberg lights cigarette after cigarette, throwing each to
the floor unsmoked. After a while my door closes, then my
mother's. Mr. Rosenberg sighs deeply and wonders if he
should pick up the smoldering cigarettes, or leave them to
burn long snaky scars in the wood, until finally he drifts off
into a dream of sleep.

Sometime before morning I hear a rustle of bodies and
voices.
—Goddamnit, my mother says, and a sharp crack of skin on
skin follows.
Mr. Rosenberg jerks his head up, startled awake by the
sound; he peers into the shadows of his room until, satisfied
that nothing is there, he slips away again. I close my eyes
and try to remember whether or not I had been sleeping.

In the morning one of my mother's eyes is dark and puffy,
but it's the other one that looks bruised.
—So, I say, unable to stop myself, —where's Nicky?

She reaches for her cigarettes wearily, as if she has been
asked this question every morning for years, and still has
not found an answer. —Don't you get tired of toast? she
asks, lighting a cigarette.

She rises, as if with great effort, and walks slowly into
the next room, the sash of her bathrobe trailing behind
her.

—Baby, she says from her chair by the window, —I could
really use a drink.

When she bends her head to look through her purse for
money, I can see the thin wires of gray running through her
hair. She looks up at me with one darkened eye, the other
as thin and transparent as a child's.

—I've been a good mother to you kids, she says, and even
though her dark eye is swollen almost shut, that's the only
one I can look at. —Haven't I? she asks. —Haven't I?

Behind her the rush-hour crowd of feet passes, too quickly
to tell anything at all about them. Finally I turn to leave, but
her voice catches me at the door. —Honey, she says to the
crowd of feet passing through the window. —You wouldn't
ever leave me, would you?

She turns to face me and her dark eye settles heavily on my
face. I shake my head. She smiles. —You can't leave me,
she says, turning back to the window. —I'm your mother.
She lights her cigarette, and I wait in the doorway a moment, until the smoke has settled in a circle around her
head.

—Sweetheart, says the boy at the liquor store. —Darling.
His new sneakers glow in the dim store, and his friends
stand closer together on the corner as the temperature falls.
They call as I pass and watch me with hungry, mean eyes.
They mark the passing of days, moving together for warmth,

glancing nervously at the sky when it threatens to snow. In our alley, the pigeons move stiffly, flying as if on mechanical wings. Upstairs, Mr. Rosenberg circles his room tirelessly, sometimes pounding for my company, sometimes forgetting me altogether. My mother sits at the window watching the last leaves blow away, until the dark bruise around her eye has faded.

—Honey, she says, —say hello to your Uncle Bill.
A tall black man smiles at me. —William, he corrects her patiently.
—William, she says.
—Nice to meet you, he says politely, but he's already lost interest in me, and turns back to my mother. His skin gleams as he lights a cigarette. His teeth gleam. His hair gleams and his eyes gleam and the material of his shirt gleams as he moves. My mother smiles and touches it with the tips of her fingers.

—Black men are different, she tells me, although I am not interested in hearing this. —They don't hate women as much as white men do. She pauses to light a cigarette.
—But they do hate them.
I watch several pairs of feet pass by the window.
—You're going to have to know all of this someday, she says. —You are.

—Honey, my mother says, —this is your Uncle Nathan. I take his hand, which he offers kindly to me. He shakes my hand kindly and he smiles kindly and lets go of my hand quickly and kindly. Everything about him is kind, and because of that he will be gone soon, before his kind eyes fill with anger.

* * *

When he has been gone a few days, my mother stands in front of the mirror and moves her head from side to side, pulling a few gray hairs away from her head.

—I need a change, she says, and soon we are at the beauty parlor on the corner, where they make a great fuss over her, how little gray she has, how young she looks to have such a tall daughter; in a soft mix of Spanish and English they hover around her while I flip through magazines. Permanent-wave solution cuts through the air and makes my eyes water. She is so beautiful, they tell her, and she smiles and says, Oh, you should see my son. They all smile and nod and talk about their own sons, their own husbands. The prettiness of men is something for which they have all suffered. The woman behind the counter watches me as I turn the pages of hairstyle magazines. —You'll be a beauty one day, too, she says, as though she is pronouncing a sentence of doom. When my mother is through, all of her hair is dark again, with a reddish tint, and she stands in front of me, looking at me as if she is trying to remember exactly where it is we met. She pats her stiff hair. —Well? How do I look? she asks, and turns around so I can see the back.

Mr. Rosenberg is sitting in front of our apartment house, taking in the last days before winter. A circle of butts surrounds him and he is tossing pieces of bread to several pigeons gathered a few feet away. The chunks of bread he throws are too big to eat at once, or to carry off, and the birds peck at them, finally abandoning the larger pieces, then drifting back to pick at them again.

—Well, ladies, he says as we come closer. —Out for a stroll? His skin looks bluish in the bright light of day.

—Watch this, he says, and he holds up his bag of bread, then empties it over his feet and on the ground around his chair. One fat pigeon comes cautiously forward, then another, and in a moment the air around him is filled with the beating of wings; as the birds settle over the crumbs Mr. Rosenberg has dropped, his legs and the bottom of his chair disappear under a bobbing blanket of gray, and he smiles as they peck at the bread. They have never come this close to me.

—Hah, he says. —Not bad for rats with wings.

As my mother passes him, she bumps his chair, and the birds scatter in a flurry. —You're going to turn to dust there, she says, —to a big heap of dust and ashes and then we'll just sweep you away.

He winks and smiles at me as I follow my mother. —Hey, sweetie, he says, but when I turn back, he is turned to ashes; the words come from a heap of dust and ashes gently smoldering on the sidewalk.

Men come in and go out and my mother waits patiently by the window, tapping a beat to the radio station, smoking. Occasionally her hand moves to her hair, running through it, patting it softly. When she is out of gin, she sends me for more.

—Hey, says the boy at the liquor store. —My cousin seen your brother.

—Your cousin, I say. —He doesn't even know my brother.

—Oh, he knows him, the boy says. —He knows him *real* good. He seen him downtown. And he says he don't look so hot.

He passes the bottle through the slot and raises one eyebrow. —*If* you know what I mean, he says.

I know what he means, but I pretend I don't, and give him my money. When he pushes my change through, he leans forward and presses his lips against the glass. The greasy shimmer of his kiss hangs between us and I turn to go.

—Hey, he says, —don't you even want to know where he seen him?

The street he named is full of men and boys, leaning against buildings, standing alert at windows, idly walking up and down past doorways. They cast out oblique glances, never looking directly into each other's faces, and when they catch glimpses of their own reflections, they stop to adjust their scarves, or their ties, or their sunglasses.

I am only here an hour or so when I see my brother walking down the street toward me. He is with a man, against whom he gently sways from time to time. Each time my brother leans into him, the man moves just slightly away, inching toward the curb. When my brother sees me, he straightens, his face changes.

—Robbie, I say, —I've been looking all over for you.

His companion looks uneasily up and down the street and takes a step back. —Listen, he says.

—No, wait, Robbie says, and looks at me, staring right into my eyes.

—I wanted to talk to you, I say. —Just for a minute.

—Listen, the man says again. —Listen, I'll call you, okay? He begins to edge away, already looking down the street.

—Okay, Robbie says. —Wait. He pulls a matchbook from his pocket, digs for a pencil, and scribbles down a number.

—Robert, he says, and hands the matchbook to the man, who puts it in his pocket without looking at it. —Don't forget, Robbie says. —I'll be home tonight.

—Yeah, the man says, and walks away. Robbie watches him for a moment, then turns to me.

—I've been looking for you, I say. —I wanted to talk to you. Now that I have his attention, I can't think of how to keep it. —Tony called, I finally say, although this was months ago.

—Tony called? He brings his fingers to his red lips and rubs them over his mouth, leaving a pinkish smear across his chin.

—He was in Buffalo. He wanted to talk to you.

—Buffalo? He looks out over the street, searching out the particular tilt of a jaw, the turn of a glance, a pair of eyes looking directly at him. —Buffalo, he says again. He catches the glance of a boy down the street who is pretending to look in the window of a bookstore, and I can feel him slipping away.

—Robbie, I say. —Listen.

—Robert, he says absently, still looking at the boy. —Remember, I go by Robert?

—Robert, I say. —Listen.

He pulls his glance back to me with some effort. His lashes are clumped together in little black spikes. —What? he says. —I have to go soon.

—Listen, I say again, and wonder what it is I am going to say, what I am going to do, but I know I have to say it quickly. —I'm going to New Jersey, to visit Dad.

—New Jersey? he says.

—I thought maybe we could move back there.

—To Jersey? he says. —With Dad? He leans backward slightly, tilting gently back and forth.

—Not *with* him. You know. Just *there*.

As I say it, it all makes a kind of sense, and I can see us in our little house, making breakfast in our sunny, yellow kitchen, bright blue curtains at the windows.

—Jersey, he says, and looks around him.

His eyes are like black holes. When I turn to wave goodbye, he is leaning against the window of a laundromat, talking to the boy from the bookstore. He smiles, running his fingers through the boy's shaggy hair.

*　*　*

Heading for New Jersey, the train rises up from underground. The man behind me rattles his paper and leans forward. I can feel his hot breath on my neck, and I keep my hand on the thin edge of the envelope holding my money and a picture of my mother and my brother.

As we cut through the gray New York neighborhoods, I catch frozen glimpses of other people's lives: behind a rusty fence, a boy leans high into the air, pushing a basketball toward a hoop, but we're gone before it falls, and he hangs there, floating in the dirty air; on a street corner, a woman lifts her baby from its carriage, stretching her long neck toward it, the baby reaching out for her face; in a cluttered alley, a cat crouches behind a garbage can, its tail whipping as it gazes at a pigeon pecking at something flattened on the ground—we are gone before it leaps.

At the station I get directions to the address I have gotten from the telephone book. The walk is no longer than those I have taken in search of my brother, but here the wide avenues are lined with trees and houses. Children and dogs and men stand around like lawn ornaments, paying almost no attention to me as I peer past them at house numbers. It is like another country. When I find my father's house, I stand across the street from it. My father leans over the engine of his car. He is tall and thin and his hair is turning gray in little patches. I watch him for a while, then cross the street and stroll past him. He looks up briefly, then back down to the engine. I stroll back and stop in front of him. He glances up, smiles politely, then bends his head again, but only for a moment. My mother once told me I have his eyes, and he has seen them. He looks up at me as if he is trying to remember the words to a song, and I wonder what it is I am supposed to call him.

—Catherine? he says, and I nod.

—Well, he says, looking around. —Well, he says again, and

then again: —Well. He wipes his hands on his khaki trousers, leaving long dark smears of grease, then looks with dismay at what he has done. He looks quickly back at me and opens his mouth to say "Well" again, but catches himself and closes it, smiling tightly.

—Well, he finally says. —What brings you to New Jersey?

—Oh, I say. —Nothing. Really.

He looks with longing at his house. His yard is neatly mowed, with little trimmed hedges all around the sides. Even the trees are neatly stripped of leaves.

—Oh, he says. —Well, how are you? He leans back against his car, settling stiffly in. All around us men rake up leaves, children wind around the legs of their mothers, dogs erupt in frantic little spasms of barking, then quiet just as suddenly.

—Fine, I say. —I'm fine.

—Good, he says. —Good. He looks again at his house. By now, several faces have appeared in the large front window. I smile at them, but they remain expressionless, and soon the curtain drops. My father watches the curtain fall, then looks back at me.

—Well, he says, —I suppose you'd like to come in? For a minute?

When I nod, he looks down at the black streaks on his pants, but does not move.

There is no one at the window when he opens the door. There is no one anywhere, but the house vibrates with human noises. Upstairs a stereo plays, from the kitchen comes the sound of running water, and somewhere a television is on. I recognize, over all the noise, the commercial jingle that is playing.

My father sighs, then calls out, —Roberta.

His new wife comes out of the kitchen, wiping her hands on

a dish towel, and smiles at me as she might smile at the paperboy. From nowhere come a boy, a girl, another boy. They are all blond, with blank puffy faces.

—This is Catherine, my father says, and he recites their names too quickly for me to catch any. The girl is closest to my age; maybe she is fourteen, clearly born before my father left us; she is not even his real daughter. Her eyes run up and down my body, and I try to remember without looking what I am wearing. The boys look at me with no real interest, just a kind of boy curiosity about what might happen next, and my father's wife continues to smile and wipe her hands on the towel. Like this we all stand until my father interrupts the silence.

—Well, he says, and we all look at him gratefully. —Well, he says again, and smooths his sweatshirt down over his pants. He looks at his wife.

—I think Catherine could use a Coke, she says. —After her long trip. My father stares at her as if she has spoken in an unfamiliar language. —Don't you, honey? she says, and he nods suddenly.

—Yes, he says. —Of course I do. Of course she could.

—You go on in the living room and sit down, she says, and waves me out of the hall. I walk a few steps into the living room and turn to wait for my father. All the children watch me, but he is staring at his wife and I realize that this is going to be harder than I thought. I try to remember or to imagine just what exactly I was going to say, but all I can think is that he has a nice house.

—You have a nice house, I say, and he and his wife stare at me, startled, until she turns and he joins me.

—Yes, he says. —I mean, thank you. Yes. I guess so. Scattered around the room are photographs in silver and wood frames. I don't look closely enough to see the faces. He sits on the edge of a chair and I sink deep into the couch.

—Well, he says, and his wife enters with a glass of Coke, which she puts carefully on a little wooden coaster. She smiles at me and leaves the room. My father watches her back until she is gone, then turns to me. When I pick up my glass, it leaves a wet ring on the coaster. My father smiles carefully.

—How's your brother? he asks.

—Oh, I say. —Fine. I try to place my glass back exactly on the ring. —He doesn't really live with us anymore.

—Oh? my father says. —What's he doing?

Upstairs doors open and close, and voices come from the kitchen. I try to hear what they're saying. While he waits for my answer, his hand reaches for a magazine on the coffee table. He strokes the cover, but does not pick it up.

—Well, I say finally. —He has a job. A good job.

—Yes, well, he says. —That's good. That's terrific.

—Yes, I say. —It is.

—And your mother, he says, not looking at me. —How is your mother? He runs his finger along the edges of the magazine, flipping the pages. When I take a sip of Coke, his eyes flick to the cover, reading the headlines.

—She's fine, I say. —Just fine. Great.

And for just one bright second, my father's eyes meet mine, and in this moment, so brief it may not even have occurred, he looks at me as my father, who loved me once, and who knows this cannot be true. But then his eyes dart away, back to his magazine, and the moment passes, gone so suddenly I will have trouble believing it happened. It leaves us in an airless silence, and I move closer to the edge of the couch. In a few minutes I will go back to New York, where, right at this moment, the basketball player stumbles to the ground, his shot clanging, unmade, off the rim of the hoop; the woman with the baby smiles up at a man who happens to be passing, her child forgotten; and in the alley, the cat springs after the pigeon, leaping right to the center of feathers and flapping wings.

My father sits back suddenly, putting his hands in his lap. A look of something almost like contentment settles on his face as he gazes across the room, and I try to think of something we have in common.

—Thanks for the birthday cards, I say. —And the money.

They have come regularly every year, more or less around the times of our birthdays, colorful impersonal cards with a ten or a twenty tucked inside, signed just *Dad*. For years I suspected that my mother was responsible for this, that she took the money from his regular child-care payments, and that this is what accounted for the rather terse signature. I suspected this even after it became clear to me that this was simply not something that would occur to my mother to do.

—Oh, my father says, embarrassed. —Well, it's the least I could do. He laughs nervously.

—It's nice of you to remember.

He looks confused, shifts in his chair. —Well, yes, he says.

—I guess it is. He looks around the room. —I guess your birthday is coming right up sometime soon, he says.

—A couple of months. I'll be seventeen.

He smiles. —Deirdre's birthday is coming right up too. She'll be fourteen. And the twins. He shakes his head, smiling. —They do grow up.

He stops suddenly, jarred by his words, and turns his attention back to the magazine. —Do you want another Coke? he says, making no move at all.

—I guess not, I say, twisting the glass round and round into the wet circle on the coaster.

—Well, he says, —it's been awfully nice of you to come all this way just to see us. Me.

He smooths his pants down over his thighs and prepares to rise and I think, *Wait*, but when I look up to say something,

he is gazing down at me, patiently waiting, and I recognize
the expression on his face, in his eyes: it is the look of every
man my mother has ever loved.

No one comes to the hall to see me off, only my father, who
says goodbye with his hand on the doorknob.
—Well, he says, and I say, —Well.
—Say hello to your brother.
—Okay.
He calls my name when I am halfway down the front walk,
but when I turn, he clearly does not know what to say. He
stares at me helplessly and opens his mouth, but nothing
comes out. He closes it and I turn again. When I reach the
sidewalk, I hear the door close. On either side of their
house, the houses look alike. A few dry leaves drift across
the lawns as the wind picks up, and the rising chill of evening has driven most of the neighborhood children inside. I
head back for the station and wonder what I could have been
thinking. What could you have been thinking? my mother
will say when I tell her and she'll turn her face to the wall.
Haven't I been a good mother to you kids? she will ask. I
count each block of cement in the sidewalk as dusk falls
over the quiet street, the quiet cars, the quiet families living
in each quiet house.

Mr. Rosenberg looks down at me through his gray window.
He is smoking and does not wave. When I knock at his door,
I hear him creak slowly across the floor. I am surprised to
see that the television is not on and that all of his window
blinds, even on the side wall, are raised.
—So, I say. —How about some TV?
He throws his cigarette on the floor and rolls back to the
window. —Oh, he says, —I don't know. Maybe your mother
was right about TV. He lights a cigarette and holds the

match up in front of his face. —It's cold in here, he says.
—Don't you think it's cold in here?

Through the uncovered windows I can see the people in the
building across the alley. An old man takes off his shirt and
stands in the cold, while next to him, only a thin wall away,
a woman pets her cat, blinded by the certainty that love will
come to her today, or tomorrow, and over them and under
them lives go on that are just the same.

—You know, Mr. Rosenberg says, staring out the window,
—you ought to do something with your life. You really ought
to. You just ought to do something.

He does not look at me when I let myself out. The streetlight
glints off the steel arms of his chair, and Brenda smiles sadly
down at him.

—Honey, my mother says as I open our door, and Nick
looks up from where he stands behind her, his hands hanging loose at her neck. She smiles as his eyes travel up along
my legs to my face, and I pull the door shut on them, but
before it closes, I see Nick pull the scarf from her neck and
let it fall to the floor.

She is in his arms again by the time I am on the street. I
look up at Mr. Rosenberg, but he doesn't see me, gazing
past me at a city full of people going on about lives that have
nothing to do with me. He drops his cigarette and wheels
away.

Right now my father is sitting down to dinner, smiling absently at the bright blond heads of his new children while
my brother sits in a dark room, turning to stone. In the alley,
pigeons rise and settle anxiously, shaking off the growing
chill. *Mother*, I want to call out, *Mother, I am dying*, but she
is falling once again into the arms of a man she loves.

At the End
of My Life

Because he is my brother, I will try to remember everything. I am waiting for him here at the edge of the campus, watching ragged clouds skid across a dirty sky. Across from me is the city, which comes right up to meet us, but we are cut off from it by a highway, cut off here with our books and our

stone buildings. Around me pass students, and above me
rises a statue of Winged Victory, its head long gone, the
enormous shadow of its wings stretched out across the black
grass. I wait here and try to remember everything.

In the neighborhood free-for-alls on the rolling lawn, he is
always the smallest, always the most vulnerable. —Glen,
Mother calls, sitting with Father and Uncle Bill and Aunt
Eileen. —Glen, she calls again, flicking her cigarette ash
onto the fresh-cut green of the lawn. —Don't break anything. Watch your glasses, watch your braces. For God's
sake, be careful if you're going to roughhouse like that.
—Elizabeth, she calls to me, —you watch him.
When I look over at her, her face is already turned up to
Father as she holds out her glass for a fresh drink, already
turned with a smile to Uncle Bill. She does not see me
watching Glennie through a pile of boys, and she never sees
me join the pile. When Glennie looks up with his myopic,
undirected gaze, I wonder what he sees. He turns his small
face to the ground, waiting for the boys to grow bored and
wander off to some other cruel game; he turns his face to
the ground to watch the beetles and ants fight it out over a
territory smaller even than his own. In front of the house,
Mother's laugh trails out over the lawn and ice clatters
against the sides of empty glasses. The boys wriggle off
eventually, and Glennie stays on his stomach, looking down
at the ground. When he raises his head, his face is cheerful,
but I know that in one way or another I will later pay for
this.

—Lizzie, he whispers. —Don't tell Mother I broke the lamp.
He looks up wildly at the sound of her car pulling into the
driveway, and looks down at the broken shard of lamp in his
hand.

—Tell her a burglar came in, he says. —Tell her that he tried to kidnap us and broke the lamp. Tell her that, he says, beginning to believe it himself. He hands me a piece of the lamp, and his eyes go sly and clever as he smiles a little half-smile. —Tell her he looked like Daddy.

When I tell my mother that our dog broke the lamp, running from window to window after a squirrel it spotted in the yard, she fingers a frosty silver streak she has just had put in her hair.

—Elizabeth, she says, already losing interest. —Did you and your brother break the lamp?

—No, Mother, I say. —Honest.

She turns to look at her new hair in the mirror. In the corner Glennie smiles, but later we are twice denied dessert: tonight for breaking the lamp, tomorrow for lying about it.

I tell Glennie that I wanted dessert, and he smiles. —Don't worry, he says. —I'll buy you a candy bar.

When I ask him with what, he opens his hand to show a few coins, a crumpled dollar bill. —With this, he says. —I got it from Mother's purse.

He closes his small fingers over the money and holds his fist against his fragile chest, smiling at Mother's purse, where it sits innocently on the counter. Our parents' bedroom door is closed and their voices are just a hum, an indistinct buzz.

Boys pass me by as I wait for Glennie here in the moonlight by the highway. Girls pass me by, and the statue casts a pale shadow against the ground.

Mother's purse sits innocently on the counter and the door to their room is closed.

—Lizzie, Glennie says, and he pulls me quietly over to the closed door. —Owlcake, he whispers, and we giggle, clamp-

ing our hands over each other's familiar mouth. —Owlcake, he breathes against my warm hand, and we run off to
our own bright rooms. —Owlcake? we offer one another;
—Madam, may I get you some owlcake?
We laugh and do not know why we are laughing. Their door
rises far above our heads, and I feel nervous as I laugh,
thinking of the owls that rise every night from the woods
behind our house.
There is something in his face I want to turn from, something strange and excited. But in the exact dark center of
his eyes, I see my own face looking out, huge and confused.
I look away from him, at the four walls of my room, painted
pink, at the white furniture, dotted with stuffed animals and
familiar fluffy things. —Owlcake, Glennie croons. His
hands are like soft little animals.

—Look, Lizzie, he says and I see that he has taped closed
the muzzle of our dog Puff. I watch her struggle for long,
domesticated minutes, until finally she comes to me, tail
wagging, dumbly begging for release. I reach for her, but
Glennie puts his hand on mine.
—Don't, Lizzie, he says. —I want to see if she can get it off
herself.
—It's mean, I say. —You'll make her mean.
He looks at me and smiles. —She loves me, he says.
—She'll always love me. He turns to Puff, who wags her tail
hopelessly. Soon she will live in the back yard, not mean but
not friendly, digging holes against the fence and watching
us from a distance.

I wait patiently, and in the windows of dorms girls hold
dresses up to their bodies and turn this way, that way,
seeing how they look, wondering what the boys they love

will think of this shirt, those shoes, the hair pulled back that way. They turn in the mirror and admire themselves and each other for the boys they love.

—Lizzie, he whispers. Like an insect he seeks the light at night, the moon coming through my window. His tiny heart beats against my hand and I tell him what I learned in science class today: that the heart is a muscle, made up of a long connected cluster of nerves. When it beats, the impulse runs down the cluster, activating each nerve ending, so that every heartbeat is nothing but a long involuntary tremor of nerves, a running impulse that can't stop itself once it's begun. He smiles and turns his face to the moon. —Look, Lizzie, he says, pointing to an owl coming up out of the woods. His heart beats, a long running pulse that feels like a cloud of moths fluttering against the wall of his chest.

Father works in the garden, digging away in the blazing sun, poking his trowel into the dirt. His blue shirt is marked with a pattern of sweat that runs wide across his shoulders and narrows as it trickles down the small of his back; it is like a butterfly pinned to his spine, spreading its wings across him as he bends to the dirt. Glennie sits rocking back and forth on his heels, staring down at the tiny mazes of life in the ground around him, looking up at Father, then back down at the grass. As he rocks, the sun glances off his glasses, so that his eyes, when he turns them on me, are like two blinding panes of flashing light. As Father digs into the lush waving flowers, Glennie watches, and hisses at me, —Lizzie, Lizzie, owlcake, and we slide into hilarious, uncomprehending collapse. Father looks up at us, Glennie rocking on his heels, me rolling backward on the grass. When Father waves his trowel, Glennie stops laughing and swats at me

with his arm. Father goes back to tending the bright heads
of roses and carnations sunk in dirt.

—Lizzie, Glennie says. —Don't you think Father will have
a heart attack? and I am shocked by this. I look away and
bright sunlight glitters off the chain-link fence. Behind it
Puff stares at us.

—Lizzie, he says again. —Don't you think he will? I do.

—That's bad luck, I say. —Don't even think about it.

He turns his eyes on me. Through the thick glass they are
the color of the ink that runs out of my fountain pen, faint
blue and brilliant both somehow.

—It's true, he says. —Look how hard he works.

I pretend he has not said this, and suddenly his hand darts
out and closes around the delicate wings of a butterfly. It is
his only talent, catching butterflies, snatching them right out
of the air, or from where they rest on the grass around him.
He catches them and brings them to me, opening his hand
to show a butterfly sitting there, like magic, until it flies
shakily off, or drops feebly from his hand.

It grows late as I wait here. A few lights go out in buildings.
Girls lie in the darkness, just a few feet away from the
strangers who are their roommates. They sleep and try to
grow accustomed to the strange patterns of breath, the
strange noises, the strange rustlings of people they don't
know lying in beds only a few feet away. Somewhere the boy
I will soon love tries to sleep. He pulls the covers up to his
chin and dreams of touching my pale skin.

What I remember: the sun stretching across my bed, the
crows quarreling in the trees, the quiet whisper of Puff's
tail against the floor as Glennie opens the door.

—Lizzie, he whispers in my ear, —time to get up. Lizzie,

he breathes. —Owl eyes, and I keep my eyes closed until I feel the pressure of his forehead against mine, his nose on my nose.

—One, two, three, he says, and I open my eyes to see his, spread like a shining mask over his face, half an inch from my own. I close my eyes again and wonder at the tiny fine bones of his face.

This is what I remember. This is all I remember and this is how I remember it.

—Lizzie, he calls. —Come. Look.

It is a late summer evening and all the children have gone home from our game of hide-and-seek. As they move away from this safe ground, under the streetlight that serves as home, I imagine they turn into monsters. Glennie is crouched under our parents' window, and when I join him, I see Mother's body and over her Father, arched backward, straining like a bone about to snap.

—Owlcake, Glennie whispers, and he lets go a high-pitched giggle. He smiles. —I watch them all the time, he says.

—Look at Father. He's going to have a heart attack.

They hear our voices and turn toward the window, ghost-faced, wondering what is there, but we back away, making noises that could be nothing more than the rustling of small animals in the bushes.

In my own bed, I cannot sleep. When I turn out the light, all I can see are their round ghost faces, glowing in the dark room.

The boy I will fall in love with wakes and walks to the mirror. He looks at himself and rubs his hand across the new stubble on his cheeks. He imagines what it must be like to touch my face.

*   *   *

At school Glennie is what they call difficult, behaving in ways that confuse teachers and administrators: he talks too loud, will not sing in his music class, breaks whatever he makes in art. Our teachers are always surprised to find we are related, and I can tell they see me differently then, watching me with sideways speculative looks. My parents shake their heads over the notes on his report cards, and put them down, fully intending to do something about it all, but time drifts away from them, and they sign them and send them back, settled by the sense that if the card has been signed, something must have been done.

Glennie is only two years younger than I. In the hallways and on the playground I watch the other children move uneasily away from him; they are deceived at first by how much he looks like them, his cheerful happy face, his neat little shoes and shirts and shorts.

In first grade he sits at the edge of the concrete playground, holding a stick; as the other children climb over the jungle gym, he whacks the stick against the ground, humming a little song and gazing intently at their arms and legs as they move like spiders over the bars.

In third grade he always wanders away from his class at recess, and I spot him, a little dark hump in the corner of the schoolyard, digging holes with his hands. He removes his shirt in the heat and his back glows, the brightest spot in the whole gray day, as he puts things in the holes, then covers them up.

I should do something, I think, there is something I should do, but I am only in the fifth grade. I am only in the fifth grade, I tell myself, and I turn to watch the children my own age, then go to join them.

* * *

Glennie's fourth-grade class is keeping a rabbit, to teach them about responsibility, and soon, the teacher has told them, they will experience the miracle of birth. Each child is given a week with the rabbit at home, but somehow Glennie's week never comes, even though he has made a bed for the rabbit in the corner of his room, and dug a little hole in the yard for it to rest in. He is already planning to bring home one of the baby rabbits as a pet, and when he tells my parents this, they nod absently in his direction. We'll see, we'll see, they murmur, and his face glows as he plans the fun he will have with his new pet.

When the children come in one morning, the rabbits have been born, five new rabbits, and one tiny dead one. The teacher picks the students who will get to keep a baby, and of course none of them is Glennie, but somehow in all the excitement and confusion he gets hold of the little dead one. A while passes before they notice the blood on his bright shirt, where he has hidden the rabbit against his chest, and when they take it away from him, he runs from the room. They find him later in the bathroom, gazing down into the toilet as he flushes it over and over.

Because my mother is shopping or at the beauty parlor or having lunch with her friends, I must walk Glennie home to change his shirt, and as I approach the office where he waits, I see him before he sees me. I stand in the hallway just out of his sight; he is bent over his knees, looking down at his feet, but even so, I can see the stain creeping across his shirt, and I run to the bathroom, where I don't have to believe this is happening.

I look at myself in the mirror. —I am in the sixth grade, I say out loud. —I am in the sixth grade, and I don't care, but the face that stares back at me does not resemble my own. For the first time I realize that he is going to get in my way. When I come back to the office for him, he smiles when he sees me. —Lizzie, he says. —Let's stop for candy on the way home. His shirt clings to his chest in dark, wet patches, but as we walk down the hall together, he takes my hand and smiles at the empty walls; behind the walls, children stare at figures on a dark board.

In the bathroom, the girl next to me, whom I would like to be my friend, says, —Your brother tried to steal that dead rabbit.
She pulls a tiny lipstick from her purse. —Didn't he?
I look at myself in the mirror. —No, I say.
She brings her face close to the glass. —He had blood all over his shirt, she says.
I watch her smear lipstick across her pink lips.
—He was bleeding, I finally say. —He has a disease that makes his chest bleed.
She looks over at the girl on her other side. Their eyes meet in the mirror and they trade their miniature cosmetics. The girl next to me draws large red circles on her cheeks and I smile at her.
I want these girls as my friends. I walk down the hall just a step behind them and grow older with each moment.
—Lizzie, Glennie calls from the water fountain where he stands alone, but I do not hear him as I walk down the hall with these girls. Our skirts rustle in the cold air.

What happens after this is what happens, and cannot be changed. Over the years only cruelties pass between us, and I do not remember them except as little flare-ups in a long glowing stretch of mirror. His cruelties are small, but dazzling in their sincerity. He calls me desperate names to get my attention, but I hear them only distantly; they are like the faint buzz of a fly caught between a window and a screen.

* * *

Glennie looks at me slyly over his cereal at the breakfast table, where I sit unwillingly, eating little, waiting to be released to school.

—Lizzie, he says, his voice rising and falling in a little song. —I saw that boy you like.

I look down at my bowl, soggy lumps of cereal floating in yellow milk. My parents do not look up from their papers, but they tilt their heads to listen, and after a moment their eyes meet.

—He was smoking pot, Glennie says, and laughs. —Right on the street corner.

My parents' heads swivel slowly toward me like heavy flowers waving on thin stalks. They gaze blindly at me, waiting for an explanation, while Glennie smiles and drowns the lumps of cereal in his bowl, pretending they are bugs clinging to crumbling boats.

When I walk by him later, he is standing in the open door, shirtless in the heat, trying to decide whether to stay in or go out. He has already forgotten the betrayal at breakfast, but I have not, and as I walk by him I am unable to stop myself. I watch my arm swing out, as though it belongs to someone else, and slap him hard on his back; it makes a horrible satisfying smack in the quiet afternoon and he turns to me with tears in his eyes. —Lizzie, he says, in horror and disbelief, touching his hand to his soft cheek. —You made me cry.

His cruel little deeds are forgotten in a moment, swallowed up in his strange days, but mine will never fade, each a testimony to the frailty of my love. This slap will resound through the years; it will draw for me all the boundaries of my past and my future, his face turning to me in slack-jawed

stunned innocence, the afternoon sun shining brightly behind him, his cheeks glittering with unaccustomed tears.

These years of closed doors–I can hardly believe they happen. I barely remember each moment even as it ends.
—Lizzie, he whispers at my door. —Let me in. I have to
talk to you. I look out the window and watch the owls gath-
ering in the trees. If he is gone before I sleep, I do not know.
I imagine him curling up outside my room, and I can hear
his slow breath through the thin door, his tiny heart beating
against the floor. I lock the door and leave him to his life.
He will get in my way and I will be left behind, mired in
whatever it is I feel for him. I have no other choice: I lock
my door and do not hear the faint scratch of his nails against
the hollow wood.

These are years that never happen. At school I look in the
mirror and meet the eyes of the other girls. We exchange
our lipsticks, and admire each other for the boys whose eyes
we will catch, the boys who will watch us in the mirrors of
their cars. Hardly a moment goes by for us that does not
pass under the gaze of those boys, and I work hard to let
them see how much I want them. They are so sleek, with
their smooth hairless chests, and I am only happy when I
find myself with one or another of them in the back seat of
his car, the moon rising all around us, the engine hissing,
our breath rising against the windows. I forget each boy's
name as we kiss, his face as he touches me, and when he
lays his body over mine, inert and inattentive, I smile with a
secret pleasure, but whenever I am careless enough to look
over some boy's shaggy head, I see Glennie there, his eyes
like little black cavities in the moon; *Owlcake*, he winks,
and turns to let a spray of butterflies into the milky sky. I

close my eyes and concentrate on the smell of a strange boy's skin, his quick breath in my ear, the unfamiliar welcome heart beating against my breast.

In the hall mirror at home, I practice looking up at boys from under my eyelashes; I practice three or four dazzling smiles before I notice a little blot at the edge of the mirror, and turn to see Glennie hunched in a corner, staring at me. Every day at school he creeps along the hallways behind me. When I turn to smile at a boy, he is there, watching us from some doorway, or half hidden by his locker. I freeze my smile and fix my eyes on the face of the boy in front of me, so he won't turn and see Glennie watching us.

As I wait here by the campus, the boy I will love closes his eyes and finally sleeps, finally dreams. His roommate raises himself up on one bony elbow and watches the boy I love sleep and dream of me.

When I am finally let free to go to college, my suitcases sit in a heap by the door. My mother becomes sentimental and adds to the pile a stuffed panda from my closet. I return it, but later it is replaced by a tiger whose face has been rubbed smooth. Glennie says nothing while all of this goes on. He hates school, and he is getting fat, swelling out of his shirts, rocking in the hot desert of the August sun.
—Glennie, I'll see you at Thanksgiving, I say. —Okay?
—Okay, he says, not looking at me. He drags a stick through the ground, disrupting an anthill, and my mother and father listen to us from behind their closed door.

Here at school I have tried not to expect anything. I go to classes and do not think of home at all. When I arrived, my new roommate suggested that we get identical bedspreads, and curtains to match. I could not think of what to say and only stared at her, fingering the rough chenille of the bed-spread that covered my bed at home for so many years. She has a boyfriend who leaves when I come in, not looking at me.

—Elizabeth, my mother says on the telephone. —You'll have to come home. Your father and I need to talk to you.
I have been here only a month. My roommate files her nails and looks at herself in the mirror.
—What about? I ask.
—Your brother, she says. Her voice is higher-pitched than usual, and it is clear she will say no more on the phone. My roommate looks at me without interest, and bites at the corner of one of her nails.

At the airport my mother stands nervously in the entrance-way, so that I have only a moment to compose a face to meet her. She kisses me quickly on the cheek.
—Let's go, she says. —I'm double-parked. She turns and I notice that she has somehow acquired a tan while I've been gone, even though it is bleak fall in Ohio.
Before she starts the car, she pulls the sun visor down to check her makeup in the mirror, using her little finger to rub away the faint smears of lipstick in the corners of her mouth. As we pull out of the airport onto the highway, she drums her long fingernails on the hard plastic of the steering wheel, and her eyes go back and forth between the rearview mirror and the road ahead, though there is almost no traffic.
—We've decided to send Glen away, she finally says. —To a school.
She glances in the side mirror. I roll my window up and

down and stare at the landscape. So quickly have I become accustomed to the gentle hills of the East that this flat stretch of ground surprises me.

—Away? I say. —What kind of school?

—A special school. She glances at me, but I look away quickly, straight ahead. —We have to, she says, changing lanes and driving right into the splat of a bug on the windshield. —Damn, she says, turning on the wipers.

—Have to? I say. She turns the wipers off, but there is still a greenish smear where the bug hit the glass.

—Well, she says, —we can't, and she pauses, pretending to search for the words they have already decided upon, —control him. He has a problem, she says, glancing at me quickly. —With girls.

I feel the world shrinking, narrowing around me, and I open my window wider. My mother has found her voice again and she goes on.

—He forced himself, she says, pausing to push in the cigarette lighter, —on a girl at school. Get me a cigarette, will you, honey?

She pushes her purse toward me.

—What do you mean? I ask her. I know what she means, but I want to make her say it again. She looks in the mirror, takes the cigarette I offer her.

—We don't exactly know what happened. The janitor caught them. It was after school one day. In the auditorium. Behind the stage. She waits for me to say something. I roll my window up, down.

—He's just different, is all I can finally come up with. —I'm sure it wasn't his fault, I say. I smile reassuringly at her, but I can imagine Glennie smiling secretly at the girl, following her secretly behind the heavy velvet curtains. I have no doubt he did it.

—Oh, honey, my mother says. —You don't understand. All

he does is eat and sit in his room, or watch your father in the garden. He doesn't even watch TV. Without you here he's impossible.

—He's your responsibility, I say, but my voice is hollow. We both know this is not true.

—Oh, honey. She reaches over to stroke my cheek. It is a gesture left over from a time I don't remember, a time that may never have actually happened. I let myself feel nothing except the touch of her hand; the smell of smoke clings to her skin and hair and clothing. I will start smoking myself soon, and that sweet compelling presence of smoke will carry my mother with me through all the gestures of my life. We drive the rest of the way in a silence broken only by the occasional drumming of her nails on the wheel and the pop of the cigarette lighter.

Glennie has grown larger in my short absence, so that, rocking on his heels in the yard, he topples backward into the leaves. He sits up suddenly, surprised by this betrayal of his body, and looks at the ground around him as if searching for some ballast to loose. His ankles are puffy and he looks up when I slam the car door.

One night is all I have agreed to spend here, and I lock my door when I go to bed, but Glennie is already in his room, his door closed. I listen all night long for him, but hear nothing, not even the whispers of my parents, or the occasional rustle of a squirrel outside my window. In the morning, I smooth the blankets up over my pillow, and go down to breakfast, eager to show the sleepless circles under my eyes.

—Elizabeth, my mother says, looking at my father, who stares glumly out at his bare, ruined garden, dreaming of summer and spring. —We want you to drive your brother to the school. It's all arranged.

I feel as if I have come home to find a pet savagely neglected
in my absence; all I can think is if only I hadn't left, and all
I can think is if only I hadn't come back. This is not something I want to see. So much is happening now. Soon I will
fall in love. Soon my father will die of a heart attack in his
garden, and my mother will turn her face to me at last.
Glennie will run away from the school, and I will wait here
until he comes. These things will all happen, but for now all
that is happening is this: we will drive together to the school.
My parents will wave us off from behind their closed door;
then they will turn and fall into each other's arms.

The boy I will love is awakened suddenly by some noise, but
when he opens his eyes, there is nothing there. He thinks of
what it must be like to touch my breasts, my white legs, and
he swoons in a dream of heat and longing, but I do not let
him touch me.

The world rushes by us as we drive across the vast, flat
waste of the Midwest.
Glennie rubs his lips against the window. —Lizzie, he says.
—I don't want to go.
—I don't want you to go either, I say.
—I want to go to school, he says. —Like you.
—You are, Glennie. You are going to school. That's where
we're going now.
I feel his head turn slowly to face me, but I keep my eyes on
the road. He closes his eyes and dreams, his head rocking
against the window, and the miles go by like minutes.

—Lizzie, he says, looking up from a book of travel games.
—I'm bored.
A huge truck pulls up on the right and slows. The driver

stares down at us for a moment, then waggles his tongue
between his teeth.

—Look, Glennie, I say. —That truck is from California.
Why don't you count license plates? Remember, you used
to love to do that.

He gives me a scornful look. —I'm not a baby, he says, and
savagely darkens a square on the page of his travel book.

I want to ask him why he did it, what was he thinking, who
was that girl, and what did he say as he held his hand to her
face, his other hand round her neck. I want to ask all this,
but already I know that answers are never really answers,
they are only more questions. He would only smile sweetly
and tell me it was me.

—Lizzie, he says, —I'm hungry. Let's stop and eat.

He points at signs along the highway, for truck stops or
restaurants, and I tell him we have sandwiches in a cooler
in the back.

—I don't want sandwiches, he says. —I hate sandwiches.

He throws his book to the floor of the car and turns his face
to the window. After a while I hear him whisper to himself:
—Ohio, Indiana, Ohio. His voice flutters against the window, and I keep my eyes on the road, the long strip of black
that will take me there and take me back.

Glennie pulls down the sunshield and looks in the mirror
that Mother uses to comb her hair. —Lizzie. Look how
round my cheeks are.

—Like apples, I say.

He looks again, turns his face from side to side, touches his
cheeks. —Do we have any apples? he asks.

—We have sandwiches. And cookies.

—No apples?

—No apples.

—Let's stop and get some apples, he says. His face bobs at the window, searching for signs to the next exit.

—Glennie, I say, —why don't you just have a cookie? You don't even like apples.

He turns on me furiously. —How would *you* know? he says. —How would you know what I like? You haven't even been here. I love apples. I *love* them.

These child's words sound strange in his changing throat. He rocks in his seat and his eyes are as slick as oysters, blue and full of tears.

—Look, Glennie, I say. —There's an exit. We can stop and get some apples.

He does not look at me, but rolls down his window and gazes at the driver of the car we must pass to get into the exit lane. The driver glances over at Glennie and looks quickly in his rearview mirror. When he slows down, we pass and move into the exit lane.

From the store, I can see Glennie blowing against the car window, then drawing sloppy hearts in the steam left by his breath. He does not see me. He breathes against the glass and draws my name, then wipes it off with his moist hand and smiles to himself as I come back with the apples.

As I wait here, it grows chilly and wet. Boys and girls turn off lights, put away books. My roommate wonders for a moment where I am, then turns out the light in our room.

Glennie's school has tall fences and a guard, who waves us in without stopping to check our forms. Glennie does not look around, but continues to draw thick circles around jumbled words in his travel book. In the office they seem somewhat surprised that I am the only one with him, but they adjust quickly, and reach out to him with kind, efficient hands. He pulls away and stands by aloofly, watching while we make arrangements. I look up from the papers and his eyes meet mine, unbelieving: surely I am not going to leave him here; surely we can regain all that we have lost.

—This will be fun, I tell him. —You're going to like it here. He nods, but we both know that this is a place in which nothing can be believed. Boys stand around sullenly, leaning against walls, waiting for someone to claim them, and now he is one of them.

We walk to his room and are left alone for a few minutes. I do not ask him what he was looking for in that girl, but as I say goodbye to him at the door of his blank white room, he turns away from me and says to the thin mesh covering his windows: —I didn't do anything to that girl, Lizzie. I just missed you.

Walls rise behind him and his hands open and close at his sides like tiny wings.

Driving home from the school, I am for the first time alone; I feel as if I have reached the end of my life, and a new life can now begin. I push Glennie from my world; he is fine, I tell myself, he will be just fine there, and all I will let myself notice from this night are the stars overhead, a sky packed full of them. I close my eyes a moment, and Glennie whispers, —Owlcake, but when I open my eyes, all I can see is a sky full of stars.

When my mother calls, I know something has gone wrong, because it is the only reason she would have to call me.

—Elizabeth, she says, —Glennie's gone.

—Gone? I repeat. My roommate looks up from her legs, then goes back to spreading lotion along the smooth dark skin.

—From the school. He ran away.

I've been waiting for this call, but I don't want it. I know he will ruin everything, and I would rather spend my life alone, unobstructed by his gaze as he stares past me into a darkness I can only see reflected in his eyes.

The library has closed now, and most of the lights have gone out in most of the buildings, but cars still rush by, on their way to Boston or New York. The drivers pay no attention to me standing here waiting. I have brought all the money I could find, and still I know it's not enough. When Glennie comes, I want to turn away or hide. I see him across the busy highway, moving closer in his dark jacket and pants. He has grown taller in his short time at the school, taller and thin, and his white face catches the moonlight. Like a raccoon or a possum, he creeps along the side of the road, waiting for a break in the traffic, and his eyes gleam in the rushing lights. He is dressed like a thief, moves like a thief, crosses the road like a thief. Our eyes meet and we both look away, suddenly shy.

—Look, I say. —I brought you some money.

I hold it out and he looks down at it, then glances around the campus, then at me. —Lizzie, he says. —I want to stay here. With you.

He looks around me at the campus, his eyes moving from lighted window to lighted window; I can tell he is wondering which room is mine, what it looks like.

—You can hide me.

He holds his fists balled up tight in the pockets of his thin jacket. —I'd be careful. I could stay in your room.

—I have a roommate, I say. —She'd tell. I make my voice as earnest as possible, but really I am not sure she would much notice him.

Glennie looks around wildly, trying to plan. —Lizzie, he says finally. —There's no place I can go. You know that.

He stares at me, his eyes the color of a piece of sky on a
snowy day, blue then gray then white, light and dark at the
same time.
I take him by the shoulders, bony and frail through the cloth
of his jacket. I wonder where he got these clothes, who
bought them for him.
—Glennie, I say. —You have to go. But listen: I'll come and
get you. When I get out of school, I'll come and get you.
He looks at me suspiciously. I stuff the money in his pocket
and tell him where to catch the bus. I do not want him here
another minute.

Awakened by my voice, the boy I love lifts his head a moment, then lays it back down.

—Lizzie, Glennie says. He stares at me, his eyes like scars
against the scared lonely white of his face. —I have to stay
here.

I am falling in love right now. He is going to get in my way.

—I have to stay here, Glennie says again. He moves past
me onto the campus and reaches up to touch the white stone
wing of the statue, gazing up at the cracked neck with a
thoughtful, considering look, as if he has nothing but time.
—You can't, I say. —I won't let you. This is my life. I don't
want you here.
He stares at me while I talk, then looks around the campus
again. It is a peaceful, sleepy place, with only a few shining
lights.

He turns and begins to walk away. I know he won't go back
to the school, and I know he won't return here. My heartbeat
rises and I wonder what it is he sees now, what the cars and

streets and lights look like to him. I turn away, back to my
world, but in front of me is only a long blind stretch of black,
and I look back at Glennie and call his name.

He stops, waits a beat, then turns around. Even from here I
can see the tears that have risen in his eyes, blue the color
of the veins on the back of my wrist. Where the head of
Winged Victory belongs sits the dead pitted face of the
moon. Glennie comes back, his body fitting against mine as
though it has always been there, as though all the years have
passed for this, and all the motions of our world are like
butterflies falling to the ground. As he leans against me, the
moon drifts away, under a cover of clouds. If I wait long
enough, it will return. I am falling in love right now, and
whatever happens, this is what I remember.

MINOR
CASUALTIES

My brother David's new car is a Toyota and it's all he wants to talk about. Even in the middle of another conversation, he'll stop abruptly.

—But you know, he'll say, looking earnestly from my

mother to me and back again, —the Japanese really do
make better cars. They really do.

Or he'll stop chewing a moment and stare down at his plate.
—Do you *know* how many miles to the gallon I'm getting?
He shakes his head almost unhappily, as though no matter
its virtues, his new car can't make up for all the misery he
suffered at the wheel of his previous car, an old yellow
Pinto.

The only problem with the new car seems to be its color, a
light bluish-green that he thinks is somehow too feminine;
it's a color his ex-wife would have loved, but since we have
all been so careful to say nothing about her, it's hard to tell
if he bought the car because of the color or in spite of it. It
is almost the exact color of the sweater he gave her for
Christmas last year, and when she opened the box, even I
could tell she couldn't stop a look of surprise from flashing
across her face. —It's lovely, she said, looking around, be-
wildered that he had gotten her something she liked so well.
We all watched her fold the sweater carefully back into its
tissue paper and replace the lid of the box; all but David,
who was gazing intently at the tree, in order to avoid meeting
the eyes of my mother, who had told him the sweater was
all wrong for his wife's coloring. Now he puts his fork down,
a piece of broccoli speared to the end.

—I don't know how I got along with that Pinto all these
years, he says, and my mother nods, rattling the ice to the
bottom of her drink.

—That's right, she says. —You shouldn't have had to keep
that Pinto to begin with.

The Pinto was all that was left my brother from his marriage
—that and a vase I gave them for Christmas. He mentioned
it when he called from Ohio to tell me about the divorce.

—That vase you gave me, he said. —I kept it. I have it right
here.

The vase was tall and thin, made of light green glass, and as he spoke, I was imagining him in a room perfectly empty but for the phone and the vase, casting green shadows over his face in the late-summer evening light.

—Yep, he said a little later, —that vase and the Pinto, that's it. —And the kids, he added after a moment, —for two weeks in the summer. He was quiet then, and I could hear the ring of emptiness in the room around him. —I'm not sure what I'll do with them, he said finally. —Maybe take them to Disneyland or something. I guess I could take them there.

He tells me now that he'd like to rent a little house somewhere, something like mine, but for the time being, he is living with my mother—a temporary arrangement, he says, until he gets back on his feet. It has been only six or seven months since his divorce, and he and my mother are taking a vacation, driving out west in David's new car—it's a good opportunity to break it in, he says, to work out the bugs. I am only a hundred miles or so out of their way, and this is the first of the two nights they'll be spending here. They are really the first people to have been here any length of time since Alan left, which was a month ago, or two months. He left almost nothing behind him, only an old desk in the corner, a few articles of clothing, and his cat. Every now and then, I expect to run across something of his, in the back of a drawer, or the corner of a closet, but there's nothing, not even a comb, or a postcard; all there really is to remind me of him are big empty stretches of space that rolled in to take up the places he once stood, or sat, or slept in. They lurk around the house like ghosts, waiting to surprise me, and I am always taken aback when I run into one of them. It is like hitting a pocket of air on a plane: my stomach dips and I have to sit down and wonder what it was like to have him here, and then I have to wonder what it means that I hardly remember him—what he looked like, how he walked, the smell of his breath. All that really comes back to me, from time to time, is his voice, a tremulous reedy string of questions that I hear sometimes at night, right before I fall asleep.

I was more shocked that he left his cat than that he left, and so, it seems, is his cat, which spends most of the time outdoors; when it comes in, it sits at the window and stares out at the street. It hardly notices me, but its ears twitch at the sound of any male voice on the television. My own cat sits on the couch and stares at Alan's, then follows when it goes outside.

My mother didn't mention Alan when she and David called about their visit. She only met him once and didn't like him, but when I told her that he was gone, she was quiet a moment and I could hear her breathe.

—Now, she said finally, —which one was Alan?

Later she said that she hated to think of me out here all alone, but she said it vaguely, as though she was watching television at the same time, and trying to keep track of a complicated plot line.

There have been others before Alan, and though I like to think otherwise, I know others will follow. They come and go like summer storms, hard to remember in the bright afternoons that follow. I never think of them, really, and they leave behind only tiny tears in the fabric of things—nothing enough to ever really notice. I suppose one day they'll all add up and I will be left with a life full of holes, but for now I have a cat, and a desk, and—for two nights—David and my mother.

This is the first time they have been to visit me here, so I waited all day at the window to watch for them; when my brother's new car, which he had described to me in great

detail over the phone, came down the street, I watched them
slow at each house, checking the address. When they crept
past mine and my mother peered out at my door, I was sure
that our eyes met, but she shook her head and they drove
on, only to edge reluctantly back into sight a few minutes
later, pulling to a stop at the curb. As they got out of the
car, I tried to imagine what they would look like if I didn't
know them, and what they looked like was a couple in need
of exact directions. They stood on the sidewalk and looked
longingly up and down the street at all the other houses—all
larger than mine, surrounded by neat lawns full of children
and flowers; then they finally started up my cracked walk,
my mother stepping carefully, glancing around at the over-
grown lawn, my brother's arm hovering at her elbow. They
seemed startled to see me when I opened the door, but after
a moment my mother spread her arms and I entered them
cautiously, smelling her powder and a new perfume. My
brother stood by uneasily, patted me clumsily on the shoulder.

—You look good, Theresa, he said. —Maybe a little thin.
He was dressed all in pastels, which turned his skin a kind
of light orange, but I told him he looked good too, and he
stared down at himself. —Oh, he said. —Well. I guess I've
put on a few pounds. I could probably stand to lose a little
weight.

My mother patted him on the arm. —You can carry it,
honey, she said. —You have big bones.

He smiled unhappily off toward the road and placed his
hand gently against his chest.

Now, in the restaurant, when he is not stopping to discuss
his car, he eats steadily, bent over his food, without talking,
and his eyes focus dreamily on the white stretch of table-
cloth in front of him. Over the rim of her glass my mother

watches the steady motion of his fork, and when he is finished eating, he looks with dismay at his empty plate and
lays his fork down next to it.
—I can't wait for you to take a drive in the Toyota, he says.
We drove to the restaurant in my car because he wanted to
give his own a rest after the long day's driving from Ohio,
but he has promised me a test ride tomorrow, so he can
point out the car's features, all of which he has already listed
for me. This is what we have talked about since their arrival:
David's new car, the weather, and the face-lift my mother is
considering when they return from their trip.
—A face-lift? I say. —Why would you want to get a face-
lift?
—Oh, she says, her fingers fluttering to her face. —Just
here, where it's puffy, and here–she strokes the soft skin at
her jaw–where it's starting to sag.
She drops her hand to the table and looks from one of us to
the other. —You think it's a bad idea, she says to David.
—Don't you? He spreads his hands out against the table-
cloth.
—It's fine, he says. —I think it's fine.
He stares down at his hands and my mother picks up her
glass. I can tell they have discussed this at least once a day
since it occurred to my mother to do it.
—No, David says, though she has said nothing. —Really.
It's fine. Why not? He smiles and she leans sideways to get
the attention of our waiter; when he sees her, she holds up
her glass.
—I mean, she says, settling back into her chair, —it's my
money.
I saw once, in a waiting-room magazine somewhere, pictures of a face-lift operation. I turned past them quickly,
then went back. I could hardly bear to look at them, but
there was something compelling about seeing this woman's

face cut neatly away from itself, the skin pulled back to show the muscle and blood and bone beneath. When her skin was trimmed and sewed back up, the stitches cleverly hidden in the curve of the jaw, the woman did look younger, I suppose, but her eyes were lit by a fear that seemed huger than in the picture taken before. My mind balks at the image of my mother there, staked down like that, but I smile at her.

—It's great, I say. —I think it's a great idea.

—Your father, she says, —thinks it's a waste of money.

My father lives with his second wife in the same city as my mother and my brother. They are not friends, but it's a small town and they run into each other often, always by accident.

—Well, she says, —I think it's a great idea.

David pushes his plate away and glances at my mother; her food is picked over, pushed around the plate, little clumps of peas and potatoes mixed in with the veal she has hardly touched.

When the waiter brings the check, he hesitates a moment, clearly uncertain as to our relationship to each other, though I imagine we look like any other young couple having dinner with the mother of one of us. Finally the waiter lays the check down in the space between David and my mother, though it is slightly closer to David. My mother smiles and waits until the waiter is gone to reach for it.

—People can't always tell we're mother and son, she tells me. —At least not now that it's just the two of us. She lays her credit card on top of the bill and slides it back across the table, leaving it next to David's elbow.

David is quiet on the way home, sitting by himself in the back seat, and my mother sketches out their itinerary for me. Their eventual destination is the Grand Canyon.

—Remember, she says, looking around at David, —how you
kids always wanted to go there?
In the rearview mirror I see him nod without looking at her,
and I try to remember wanting to go to the Grand Canyon,
but all I can really recall of any of our family vacations is the
back of my father's head in front of me and in front of him a
dismal stretch of road dotted with cars just like ours, filled
with families just like ours: a mother with her head bent
over a book in front and a few bored children in the back.
—I don't remember wanting to go there, I say.
—Oh, Jesus, she says. —You kids were always nagging to
go, every summer.
—Well, then why didn't you take us?
—I don't know, she says, patting at the side of the door,
looking for an automatic window switch, which my car does
not have. —Probably something to do with your father. Finally she rolls the window down by hand. —But we're going
now.
I try to catch my brother's eye in the mirror, but he is gazing
into the eyes of his own reflection in the window beside him.
His reflected face looks paler and puffier than his real face.
When we pull into the driveway, there is a sudden quick
flash of cat eyes caught in the headlights as they swing
across the yard; they're gone too soon to tell which cat it is,
but it's all I'll see of either until morning. Now that it's
spring, they stay out all night, prowling around after nests
of newborn animals. They kill whatever they find, appar-
ently–voles, field mice, baby chipmunks. Sometimes the
animals are partly eaten, but mostly they look almost untouched, perfectly intact but for a smear of red at the mouth
or a tiny rip in the back of the neck. My own cat was never
much of a killer before, and I would like to blame all of this
on Alan, but I know there are too many dead to be the work
of only one cat. The vet tells me that it's not their fault, it's

in their nature to kill; in fact, he says, they think they're bringing me something I will like. I try to look at it from that perspective, but even so, there seems something willful about the sheer numbers. There's nothing I can do about it, the vet told me, except leave them inside all the time, which I tried, but they scrabbled at the door and raced around the house all night, howling miserably; when I let them out in the morning, they were gone for two days, for fear, I suppose, that once I got them back in, they'd have to stay there forever. So I let them out at night, counting the months until winter, and in the morning my neighbors sit at their windows watching me as I walk around the yard collecting the bodies.

—You know, my neighbor to the right said a few weeks ago, —it's not good to just let animals roam around and kill whatever they want. I remember, she went on wistfully, —when there were seven kinds of birds that came to my feeder alone.

I didn't believe this, but I nodded, and together we glared at my cat, who lay innocently in a strip of sunlight on the driveway.

—That was before you came, she added unnecessarily. Now her bird feeder creaks emptily from the rain gutter of her house, and the cats' ears flick back and forth at the noise it makes in the wind.

The miserable little deaths go on, and I try to tell myself that they don't matter, they are so small, only minor casualties, really, but as I walk around my yard, I want to apologize to each stiff little sad body I retrieve. I remind myself now to get up early, before David and my mother, to spare them the sight of the evening's death toll.

Before we go to bed, my mother has a nightcap and David walks around the kitchen opening and closing cabinets. —Don't you have any cookies? he asks. He pats his stomach and smiles. —I've developed kind of a sweet tooth.

He finds a box of crackers, and takes them into the living room, where he sits and eats them while I make up the couch for his bed. My mother sits at the kitchen table watching us, and I wonder for a moment what it must be like for her to have us as her children. Perhaps it's something like winning a prize for which you have no use–a minor, fleeting disappointment, forgotten until provoked by the sight of the useless object.

By the time I have brushed my teeth and gotten into bed with her, she is asleep, drawn stiffly up on her side, taking up only a tiny corner of the available space, her nightgown buttoned tight up to her neck.

I wake later to the shrill panicky cry of an animal just outside the window, and my mother opens her eyes and stares at me.

—Honey? she says.

—It's okay, I say. —It's just the cats. They caught something.

—Theresa? she says. —What are you doing here? But she is asleep before I can answer. In the bars of moonlight that stretch across the bed, I see the muscles in her jaw relax, and the lines disappear. After her operation, some of the skin I am looking at right now will be gone, sliced off and dropped into a bucket somewhere. I wonder what she is dreaming about. I put my head down. In a few minutes everything is quiet again; the cats go back to prowling through the bushes, and the neighbors turn and mutter under their blankets.

In the morning my mother's side of the bed is empty; her sheets are tucked neatly into the mattress, and except for the faint scent of her perfume on the pillow, it is as though no one has been here at all. When I come into the kitchen, she turns from where she is standing by the stove.

—Oh, Theresa, she says, —I was sure you were a late sleeper, so I made coffee already.

David looks up from the paper. —What's wrong with your cats? he asks. —They kept me awake all night.

—Nothing's wrong with them, I say. —They like to prowl.

—Well, my mother says, —it's only one more night. She opens a cabinet and gazes into it for longer than is merited by the few cans and boxes there. —You don't seem to have much food, she says finally. —Is that why you've gotten so thin?

She scrutinizes my body, though she herself is tiny, with bones like a sparrow. She opens another cabinet. —All you have is condiments. What do you eat? Do you ever cook anything?

In fact, after Alan left I went right on preparing the kind of meals I had cooked for the two of us—out of habit, I suppose, but without anyone to share it the food looked distasteful, and somehow artificial, like plastic refrigerator magnets shaped to resemble cookies and orange slices. I saved the leftovers at first, piling it all into plastic containers in the icebox, then freezing it, until finally I just threw everything away, which is not something I want to tell my mother.

—I eat, I finally say. —I've just been exercising a lot. That's probably why I'm thinner.

David puts his finger on a word in the article he's reading and looks up. —What kind of exercise?

—Oh, I say, —I joined a health club. As I say this, I can see that it is exactly what I should have done, months ago. It is something I've always meant to do, and now I think of all the things I could do there if this were true.

—I swim. And run. And lift weights. My mother looks at my thin arms. —Light weights, I say. —It's aerobic. I do aerobics, too. They have classes.

As I talk, the health club rises in a gleaming surge against the sky; it is full of beautiful men and women who don't even bother to look at each other; instead they gaze lovingly down at their shining skin, and run their hands over their own fine muscles and bones. When my brother says it sounds nice, I nod.

—It is, I say. —I eat there, too. Sprouts. Raw juices.

—I've been meaning to get some exercise myself, he says. —Maybe we could go there today.

My mother nods. —That would be nice, she says, and I almost agree to take them, so real has the health club become, so essential to my well-being.

—We can't, I finally say. —It's closed right now. They're fixing the pool.

My mother turns from the sink. —What's wrong with it? she asks, and her interest seems so genuine that I feel ashamed for having provoked it.

—Oh, I tell her, —I don't know. It was too small. It got dirty too fast.

They gaze at me, waiting for more. —Actually, I say, —it's not a very good health club at all. It's sort of run down, and the equipment is old. I've been thinking about maybe joining a different one.

With every word, the beautiful club begins to crumble: the chrome flakes to rust, the sparkling walls clot with mildew, and the foundation weakens and collapses; from the dust rises a wormy Y, and inside it all the men and women slow to a creep around a warped track, or splash heavily through the murky water of an ancient pool. My back stings from the dirty water, and I grow weary of the aging spotted men who follow me from rusty weight to rusty weight.

—Well, anyways, David says, —it's good you're getting some exercise. I really ought to lose some of this weight.
—Oh, honey, my mother says. —You look fine. It's just a few pounds, she says to me. —Now that he's eating better. David stares down at the paper, moving his hand up and down each column as he reads.
—Anyway, I say to my mother, —I do have food. Look.
I open the icebox to show her the food I bought for their visit, eggs and bacon, the food we grew up on.
—Don't you have any oat bran? David asks. —Or cereal?
—No. Just eggs and bacon. American food. I close the icebox. —I could go to the store.
—That's okay, he says quickly. —I like eggs and bacon. Barbara never let me eat anything like that. She was always giving me oat bran.
My mother rotates each of the rings on her fingers. —Well, it *is* better for you, she says abruptly, as if it pains her to agree with Barbara on even so simple a matter as food. She opens another cabinet, closes it, and sighs. —I suppose a few eggs won't kill us, she says. She bends to find a pan in one of the cupboards under the stove.
—Mom, David says, —listen to this. He reads to her from the newspaper as she rinses and dries the pans she has pulled from the cupboard.
Outside on my neighbor's lawn, a bird hops through the grass; somewhere my cats are crouched, watching it, too. When my mother has bacon frying and water boiling for soft-boiled eggs, she wipes the counter with a paper towel.
—Well, she says brightly, —what shall we do today?
This–what to do with them–was the bridge I figured I'd cross when I came to it, and now it is here. David looks up from the paper, and they both smile at me expectantly. After a moment my mother says helpfully, —We just want you to do your usual routine. We don't want to be in the way.

—Oh, I say, —I don't know. With the health club closed
. . . I trail off and look out the window; I'm sure they take
this opportunity to exchange a glance. —I guess I could go
to the store. I *have* been meaning to get some food.
—Perfect, my mother says. —And we can get some cereal
for breakfast tomorrow.
She drains the bacon on a paper towel and pats the grease
from the top before she brings it to the table, then sits and
watches David eat as he reads. When he reaches for his
fourth piece, she clears her throat, and he looks up, surprised, his hand still hovering over the bacon.
—That's your fourth, she says, and he stares at his hand as
though someone else has put it there. He looks at me as he
withdraws his hand.
—Cholesterol, he says. He gazes at the bacon a moment,
then goes back to the paper. —Listen to this, he says, and
begins reading from a story about the level of radioactivity
found in the pets of people who live near nuclear reactors.
He looks up at me. —Those people's cats are radioactive,
he says, and shakes his head. —Jesus. You can't even trust
your own pets anymore. He looks back at the article, then
up again at us. —I wonder if they glow in the dark, so at
least you'd know.
My mother nods and I look out the window. From here I can
see a small spot of gray in the grass by David's car; it could
be a stone, perhaps, or a patch of dirt.
—I guess I'll check up on them anyways, I say, but my
mother pats the air for silence as David reads a letter to the
advice columnist.

The gray spot by David's car is a field mouse; it stares forlornly up at me with its tiny black eyes, its paws drawn
stiffly to its mouth. I sit on the hood of David's car and light
a cigarette. Already the neighbors have clumped at their

windows to shake their heads over me, my cats, the careless
and shameful way they seem to think we live. They must
wonder whose car this is, speculating over it all day as they
clean their houses and mow their lawns.

I toss my cigarette out into the street as David comes out of
the house, carrying the newspaper. He looks dismayed to
see me on his car.

—I thought you might want to keep this article, he says.
—About the cats. Just in case.

I take the paper from him. The article is accompanied by a
picture of a woman gazing at a cat who sits hunched inside
a little glass cage.

—So, David says, leaning carefully back against his car.
—This is a nice place.

—It's okay, I say. —For now.

He wipes his hand across the hood of the car and looks at it
for dirt, but his palm comes up clean.

—Hey, he says casually, as though this is just occurring to
him, —why don't you come with us? There's plenty of room
in the car.

I envision them traveling together across the country; they
are always sitting someplace–in the deserted parking lots of
Dairy Queens, the dark lounges of highway motels; even at
the Grand Canyon they're sitting, perched on little burros in
the middle of a herd of tourists crawling down the rocks. I
try to put myself into any one of these pictures, but I don't
fit, like something with too many corners.

—I don't know, I say. —I don't really want to go to the
Grand Canyon.

—Well, you sure used to. I'm surprised you don't remember.

—Why are you going now?

—I don't know. It just seems like a good idea. He looks at
the house, and around at the quiet neighborhood. —I don't

see why I have to have a reason. He licks his finger and rubs
at a spot on the hood of the car, but it's a flaw in the paint,
and doesn't rub away.
—Really, he says, —you should come.
He looks at me hopefully, and I look out across the street.
Curtains flutter in the windows of the houses that face us.
—I would, I say. —I really would, but I don't think I can
leave the cats that long.
He nods and eases himself away from the car. —Well, he
says, —if you change your mind. He turns toward the house
and stops. —Theresa, he says. —There's a dead animal
here.
—There is? I say. —Oh my God.
I jump down and stand next to him; together we stare down
at the mouse. —Oh my God, I say again. —Alan's cat must
have done that.
David looks up and around at the yard, and at the same
moment we spot a small chipmunk in the driveway, and near
that some other little brown thing.
—Look, he says, —there's more. Jesus. It's like a battle-
field.
—It's not that bad, I say. —It's Alan's cat. I can't stop it.
David shakes his head as we go into the house. —You
should at least pick them up, he says. —You shouldn't just
leave them there.
My mother looks up when we come into the kitchen.
—Mom, David says, —Theresa's got dead things all over
her yard.
She turns the water off, and I see that she is rewashing all
of my coffee cups. —Dead things? she says.
—Mice, he says. —Chipmunks. Birds. You name it.
—Birds? she says, and I say, —They don't kill birds. Just
mice, really. Field mice.

Their eyes meet. —It's Alan's cat, I say. —I'm pretty sure it's just Alan's cat.

—Well, my mother says, drying her hands on a paper towel. —That's easy enough to stop. Just have them declawed. Remember Fuzzy? Fuzzy was declawed and he never killed anything.

—Fluffy, David says, and my mother looks at him. —Her name was Fluffy, he says.

—Oh. Well, anyway. He was declawed and he never killed anything.

—She, David says. —And she never went out, so how could she kill anything?

—Well, my mother says. —Whatever. My point is, if you have them declawed, they won't be able to kill things. And, she adds, looking around pointedly, —it's better on your furniture.

—I don't think, David says, —that if Fluffy *had* gone out, she would have killed anything. She wasn't that kind of cat. My mother looks down at the paper towel in her hands and folds it neatly into quarters before she throws it away.

I hardly remember Fluffy except as a furry white blot at the end of the couch. —What kind of cat was she? I ask.

David goes to the window and looks around at the yard. —I don't know, he says. —I don't know what kind of cat she was. I don't even like cats. Barbara was the one that liked cats. He puts his hands flat against the window and brings his face to the glass. —I hate cats, he says bitterly. —I've always hated cats.

My mother clears her throat. —Well, she says, —I just think you ought to consider it. Declawing, I mean. It's perfectly harmless.

In fact, I did consider declawing when Alan first brought his cat here; it clawed everything–the furniture, the curtains,

the stereo speakers–and my cat, who had never clawed
much of anything, took it up, too. When I asked the vet
about it, he said, —Sure, then took my hand and pinched
my finger just above the middle joint. —That's where it
would be on a cat, he said. —We just cut it right off. On the
way home I could still feel the pressure of his fingers on my
bone, and I wondered all day what it would be like to go
around without any fingernails, without any fingertips.
—I'll think about it, I say, but my mother is watching David
draw circles in the dust of the window. He has drawn a large
circle around his car and smaller circles around each dead
animal he has spotted in the yard.
—Maybe we should go to the store now, she says, and when
I offer to drive, David turns around with a look of horror.
—Oh no, he says. —Let's take the Toyota. You haven't
ridden in it yet.

We wait at the curb while David unlocks the doors for us,
and my mother looks at all the houses lining my street; when
she realizes that the dark lumps in the windows are people
looking out at her, she is startled and pulls her purse to her
chest. She steps delicately around the mouse to get into the
car.
As we drive David points out the Toyota's features.
—Feel that, he says, turning on the air conditioner. A tepid
rush of stale air comes back to me, and he turns it down.
—Well, he says, —it takes a minute to get cranked up. And
look–he pulls down the sun visor on my mother's side
and flicks a tiny switch under the mirror, which turns on
a light. My mother smiles and lifts her chin a bit as she
looks up at her reflection, and when David flips the visor
back, she brushes her fingertips lightly along the edge of
her jaw.
—And see this? Suddenly David's seat tilts almost straight

back, and the car takes an alarming lurch toward the curb;
then he pops the seat back upright. —In case I want to pull
over and take a nap.
My mother turns around in her seat. —It's just perfect for a
long drive, she tells me. —It's so comfortable.
—And roomy, David says. —In case you decide to come.
—Yes, my mother says, and turns back to face the road.
—But of course you'd be much too busy for that.

David parks the car two or three spaces away from any
others, and at the door he turns back to smile at it. Inside,
we are all struck a little numb by the frozen air, and we drift
along the aisles gazing at food until my mother stops at the
meat case.
—We'll need something for dinner, she says, looking doubt-
fully down at the meat.
—You pick it out, David says. —I'm going to get some cookies or something.
He wanders off, and I watch him stop at the end of each
aisle to read the signs. From here I can see the checkout,
and in the middle of the express lane is a man I saw a few
times a year or two ago. His name is Richard, and all I can
remember about him is that he wanted the television on all
the time, even when he wasn't watching it. I can hardly
remember his face without the light from the TV flickering
like a changing wind across its surface. He stares around
vacantly while he waits, leaning against a large cart, though
he has only a few items rattling around in the bottom. Before
I can turn my head away, he spots me, then looks quickly to
see how many people are in line ahead of him. Unwilling to
give up his position so close to the cashier, he calls my
name, but I look away, down at all the red-and-white lumps
of meat.
—Terry, he calls, with a kind of suppressed urgency. I

reach out and pick up the first thing I touch, which turns
out to be a Rock Cornish game hen.

—Let's have this, I say.

—Well, my mother says, looking down at the package of
fish she is holding.

—Terry, Richard calls again, and she looks toward the
sound of his voice.

—Theresa, that man seems to be trying to get your attention, she says.

I pick up another hen. —Chicken is supposed to be good for
you, I say. —No cholesterol.

My mother looks down at the two hens I have in my hands.

—That's true, she says. —And David does like chicken.

She lays her package of fish on top of a steak and bends into
the meat case. As she pushes the hens around to find the
largest, I feel a presence behind me and turn to see Richard,
holding his bag in a little bundle against his chest. I'm
amazed that he got through the checkout and down to us so
quickly. He never struck me as speedy.

—Hi, Terry, he says. —I guess you didn't hear me.

My mother straightens and smiles as Richard sways in time
to the store music, waiting to be introduced, then shifts his
bag to one arm to shake my mother's hand.

—I'd introduce you to my brother, too, I say, —but he's
disappeared.

—Oh, Richard says. —I'd like to meet him. I'd really like
that. He smiles at my mother. —I really would.

—Well, she says, —we're leaving in the morning. Early.
She looks down at the hens in her hand, and though I will
her not to say it, she does: —I suppose you could come for
dinner.

I keep my face free of any expression at all, so as not to
encourage him, but he smiles happily. —I could, he says.
—I'm free tonight.

They arrange a time, and when he goes, my mother watches him walk all the way to the front of the store. —He seems very nice, she says. —He seems to like you.

She doesn't wait for a reply, and leans back into the meat case.

As she roots around for another hen, David reappears, holding out a package of frozen French fries; his other arm is behind his back.

—I got you a present, he says to me, and holds his hand out to show us two little collars, one red, one blue, each with a tiny bell attached. —For the cats. The bells are to warn the animals they're coming. He presses the collars into my hand. —This could solve all your problems, he says.

When we get home, David unwraps the collars immediately and goes outside to find the cats, while my mother stands at the sink, preparing the hens.

—Yes, she says, —that Richard seems very nice. Not at all like Alan.

I try to remember what it was she didn't like about Alan, but by now it has become hard to remember even what I didn't like about him. I close my eyes to picture him, but his face is blurry and shapeless, like clay or dough; finally it resolves into Richard's, a face with no real expression of its own.

—Actually, I say, —he's a lot like Alan. He was Alan's best friend.

This is not true, but it does disappoint her, and she turns back to cleaning out the insides of the hens. We sit stranded in this uneasiness until David returns.

—Look, he says, standing in the doorway, his hand behind his back. —I brought you another present. He lifts his arm up high, dangling a dead mouse, which swings stiffly back and forth from his fingers.

My mother opens her mouth, but nothing comes out, and she turns abruptly back to the sink. David gazes at her back a moment, then at the mouse, as if he has only just noticed it; then he turns and tosses it out into the yard.
—Sorry, he says. He goes to the sink to wash his hands and smiles down at my mother, but she lifts the hens out and steps aside without looking at him.
—I couldn't find the cats, he says to me. —They must have heard me coming with the bells.
I leave them in the kitchen and go outside to pick up the mouse, as well as any other prey I may have missed earlier. My neighbor to the right doesn't even pretend not to have been watching when I look up and see her. She shakes her head and calls her husband over; they watch me as I walk through the yard, putting the little bodies in a plastic bag.

When I come back inside, David and my mother are sitting quietly in front of the television watching a game show.
—I couldn't find them either, I say, and my mother looks up. —The cats, I mean.
—Shhh, she says, and looks back at the television. —We like to watch this every evening.
My brother stares intently at the screen as the host asks a question about geography. —Zanzibar, David says urgently before the host has even finished the question, but the answer turns out to be Zaire. —Damn, he says. —I knew it began with a Z.
My mother pats him on the knee. —That's okay, honey, she says. —Who'd have guessed Zaire?
David watches the screen, the muscles in his jaw working as he waits for the next question, and I go into the kitchen for a cigarette. The hens are on the counter, sitting in pairs side by side on a baking sheet.
In the other room, my mother congratulates David on every

correct answer, and I imagine them in their living room, settling down together every evening to watch this program, sitting next to each other, David in the chair my father once occupied. Outside, the light is beginning to fade and somewhere my cats are lurking, their eyes gleaming like bits of glass in the dusk. My neighbors drag in their lawn mowers, and shake their heads at my own shaggy grass. Inside, they settle into their evenings; I see them through their windows at night, cooking dinner, washing dishes; they probably sit in front of the same game show that my mother and David watch, alternately congratulating and consoling each other as they compete. When the show is over, my mother goes upstairs to get ready for dinner and David comes into the kitchen, joining me at the table.

—Got an extra cigarette? he asks.

—I thought you quit, I say, but I hand him one.

—Sort of. I don't smoke around Mom. I go outside.

—You go outside to smoke?

He shrugs. —It's not so bad. It beats what I had before. Barbara used to smell my breath every night when I came to bed. I used to brush my teeth, gargle, chew gum. She always knew.

He lights the cigarette and holds the match up until it burns out. —I don't know, he says. —It was like she had spies. He puts the match on the table even though there is an ashtray in front of me. —Maybe the kids, he says. —Maybe she trained them to spy on me.

—So, I say, —when do you think you'll get your own place? He looks at his cigarette as if he has never seen one before, turning it around and around in his long fingers before he takes a drag. When he speaks, each word comes out with a little puff of smoke.

—I don't know. He blows the rest of the smoke out in a steady blue stream. —I don't see what's so bad about living

there. I mean, he says, looking around the room, —I don't
see what's so great about living alone. What do you have?
Just some cats and a bunch of dead things in your yard.
—Those dead things aren't there all the time, I say. —It's
just a phase. I'm sure they'll stop soon.
He taps his cigarette against the ashtray. —I don't know, he
says again. —I just don't see what's so bad about it.
Behind us my mother clears her throat and we both turn to
see her hovering in the doorway. —Oh, she says, —you two
are smoking. You know, she says, looking at me, —smoking
causes wrinkles.
She is wearing a purple sweater covered with bright geomet-
ric designs. It is so ugly I feel I must compliment her on it
and she smiles.
—David got it for me. For the trip.
David grinds his cigarette out and stands. —I'm going to go
look for those cats again, he says. It's dusk now, and I know
he'll never find them; I can hear the soft jingle of bells as he
circles the house.

We sit down to eat almost as soon as Richard arrives, and
when my mother brings the four hens to the table, he smiles
up at her.
—That looks great, he says. —I love chicken.
—They're not chickens, I say. —They're Rock Cornish
game hens.
He turns his soft blue eyes on me, and immediately I regret
saying what was, after all, just a statement of fact.
—Oh, he says sadly. —Well, whatever.
He pokes gently at his hen with his fork and waits to see
how my mother eats hers. When she peels the skin away
from the flesh, he does the same, and they both take small,
delicate bites. Like my mother, he takes only a few of the
French fries David bought, but David has a heap of them

piled on his plate; my mother watches him eat each one.
The cat collars sit on the table by his elbow, and he lifts his
head at every sound of the wind through the trees.
—So, Richard says. —What brings you two to town?
My mother responds with their itinerary, and when she fin-
ishes, he nods.
—The Grand Canyon, he says. —You're going to love it
there, Dave. I went there when I was a kid.
He watches as my mother carefully pulls one of the legs
from her hen, then looks down at his own plate. —Lots of
people, he goes on, —you know, want to go to Disneyland
and places like that, but I say go to the source.
David looks up from his food. —The source of what? he
asks.
—Oh, I don't know. Richard waves his fork in the air.
—Nature. You know.
My mother smiles. —I know what you mean, she says.
—It's not man-made.
—Oh, David says. He turns to me. —So where do your cats
usually *go* at night? He lays his hand over the collars. —You
know, he says, —if they *were* radioactive, they'd glow in the
dark and you could always find them.
—Dave, Richard says, —your mom says you got a new car.
David brightens. —You bet, he says.—A Toyota. It's the
smartest thing I've ever done, buying that car.
—It is, my mother says. —It's been so comfortable.
—And roomy, David adds. —In case Theresa comes with
us.
My mother slides the little heap of skin to the side of her
plate. —Yes, she says, —well. She looks at Richard.
—What kind of car do you drive, Richard? she asks.
As Richard lays down his fork to tell her, David rises, then
comes back to the table with the rest of the French fries,
which he scrapes from the pan onto his plate. He takes the

pan to the sink and turns the water on, which hisses as it hits the hot metal. Right now Richard is nodding at whatever my mother is saying and when he sees that I am watching him, panic skitters into his face, his attention torn between us, and finally he settles on a smile that stops before it reaches his eyes, which pass unhappily from her face to mine and back.

—Theresa, David says, —don't you have any ketchup?

When I give him the ketchup, he pours it onto his plate, and puts the bottle on the table in front of him.

—You know, he says, looking at the bottle, —that was one of the things Barbara was always getting on me for, leaving the ketchup bottle on the table. She said people would say we had no class. He drags a French fry through the puddle of ketchup on his plate. —But the thing was, he says, —we never really had anyone over. We never really seemed to have any friends. He looks around at us. —No one really seemed to notice when we broke up.

My mother reaches over and touches him on the wrist.

—That's all over now, honey, she says. —You don't have to worry about that anymore.

Richard pats his fork against the small pile of skin at the edge of his plate; he presses against it until he's shaped it into a small square, then looks up.

—So, Dave, he says, —what made you choose Toyota?

David looks confused a moment, then sighs and begins to list all of the car's features. Richard nods at each one, and my mother lifts her head and gently strokes the skin under her chin. Outside, something rustles in the leaves; it could be a cat following the trail of a bird to its nest, or it could simply be a trick of the wind through the branches.

When we're done, our plates are covered with tiny bones and brownish juice, dotted with beads of fat. My mother rises and Richard quickly stands. He reaches for my plate and allows his fingers to brush mine, but I stand and carry my own dishes to the sink. I can feel his eyes on my back as I walk. David goes outside with the cat collars as we clear the table silently. When all the dishes are in the sink, my mother turns on the water.

—You dry, Richard, she says, and Richard looks around happily for a towel. I hand him the roll of paper towels and go into the living room.

David has come back in; he is standing at my desk, flipping through the papers on top of it. I can't see his face in the light, but he seems uninterested in the contents of what he looks at; he glances at each page for only a moment, then puts it down and picks up another. He looks up when he hears me and smiles faintly.

—They seem to be hitting it off, he says, and I nod.

—Like old friends, I say, trying for a cheery tone.

He puts down the envelope he is holding and picks up a small jar that contains stamps and paper clips. —Do you do much at this desk?

—Not really. Bills. Letters. It's just there. Alan left it.

He nods. —I know, he says. —It's hard to get much done anymore. He twists the lid of the jar back and forth. —I have this feeling, he says, —that I should be doing things. But I don't know what they are. He puts the jar down and looks at me. —But you, he says. —You should be doing things. You were always doing things.

My mother laughs in the kitchen, over the sound of running water, and he stops to listen.

—So you and—what's that guy's name?

—Richard.

—Richard. So you and Richard. Are you going to move in together?

—I hardly know him, I say, but even as the idea is raised, I can almost feel myself becoming resigned to it. Richard could use Alan's desk and play with Alan's cat, and the television could be on all the time.

David nods. —Well, you can always move back home. There's plenty of room there.

My room at my mother's house has high yellow walls, with stuffed toys still arranged in little animal groupings on top of the bureau and bookshelves.

—Oh, I say, —I'm happy here. Really.

David stares down at the desk, then picks up a flyer advertising a lecture I meant to go to a few weeks ago.

—I don't know, he says. He turns his head quickly toward the window, as if he has heard something, but there is nothing there, only the wind and the occasional tick of a branch against the glass.

—Sometimes, he goes on, —sometimes I just can't seem to move. You know? I wake up in the middle of the night and I just can't even, he stops and looks into the kitchen, listens a moment. —Well, I just can't even, you know, lift my legs off the bed and onto the floor.

He drops the flyer and lets it drift to the floor before he bends to pick it up. —Are you sure you don't want to come with us? he asks. —You might just as well.

He looks at me and I realize he is right: I might just as well. I think for a moment, searching out some compelling reason I must stay—something that might go wrong in my absence. But all that occurs to me is that the newspapers would pile up on my step, and the grass would continue to go un-mowed, lopping over onto the sidewalk. The neighbors would probably miss me in their way, drifting aimlessly to their windows, and the cats would just go on littering the lawn with tiny corpses. After a day or two of scratching at the door for their dinner, they'd realize the little bodies were

food, and they'd eat them. This is all that would happen. I
try to think of something to say to David, but I am struck
suddenly by the sense that I am living inside one of those
pockets of air left by everyone who has been here. When
David and my mother go, they will leave behind them empty
spaces of their own for me to maneuver around; my life will
be like an obstacle course.

David is still gazing at me when Richard and my mother
come into the room.

—Well, Richard says, —I guess I should be going.

He stands at the door and my mother backs tactfully away.

—I'll give you two a minute to say goodbye, she says.

I stand on the front porch with Richard and watch his face
as he tries to think of the right thing to say.

—Well, he finally offers, —I really enjoyed that.

—Good, I say. —Thanks for coming.

—Oh, I was glad to. He looks out at the black street.
—Really glad.

As he leaves, he stops at David's car and walks all the way
around it, looking it over and nodding; when he gets to his
own car, he gives me a little wave before he gets in.

His brake lights blink like eyes, all the way down the street.
When I turn to go inside, I am for a moment surprised to
see David and my mother through the window; it seems odd
to see people there, and, watching them, I feel like a spy.
David sits at the desk, my mother stands behind him; his
eyes close as he leans his head back against her, and she
smiles, stroking his thin hair. Her mouth moves with whatever words a mother would say to a son at such a moment,
and it is clear to me that they could be anywhere: in their
own home, or in any motel in any city along their route. I
turn away from the window. It's late, and the wind carries a
faint sound as it moves through the trees. It could be any-

thing: the jingling of little bells, perhaps, or the tiny flickering out of tiny lives. I close my eyes and try to think of all I
have, but all I can see is David and my mother; their voices
echo in the deep canyons, and rocks are falling all around
them as they look up at me, their faces dizzy with the steep-
ness of the descent.

Abattoir

—Look, Teddy says, and when he turns to me, his eyes are the unquiet blue of the television, his skin lit by the reflected glare.

—Look, he says again. —You've got to see this, so I put my finger on a word to mark my place in the magazine article I

am reading and look up to see a tangled heap of men on a
baseball field.

—Not that, he says. —Wait. They'll show it again. He leans
forward on his knees, his face a foot away from the television. —Watch, he says; then, —Okay.

The slow-motion replay begins, and we watch the man on
third base run several yards into a dramatic collision with
the catcher, the pitcher, and the umpire. Somewhere in the
confusion, the baseball is thrown, and out of the pile the
catcher's arm emerges, miraculously holding the ball.

—Amazing, Teddy says. —Amazing. He turns to me.
—You'll never see a better play at the plate. That guy
should have been safe. Anyone else would have dropped the
ball.

He looks back at the TV. —You're looking at one of the best
catchers in baseball, he says. —I don't care what they say.

The catcher stands, and walks around, shaking out his legs.
His thighs are enormous, one of them alone the size of the
waist of any model in the magazine I am reading.

—His thighs are huge, I say, and Teddy looks at me.

—He has to have those thighs, he says. —He's got baseballs
coming at him ninety miles an hour. He nods. —You'd want
thighs like that, too.

The men on the screen untangle themselves, coaches hurtle
out of dugouts, and everyone's mouth is moving, but no one
appears to be listening. I turn back to my magazine article
about the things women do when they are on the rebound
from love.

—If I'd had thighs like that, Teddy says, —I could have
been a catcher in high school, instead of playing first base.
I might have gone to the minors. They always need catchers.
He sighs and turns back to the television. —That would
have been a good career.

He rubs his hands up and down his thighs; even bent double, they aren't as wide as those of the catcher on TV.

—You have a career, I say. —At the Safeway.

He turns to look at me. —I don't think, he says, —that being an assistant manager in the produce section at the Safeway is exactly a career.

He watches the next batter swing and miss to end the inning. —Shit, he says, then turns back to me. —At least not yet, anyways. He watches the commercial a moment, then says, —But maybe someday. Maybe someday I might just manage the whole place.

He nods thoughtfully as the game comes back on. He says this often, that he might someday manage the store; in fact, he has promised me that when I am ready, he will get me a job at the Safeway, and together we will move slowly up the ranks, so that one day we will be at the top, a brother-and-sister management team. It will happen when things settle down, he always says, but he never says what this means, or when it will be. In the meantime, he reads books to prepare himself for that day, books on cost accounting and finance management, books by millionaires and businessmen. He's going to be ready, he says; he is going to make his future happen. And mine. But for now, he smooths his pants down over his thin legs and leans forward to watch the failed play at the plate one more time.

It is early in the baseball season, and this year, as every year, Teddy believes that the Yankees are going to go all the way and recapture their past glory; this year he is so sure of it that he has spent what little money we have on a video recorder, so that he can record all the games he misses while he is at work.

—Consider it an investment, he said when he took the machine out of the box, —for the future. He untangled wires, bent to attach the VCR to the television, and smiled up at me. —We'll have all the games on tape, and maybe someday they'll be worth something. Market and supply, he said, nodding seriously. It didn't seem to occur to him that anyone at all could record these games; that, in fact, New York was probably full of people who were, at that moment, recording a ball game; and that all of those recordings would be worthless. It also didn't occur to him to consider the cost of videotapes, and I didn't remind him of it, but they do cost money, and we have only a couple, so that, instead of recording all the games, he has had to record every new game over an old one; at any one time the most he has is four or five games on tape.

To me, it is not a wise investment, but I keep this to myself, and I have almost gotten used to the sound of the VCR coming on when Teddy's at work. I might be reading, or sitting at the kitchen table, or even watching television myself, when suddenly from the machine will come a click, a whirr, and I know that somewhere, at this moment, the Yankees are playing a baseball game, moving like tiny little toys across the neat green square of a baseball field. The VCR is like having another person in the apartment, someone who does things for you that you don't particularly want done—someone I never see, but who always seems to be around, sneaking by me to turn on the VCR, then, when I look up, disappearing into the walls until the game is over.

The game Teddy is watching now was played this afternoon; it has already been lost by the Yankees, and discussed thoroughly by the men who stand around on the sidewalk just below our window. As Teddy watches the Yankees hit and catch and run, the team is already back in New York, resting for tomorrow's game. At work, Teddy puts his hands over his ears if he thinks anyone is going to talk about a game he's recording, for fear of hearing the score. His pleasure in watching is lost if he knows the outcome–every hit, every pitch, every play becomes meaningless if Teddy's presence in front of the television cannot somehow affect what has already happened. He is superstitious in this way, and he takes it almost personally when they lose: he did not cheer enough, he was not paying close enough attention, his mind was wandering. The Yankees lost today's game by only one run, and Teddy watches patiently as they build up a four-run lead that they will blow in the bottom of the ninth.

I skim through an article by a man who writes that his girl-friend never buys him the right present for his birthday; she is always getting him things like pillows for his couch and books of photographs, beautiful things for which, he says, men have no place in their homes. He follows his complaint with a list of appropriate gifts: Super Bowl tickets, a camera, sunglasses for skiing. None of these gifts would be suitable for Teddy, who cares only about our future and the Yankees; otherwise he seems to exist without interests, without desires. For his birthday I plan to buy him more videocassettes, so that he can record more games and have something to watch during the long winter, when he wanders aimlessly through our apartment, waiting for spring training to begin. Winter is a long way off, but when it comes, I seem never to be alone; sometimes Teddy adds an extra shift, and he does spend time studying, but mostly, when we're together, he is watching me, what I am doing, where I sit, when I go to bed.

—Hah, he says, and when the game cuts to a commercial, he rewinds the tape to watch the outfielder leap high against the fence to save a run. He rewinds and rewatches every important play; it can take him hours to get through a game, and when I once suggested to him that he advance the tape through the commercials, he smiled and shook his head. — You don't understand, he said. —That's part of the game.

That's why it's so relaxing–but he is always tense and hunched over on the floor as he watches, waiting for his team to lose again.

Downstairs a door slams; I turn to look out the window, and from the door below us a man emerges out onto the street; he struggles to breathe the summer air and walks uneasily toward the newsstand on the corner, then looks up and down Broadway, tracking the path of each cab that passes, but hailing none. He is coming from Madame Renalda's, whose business is directly below our apartment. MADAME RENALDA'S, it says on the door, over a large blue eye, and under that: FORTUNES TOLD. PALMS READ. I asked Teddy once if it might be a good idea to visit her and find out what lay ahead for us, but he just laughed.

—You are so naive, he said. —It's nothing but hookers. A massage joint. There are a thousand places like that in New York alone. He went back to his book on cost accounting, then held it up to me. —This is our future, he said.

—But she could read our palms, I told him, and looked down at my own hands. I couldn't imagine anyone reading a future in the smooth pink surface of my skin. He laughed again.

—She doesn't read palms, he said. —No one down there reads palms. There may not even really *be* such a thing as a palm reader.

He seemed so sure of himself, but I have seen the men who come out of there looking different from when they went in. When I told him this, he closed his book and looked at me.

—It's sex, he said. —That's what sex does. That's what it's for. It makes you feel different. It makes you feel like somebody else.

He said this as though he knew, though he is not much older than I, and he is always either at work or here with me. Sometimes since then I have looked at his dark hair slicked

back, and his thin eyebrows, and tried to imagine him with
a woman, his breath against her skin, his face pressed into
her breast, but my mind closes at the thought. That down
there, he told me once, was what he was protecting me
from, a life in a place like that, which is where he seems to
think I would surely have ended up on my own. Somebody
has to take care of me, he says, and he guesses it has to be
him, and I guess he is right. He is really all I have; he is
really all I remember having. Our father I can only vaguely
picture, a short dark man who stared at us uncomfortably,
an absence in our life for many years more than a presence,
and our mother lives in a small apartment on the East Side
with her new husband, Stan, her cat Smokey, and a dreamy
green aquarium full of tropical fish. They live there in the
light of a thousand bright ampules of morphine that Stan
keeps in the refrigerator; he brings them home from the
hospital where he works, which is why my mother loves him
as she does.
—Can I help it? she said when she left us to marry him. She
touched my face with her long dry fingers. —No, she
said. —I can't. Teddy will take care of you.
We visited her only once, and the whole time we were there,
she gazed right past us at the aquarium, Smokey in her lap,
Stan hovering unhappily behind her chair. When Stan
opened the icebox to try to find us something to drink,
Teddy didn't take his eyes away, looking in at all the vials
of morphine with a look of concentration so intense that I
thought even my mother might notice. It was only later that
I realized he was counting them, though for what purpose I
couldn't imagine; perhaps since he started working at the
store it had become second nature for him to keep track of
inventory, whatever it was. On the train home, Teddy stood
staring at the subway map, tracing all the various routes
with his finger; he didn't say a word about Stan or my

mother or the visit, and we have never gone back, but occasionally my mother calls, or Stan calls for her.

—Your mother wants to talk to you, Stan will say, hovering behind her while her mind tries to find its way back to the idea of talking to us. In the silence I can hear him breathing, and I can see my mother's sad gray face as she holds Smokey in her lap; together she and Smokey watch the blue fish flick across the surface of the aquarium, in and out of the tiny silver castle, behind the deep-sea diver. Their eyes narrow and widen with the glitter of light against the fish. —Honey? she says to me. —Honey? And after a few minutes Stan will take the phone from her hand and her long arms will fall back to her lap. —Goodbye, Stan always says politely. —It was nice talking to you. He watches her stroke Smokey. He worships her white arms and dreams of them at night. She touches Smokey's soft fur and feels his blood beat through his skin.

—She's as happy as she can be for now, Teddy always says. —She has everything she needs.

Teddy promises me that someday we will buy a big house in the mountains upstate, and she can come live with us, and Stan, too, if he wants, but for now he will not talk to her on the phone, and when she calls, he lifts his head halfway from his book and stares at the table until it is clear Stan has come on the line with me. —We have to take care of ourselves, Teddy says. —I have to keep an eye on you.

And he does. He keeps careful track of me as I grow older; he sits at the kitchen table and watches suspiciously as I cut away bruises from the discarded fruits and vegetables he brings home from the store; he glances up at me as I look out the window at the men down on the street; they smile at me as he turns each page of his book slowly, unread. There is not a moment I spend that he does not watch, and when he is at work, there is the VCR, keeping track of my day.

When I leave him, he will sit at the table and turn the pages of his book, and every now and then he will look at the couch in front of the window, but I will be gone. I will smile at him from the slick pages of magazines. Men will turn to watch me walk down the street, and I will have many lovers. He watches to see that this does not happen. Sometimes at night with him, I feel as if I am being born all over again, emerging abruptly into the blue light of the television screen and Teddy's anxious attention.

Downstairs the door slams again. Teddy does not move his thin back; he begins to relax as the Yankees continue to build their lead, and I look at the women in my magazine. Their faces are like the faces of birds, without expression, and I imagine what it would be like to have such red fingernails, how I would go to the grocery store with lips as red as these, how Teddy would look at me if suddenly my hair were to assume such strange shapes.

I go to bed before the catastrophe of the ninth inning. Teddy watches me walk to my room and turns down the television, but I can still hear the confusion when the game begins to slip away.

—Jesus, he says in a dull sigh, then later, again, —Jesus. Downstairs men move quietly through the rooms; I wonder what they read in the eyes of the women who gaze down into their palms.

Teddy stands at the mirror and straightens the black tie that is part of his uniform at the Safeway.

—There, he says, and smiles, then turns to me. —Listen, he says, —I'm taping a game, so don't use the VCR.

I have never used the VCR, but I nod and when he leaves I watch him walk down the street to work. He walks in the exact center of the sidewalk, not once looking around him.

Downstairs, on the pavement in front of Madame Renalda's, two men look up at me, brave in the daylight.

—Hey, one of them says. —Hey, girl.

They smile when I look down at them.

—Hey, says the other, —come on down here. You come on down here.

I stare at them, and they grin at each other; but they're not really smiling. Something hard and frightened waits behind their faces.

—What's wrong, honey, one says. —You deaf?

They laugh at this, and I watch Teddy turn the corner by the newsstand where young couples line up to buy the Saturday-evening edition of the Sunday paper, which they will carry home to spread across their shining wood floors. They will kneel over it and kiss across the fine print.

I close the window and the men laugh as it goes down. But when they can no longer see me, they lose interest, and look nervously at Madame Renalda's door.

I fall asleep in front of the game Teddy is taping, my hand resting on the shiny face of a beautiful woman. As I sleep or as I dream, the men from Madame Renalda's enter my apartment. They are followed by a herd of boys, jumpy in tight jeans and big sneakers. Slowly the men remove my clothes, slowly take their turns with me, while the boys anxiously watch but do not touch. When they leave, my blood trickles out into the streets behind them. The men pay no attention, but the boys stop and turn; they mix my blood with the sand and grit and glass in the streets to make tiny cakes. As they eat, blood stains their hands, their mouths, and when they finish, they stand in line at Madame Renalda's, nervously wiping at their red lips with their long red fingers. When I wake, a storm has come up, flapping the loose screen against the window. The game is on, but whether it is the tape of the earlier game, or the game itself, I can't

tell. Teddy is home and I listen as he pours himself a glass of milk. It's dark, but it could be any time. He comes into the room and smiles at me, a thin line of milk across his mouth, and downstairs a door opens, closes. Men move uneasily through the rooms below, and in the streets young boys cruise up and down, following a fading trail of blood.
—So, Teddy says, —why don't you come to the store tomorrow?
I nod and walk stiffly to my room. Teddy watches me for a moment, then turns to the baseball game.

Though it's only early summer, the heat is already suffocating; I hear the men on the street talking about it constantly, trying to explain to each other what they have not understood from the television news. —It's this greenhouse thing, they say knowledgeably, —it's just going to get hotter and hotter, and there's nothing anyone can do about it. They nod and wipe at their necks and faces, trying not to move too much in the airless heat. In the summer here, only insects move freely; they seem to thrive in the heat. Already they are breeding and being born, and the men watch with glazed eyes as insects crawl through their apartments, into their food, across the blank faces of their babies.
Women sit at windows and on fire escapes, looking down at the men, who are too hot to offer them more than a joyless attention, punctuated by an occasional spasm of anger or interest. Surrounded by the empty face of their future, the men can do no more than what's expected of them as they wait anxiously at Madame Renalda's door.
I stay inside most of the summer, reading the magazines Teddy brings me from work, except when he invites me to the store, where I sit in the air conditioning and watch him stack fruit.
Today when I come out of the apartment into the heat, the

men watch me without interest, mouth words without meaning. —Hey, baby, they say. —Hey, girl.
A man stands at the corner, handing out flyers. He flicks
them into the faces of people who pass, so they must take
one or brush his arm away. —Hey, he says. —Check it out.
He winks at me and hands me a flyer. MADAME RENALDA, it
says; A TRULY AMAZING PSYCHIC. —Check it out, the man says
again, and smiles a smile not meant for me, but he follows
me with his green eyes as I walk to the Safeway. Insects
flicker in front of me, across the hot sidewalk; underneath
the concrete there is a thin layer of them, moving gently
over the surface of the whole world, untouched by the feet
of men.

At the Safeway, women roam from line to line, looking for
the shortest, though even then there is always something to
slow things down, someone who has forgotten her check-
book, or hasn't brought enough money. As each woman settles finally into a line, she watches the progress of those
ahead of her for a while, then pulls down a magazine and
becomes lost in the enormous lives of people she does not
know: movie stars and rock singers and athletes. For a moment she reads and forgets herself, her cart, her child, and
when the time comes to pay, she looks up, startled away
from a world she can never inhabit, never even imagine
without the magazines to inspire her. She looks at the boxes
of cereal and bags of potato chips in her cart, at her child's
dirty face and cheap shoes, already too small, and puts the
magazine back, to enter, once again, with a kind of dull
surprise, her life.

In the produce department, Teddy arranges fruit in colorful
piles, stacking light green apples next to yellow ones, high

in a slant toward the mirror. His thin arms move smoothly
from the boxes to the neat banks of apples. His apron is
bright white, and his face looks tired and old under the glare
of the supermarket lights; fruits and vegetables rise neatly
around him. Suddenly a hand appears in front of my face,
holding a large red apple. I turn, and it is Donny, Teddy's
manager in the produce department. He smiles.
—Here, he says. —For you.
Donny and Teddy had been, for a brief while, a kind of
friends. Donny came over once or twice to watch ball games,
but he was a Mets fan, and seemed to take special pleasure
in every Yankee loss. As abruptly as he had begun to come,
he stopped; when I asked Teddy about it, he only said
that he didn't really like Donny's kind of person. —No ambi-
tion, he said, —he doesn't want to *be* anything. And besides,
he talks too much. This was true; the times he came over,
he sat on the couch and drank beer and talked all the way
through every game while Teddy stared straight ahead at
the television. Now he stands right in front of me, so close I
can smell something damp and fruity on his breath. Teddy
turns slightly, and in the mirror I can see him watching us.
—So, Donny says. —When did you get to be so cute?
His eyes close and open in a slow blink. I can see the outline
of a contact lens in the white of his eye, and when his lids
rise, the lenses shift, slipping around until they settle again.
—Huh? he says, and this is what I remember most about
his visits to our house, that he said —Huh? all the time.
—How about that Gooden, he'd say, —he's got any Yankee
pitcher all beat to hell, huh? And Teddy would crouch closer
to the screen. —Huh? Donny would say again. —How about
him?
—I don't remember you being so cute, he says now. —How
did that happen?

—I don't know, I say. —I guess it just did. I bring my hand
to my throat and leave it there, a gesture I have seen on
models in my magazines.

—Well, he says, —maybe I'll just have to come by sometime. He looks over at Teddy, then down at my hand against
my throat. —How about that? he says. —Huh?

—I don't know, I say. Teddy has gone back to putting apples in neat rows, but in the mirror his eyes meet mine.
Donny watches him for a moment, then smiles at me.

—Here, he says, and hands me the apple. It is perfect,
without a bruise.

As Donny walks away, Teddy's eyes follow, his hand resting
on a bank of pale yellow apples.

—So, he says, —what were you talking to Donny about?

—Nothing, I say, and he wipes his hands on his white apron.

—What's wrong with your neck? he asks. —I saw you rubbing your neck.

—Nothing, I say. —It itches.

—Well, he says, —okay. Here. He hands me one of the
apples he has arranged. —These green ones are better than
the red. They're not so big but they taste better.

Donny looks at me from his corner by the avocados, and as
I leave, I can feel his eyes on me all the way out of the store.

—Look, Teddy says when he comes home, and he pulls
from his grocery bag a loaf of store bread, a few spotted
bananas, and finally, carefully, an avocado. He smiles.

—We can have this for dinner, he says, —in a salad or
something. The avocado is perfectly ripe and green, and we
eat it with salt.

—When I'm promoted, Teddy says, —we'll eat like this all
the time. As he gently peels the skin away from a piece of
avocado, the buzzer rings. We look at each other and at the

door; finally Teddy puts down his avocado and answers the
door. It is Donny, smiling, holding a six-pack of beer.

—Hey, he says, and looks past Teddy at me. —Hey, he says
to me.

—We're eating, Teddy says. —We just started eating.

—Oh, Donny says, and looks past Teddy again, at the table. —And eating pretty well, too, he says, —huh? He
winks at me, and Teddy turns to look at the avocado.

—Well, Donny says, —I was just in the neighborhood, and
I thought I'd come by to, you know, watch the game.

—It's over, Teddy says. —They played this afternoon.
Donny steps forward. —I thought you recorded all the
games.

—No, Teddy says. —Not all of them. He backs up a step,
starts to smooth his hands down the front of his shirt, then
looks down at his green fingers and stops.

—Well, says Donny, —okay. I was just in the neighborhood. Anyways, he adds, —they lost. He winks at me
again. —See *you* later, he says, and turns.
Teddy locks the door behind him and pulls the chain across,
even though it is not yet fully dark out. He sits down and
gazes at the avocado on his plate.

—You know, he says. —I don't really like him.

—I thought he was your friend, I say.

—He's not my friend. Seems like he's more your friend,
Teddy says.
He mashes his avocado with his fork and we watch as it
squeezes greenly through the tines. Finally he stands and
takes his plate to the garbage and scrapes it clean. The
avocado leaves a green streak across the white plate.

—You know, Teddy says, and turns to the sink to wash his
plate, —I might like to have a friend too.

—You could have friends, I say. —At work. There are lots
of people there.

—No, he says, —I don't have time. I have responsibilities.

I salt the last piece of avocado. —What responsibilities? I ask.

—To you, he says. —I have responsibilities to you.

He turns from the sink. His shirt is wet where water has splashed on it, and through the cheap white cotton I can see the skin and the few dark hairs of his stomach.

He turns on the television and the VCR, then sits down, patiently waiting as today's game rewinds. By now Donny will be entering the subway, pushing money through the window for a token, pressing against the turnstile. Teddy finishes rewinding the tape and settles back on his knees to watch the game, though Donny has spoiled it for him by telling him the outcome. As the first batter comes to the plate, Donny is staring out the dirty window of his train and the Yankees are flying back to New York. Teddy watches each meaningless play without expression, and I open my magazine. Finally he leans forward and snaps the television off.

—Shit, he says. He goes to the window, then comes to sit beside me on the couch. He stares down at the article I'm reading, about young girls with anorexia nervosa.

—Why do you read that stuff? he says. —It's not learning anything.

—Well, I say. —It is, kind of. This article, for example, is about girls who starve to death.

He looks at me. —I know what anorexia is, he says. —I can *read*. But so what? What do you know that you didn't know before? How is that going to get you anywhere? He stands up and walks to the television. —I mean, he says, —it's not really important.

He lies down on the floor in front of the television and holds his hands above his head. —You want to learn things that

are important, he says, gazing up at his pale palms, —not
that stuff from women's magazines. He looks at me.
—You're not even a woman, he says. —Not really.
Finally he gets up and pulls down one of his books, a red
one on cost accounting. He sits at the table and opens it,
but I can feel his eyes on me. I put my hand on the mouth
of a beautiful woman in an advertisement for French champagne. I imagine myself drinking champagne, speaking
French. I imagine myself slowly starving to death. Teddy
leans over his book and stares at me; from time to time he
bats at one of the bugs circling in the white light above him.
He bends his head to read, but he turns the pages too
quickly, page after page until he snaps the book closed and
pulls down another.
By this time Donny has reached his home, and sits vacantly
in front of his television. When I go to bed, Teddy stands
just outside my door. I can hear his fingernails click against
the coins in his pocket. The Yankees have arrived safely at
LaGuardia by now, and for a long time Teddy stands in front
of the dark screen of the television, listening to the men
move restlessly from room to room below him. Once or twice
before I fall asleep, I hear the occasional quick clamor of a
crowd, as Teddy turns the game on, then right back off.

When Teddy comes home from work, his face is pale and
his eyes look like pieces of bruised fruit.
—Well, he says, glancing at the VCR to make sure it is still
recording today's game. —Well, I got transferred today. He
stands at the sink and watches me put spaghetti on the table
before he sits down.
—To the meat department, he says. —Now I'm in the meat
department.
He tries to twirl his spaghetti around his fork, but ends up

with either too large or too small a bite. Finally he gives up twirling and begins to cut the spaghetti with his knife.

—I guess, he says, —I wasn't stacking the fruit right. Donny told me today. See, he says, and puts down his fork, leaning forward, over his plate. —See, if you put bananas, for example, too close to something, they make it get ripe too fast. They emit some kind of gas.

—Gas? I say.

—Gas, he says. —At least that's what Donny says. He says if you put a banana next to an apple or something, one of them gets ripe too fast.

He stares for a moment at the tiny arrows running forward on the VCR. —I don't know, he says. —I think it sounds kind of weird. I never heard of any gas.

He sighs and sinks his fork into the spaghetti on his plate. —You know, he says after a minute, glancing up at me, then back down at his food, —Donny never said there was anything wrong with my work before. There is something suspicious in his voice, and his eyes flicker up to me again, then back to his plate, then to me.

—Well, I finally say, —maybe you're looking at it wrong.

—Looking at it wrong?

—You could be, I say. —Maybe there are more opportunities for advancement in the meat department.

"Opportunities for advancement" is one of Teddy's favorite phrases. In fact, he tells me, the key to our eventual success in the Safeway is going to depend on his ability to take advantage of opportunities for advancement.

He moves his spaghetti around in a big clump on his plate, then lays down his fork. —You know, he says. —Maybe you're right. Maybe Donny's doing me a favor. I'm not so sure I was going anywhere in the produce department.

He looks at me almost hopefully. —Maybe it's a lateral

move, he says and pushes his plate away, nodding. —Yeah, he says, —a lateral move. Maybe this is what I've been waiting for. I just have to make something of it.

He carries his plate to the sink, and turns. —I don't know, though, he says. —I kind of liked the produce department. I wish I'd known that thing about the gas.

He goes to the TV and squats in front of it, watching the arrows. The game he is recording started in late afternoon. It should be over now, so he flicks the television on, just for a second, to check, but at the moment the picture appears, the score flashes on the screen.

—Shit, he says, and snaps the television off, but it's too late: he's seen the score. —Damn, he says. He sits on the floor and stares at the VCR, while I clean the rest of the dishes.

—You know what we need? he asks, then answers: —Cable. If we had cable, we could watch games all the time. They have that twenty-four-hour sports channel, and all those teams have their own stations. The Cubs. He stops for a moment to think. —The Braves. There would be baseball games all day.

—Isn't cable expensive? I ask.

—I don't know, he says. —It would be worth it. At least we could see some teams that win once in a while.

He rewinds the tape and turns on the game, but I can feel him watching me clean up the kitchen. When I turn back around, he is on the couch, flipping through my magazine, while in front of him the Yankees are laboring to lose another game. Downstairs the door to Madame Renalda's opens, and he looks up. On the television, the Yankee first baseman hits a long fly ball to knock in a run, but Teddy watches for only a moment, then looks back at the magazine. As he reads, his feet shuffle against the floor, and his hand taps the back of the magazine. After I dry the dishes, I join him on the couch, but he ignores me, staring down at the article on anorexia.

—There might be something on TV, I say. —Maybe another ball game.

He looks up. —I don't care, he says. —You can turn it to something else.

—Don't you want to study? I ask. He looks up again and stares at me for a moment, then puts the magazine down and goes to the table. He sighs as he sets a pile of books on the table, then opens one and begins to read. Tiny insects crawl across the pages of his book, insects fly in front of his eyes, and downstairs insects crawl in and out of the mouths of men.

—Well, says Teddy when he comes home from his first day in the meat department, —my first day on the job.

He looks hopefully at the television, though the Yankees did not play today, then puts his bag on the counter. He pulls out store milk, store bread, and, from the bottom, a package of hamburger.

—A bonus, he says. —A first-day bonus.

He puts the hamburger on the table, and stands back to admire it. The meat is covered with a skin of plastic, stretched tight except where it is caught and bunched up by the label.

—I wrapped this, he says. —I didn't grind the meat, but I wrapped it.

He squares the package of meat with the corner of the table, lining it up neatly. —I guess the label's a little messy, he says.

—It looks good, I say. —Really great.

He smiles. —I'm a natural, he says, and pokes at the tight plastic. —Look at that. No slack.

He looks into the bag. There is nothing else there, so he folds it neatly and slides it into the space between the counter and the icebox.

—You know, he says, —there's really a lot to learn at this job. This is just the start. Tomorrow I learn how to grind it up, cut steaks, all that. He runs his finger across the smooth surface of the plastic that covers the meat. —This is just the start.

He turns on the television and switches through the few channels we get; the screen casts a faint glow against his face, turning it green, then red, then blue. I unwrap the tight plastic from the hamburger, and underneath the cellophane the meat is soft and smells of blood. When I fry it, bits of grease pop up out of the pan at me, and when I'm done, a fine brown spray covers the back of the stove.

Teddy touches his hamburger gently with his fork, as if he had expected it to look different. We seldom have meat, and the hamburgers are overcooked, shriveled little tough things next to the yellow wax beans on our plates; I thought the beans would make a nice balance with the meat, but Teddy only pushes them about with his fork, making a little circle around his hamburger.

—You know, he says, —I kind of miss the produce department. He puts a bean on top of his hamburger. —I don't really know if I'm going to like working with meat. —All those knives and things. He looks at the blank television screen. Somewhere a baseball game is being played.

—Well, he says, —I think I'll go get a paper or something. He carries his food to the garbage, and as the hamburger slips into the bag, it leaves a dark, shimmering trail on the plate.

I watch him from the window, but he walks straight to the newsstand on the corner; after he buys his paper, he stands for a moment, looking up Broadway. Around him men stir, young women buy fresh whole pieces of fruit at the stands, couples rotate in and out of the light, but he turns and comes back to our apartment, looking neither to the left nor to the right. He walks right past the men on the sidewalk downstairs. When I put the plates and the pan in the sink, the water turns brown and oily. The smell of meat lingers in our apartment, and all evening as Teddy stares at his books, I can feel a thin layer of grease on my hands, coming between me and everything I touch.

I wake up from my nap on the couch to the sound of the buzzer.

—Cable, says a voice from the door, and a young black man with a toolbox smiles at me when I open the door. He comes in, looks around the apartment, pats at the walls.

—So, he says, going to the window, —you want cable.

—No, I say. —My brother does.

—Uh-huh, he says, and begins to pull out tools. —What do you want, better reception, probably, huh?

—No, I say. —My brother wants the twenty-four-hour sports channel.

He walks to the window and looks out. The men on the sidewalk look up with mild interest, but he pays them no attention. They watch as he drills a hole in the wall, runs a white cable through it, then attaches the white cable to a black one outside the window.

—You're lucky, he says, and turns away from the window. —A lot of these old buildings aren't wired for cable. I guess they don't want people putting any more holes in the walls.

He pulls out a long stretch of cable from a box, cuts it off, and begins running it along the wall, stapling it every foot or so, until it runs out, more than a yard away from the television set. He looks at the end of the cable, looks at the television, then at the window and back to the cable.

—Shit, he says. —Goddamn. He looks at me. —Sorry, he says, and laughs. —I can't believe I did that. I've been doing this job for over two years. He shakes his head and smiles as he goes back and undoes everything he's just done. The men on the sidewalk look up and watch him.

—You know, he says, —I'm having a day like this. Ever have a day like this, where you just make a lot of stupid mistakes?

I try to think of mistakes, or even opportunities for mistakes in my days. —I guess so, I say. —All the time. But he is threading more white cable through the hole again.

—I don't know, he says. —Maybe I'm just tired of this job. He looks at me. —I've been doing it for two years. Know what I mean?

—I guess so, I say. —Two years is a long time.

He winds out cable again, and begins the process of stapling it to the wall. —You got that right, he says. —Two years *is* a long time. Maybe too long. He attaches the cable to a little box, hooks up some wires, and stands back.

—You know, he says, —maybe you're right. Maybe I'm just tired of this job. Stale, you know? Got to move on to something new.

He pulls a lever on the cable box and the unused cable snaps in, winding like a snake across the floor. The man pulls a little book from his bag.

—Okay, he says. —Here's your book. He flips through it and stops at a page full of numbers and letters. —This tells you what your channels are, see?

—Which is the one with sports all day? I ask, and he runs his long finger down the page.

—Okay, he says, —this here's your sports channel. He looks up at me. —That's a lot of sports.

—It's for my brother, I say. —He wanted it.

—Uh-huh, he says, and hands me the book, then looks around for his things.

—Oh man, he says, and turns back to the television. —We got to try it out and see if it works.

He crouches in front of the television and turns it on, tapping the top of the set as he waits for the picture. —Okay, he says when a picture appears, and he flicks the dial of the cable box from one end to the other. —Okay, he says again, and stands, turning off the television.

He stops at the door. —Hey, he says, —nice talking to you. Thanks. And who knows? Maybe I'll be doing something different next week. He laughs. —You never know, he says. —I could do anything.

He walks out into the bright light of the city and I turn to the television. When I put it on, the room darkens and the city fades away. Downstairs the women pause, listen for a moment, then turn back to the men in front of them. Madame Renalda stops and waits as I run through all the channels. She is quiet a moment, then looks into the eyes of the man in front of her. —Don't marry, she says to him. —Never marry.

I find a game between the Cubs and a team whose uniform I don't recognize, and I turn down the sound. Silence settles again over our apartment, and in the bright Chicago afternoon, fans smile as they watch their team.

When Teddy comes home, he looks immediately at the television, and smiles at the cable box on top.

—Great, he says, turning it on. —This is going to be great. He looks at me with shining, hopeful eyes. —Now we can watch games all the time.

From the grocery bag he's left on the counter, I take a box

of cookies and a steak, tightly wrapped, but without a label.
Teddy glances at me.

—Second-day bonus, he says.

—I don't know how to cook a steak, I say. —I never cooked
a steak.

—You cook it like you cook anything else, he says, looking
back to the TV. —Steak is basically just hamburger before
you grind it up. He switches happily from channel to channel. —Basically, he says, —that's what it is.

—You can fry steak? I ask.

—Sure, he says. —Fry it, bake it, whatever you want.

He stops at the sports channel, and watches as two men
discuss the day's events in sports, then he changes the
channel again, up and down the dial until he finds a baseball
game, which he watches while I fry the steak. The steak
turns brown as it cooks, and tiny balls of fat bead up on its
surface.

Teddy eats only a few bites. —It's a little tough, he says
finally, putting down his fork. —Maybe this isn't how you're
supposed to cook it.

—Don't they tell you how to cook it there? I ask.

—Of course not, he says. —I just cut it up. He stares into
the living room, at the game, which plays as we eat.

—So who's winning? I ask.

—What? he says.

—The game. Who's winning the game?

—Oh, he says. —I don't know. He thinks a moment.
—I don't know, he says. —They'll have the score in a
minute.

—So, I say. —How do you like the meat department?

—Oh, he says. —I guess it's okay.

He chews for a while and finally pushes his plate back, most of his steak uneaten. —Listen, he says. —Do you know what an abattoir is?

I know I have heard this word before, and I think until it comes to me. —A bedroom, I say. —It's a bedroom. In French.

He stares at me, then shakes his head. —A bedroom. He laughs. —You don't learn much from those magazines.

I put a piece of steak in my mouth and chew until it's soft enough to swallow. It tastes dark and unpleasant.

—An abattoir, he says, —is the technical name for a slaughterhouse. He shakes his head. —A bedroom, he says again. He gazes at the television for a moment. The Yankees are scheduled to play a late game tonight, sometime after this ball game ends.

—Anyways, he says, —my boss in the meat department says I can make more money if I transfer there. He says they always need people. I guess the store has one just out of town. Or something like that.

He stares down at the flat black piece of steak on his plate. —It's the same job, pretty much, just cutting up meat. Like I do now. I wouldn't be killing them, he says, his eyes on the television. —Just cutting them up after they're already dead.

A score flashes on the screen to report that the Mets are winning their game. —Shit, Teddy says, then looks at me. —I don't know. It might be a quicker way to the top.

—Well, I say, —if it's the same job.

—I guess it is, he says. —Anyways, I'm going to check it out. What's to lose? He smiles. —This could be the start of something. Really it could. You never know.

He stands, leaving his steak on the table, and, with his future ahead of him, he lies in front of the television to wait patiently for the game. I chew my steak until my jaws grow

tired, then wash the dishes and sit on the couch behind
Teddy.
—Well, I say, —so I guess everything's looking up at work.
But he says nothing.
—I guess the meat department must be a lot cleaner than
the produce section, I say. Teddy has complained about how
bugs get into the produce, and once or twice I think I've
seen them, tiny little black specks skimming speedily over
the bright skins of the fruit.
—Cleaner? he says. —I guess it's cleaner.
He looks at his hands. —It looks cleaner, he says. —On the
outside, where the meat is sold. He glances at the game on
the television. —But behind the glass, you know what they
have? About a thousand hunks of animals. And I have to cut
them up. You should see those things. Big huge cows. Pigs.
Lambs. He sits up and looks at me. —They have lambs.
And chickens.
He lies back down. When the door to Madame Renalda's
slams, his head moves. He listens, staring at the window,
and just as I lean back to look out the window, a man comes
out onto the sidewalk. He looks up and down the street, but
sees nothing familiar in a city in which he has lived his entire
life; finally he sets off uncertainly up Broadway, going north.
When I turn back to Teddy, he is watching me with round,
hollow eyes.

On Teddy's first day at the abattoir, I practice the word all
afternoon.
—Abattoir, I say to the men on the street, and they look up,
watching my lips move, wondering what I might be saying
to them. —Abattoir, I say, and they look off to watch the
long legs of girls bending to get in and out of cars. Their
faces register nothing, their minds move for a moment

against the smooth skin of the girls' legs, then return without interest to my face, my lips, the words they can't hear. The door to Madame Renalda's opens and closes, and they step in and out. Longing for the simple legs of the young girls, they move instead toward the beautiful women inside. —Abattoir, I whisper to them as they enter, and for a moment they pause, then go inside.

By the time Teddy comes home from work, his shirt damp, his black tie unknotted, the word is mine. —So, I say carelessly, —how was your day at the abattoir?

I stir the spaghetti on the stove to show my nonchalance. He walks to the counter, but when he gets there, he realizes he has no grocery bag, so he just stands and watches me stir. Finally he turns on the water in the sink and holds his hands under it.

—Abattoir, he says, and laughs. He dries his hands and pulls from his pocket a small jar of something red.

—Here, he says, and holds it up. —It's caviar. It was on sale. I couldn't pass it up. He reads the label. —It's from Russia. Russian caviar. That's the best kind.

He puts the jar on the table and looks around, as if he is expecting more. —I don't want that job, he says. —I'm not going to take it. That's the dirtiest place I ever saw.

He picks up the caviar and looks at it closely. —You'd never know these were fish eggs, he says. —I wonder how they even lay eggs in the water. You'd think they'd float away.

He puts the jar down and watches me drain the spaghetti. —I'm not going to tell you how they kill the animals, he says. —No one should have to know that.

He leans against the counter and watches me while I finish cooking, while I set out plates, while I sit to eat. He opens the jar of caviar and puts it on the table between us. It smells fishy, and when I take a bite of it, I can feel all the

tiny eggs burst open between my teeth, a thousand fish
loosed in my mouth.

—You don't have to eat it if you don't like it, Teddy says.

—I like it, I say. —It would just be better on crackers or
something.

Teddy picks up the jar. —I mean, he says, —how do they
even catch all these little eggs? They must have to use tiny
nets.

—Maybe they stick to rocks, I say. —Or maybe they lay
them in little sacs, and *they* stick to the rocks.

He nods. —Little sacs, he says. —That's probably it.

He pushes his plate away and gazes over at the television.
Now that his schedule has changed, he says it's harder to
keep up with the games. The Yankees are in California tonight and they don't play until later, but Teddy lies down in
front of the television, turns it on, and flicks the switch up
and down the cable box, stopping at a horse race, which he
watches while I clean up our dishes. I sit behind him on the
couch just as another race is about to start. Teddy watches
closely, as though he cares anything about horse racing.

—Listen, he says abruptly, not looking back at me. In front
of him, the jockeys raise up on their horses. —You should
see this place.

The horses come out of the gates and one pulls ahead
quickly, but just as another comes up beside it, Teddy
changes the channel, running the switch up and down, so
fast all the stations come through only as a blur of images;
then he goes back through them, more slowly this time, and
from what I can tell, there are at least five channels playing
sports, all different. Teddy passes by a tennis match, bowl-
ing, some sort of track event, golf, and finally pauses at a
hockey game.

—Hockey, he says. —What a stupid sport. But he leans

back on his elbows to watch it. On the screen, two of the hockey players, dressed in bulky clownish uniforms, have squared off to fight, but because each has hold of the other's shirt, they can only spin around and around, almost gracefully, locked together. When the referee skates over to break up the fight, Teddy leans forward and changes the channel. He passes right by a fashion show, which I would like to watch, and finally stops at the station that broadcasts only weather reports. He turns the sound down and sits back.

—They herd the cows in a long line right into this building, he says, —into this big room. They call it the kill room.

The man on the weather channel gestures cheerfully up at a chart, smiling as he uses a stick to trace the path of a big white blur across a map of New York.

—Then they kill them, Teddy says. —Well, first they knock them out. Then they kill them. This guy stands there while they come down the line, and he hits them in the head.

He watches intently as the blur travels toward New York, and I pick up my magazine. —He knocks most of them out with just one hit, Teddy says. —Just like that. Wham. Right between the eyes.

He looks around at me. —This guy must do fifty cows an hour. You should see his arms. I guess, he says, turning back to the television, —I guess it's the cheapest way.

I try to concentrate on the article I am reading, about how to love again after an unhappy affair.

—This one cow, Teddy says, —he didn't knock out right away.

He is silent as the weather report shows a chart giving the temperatures in cities all over the world: Paris, Moscow, Berlin. I try to imagine what it would be like to live in one of these cities, what I would wear, how my voice would sound in a different language.

—It just kind of kept on trying to move, Teddy says. —But it couldn't really go anywhere.

In Frankfurt it is sixty-five degrees, but I don't remember what country Frankfurt is in. I close my eyes and try to remember. Germany, it comes to me. I go back to my magazine.

—So he hit him again. Wham.

After a loss or a breakup, the article says, it is natural never to want to love again.

—There was nothing I could do, Teddy says. —Nothing.

A commercial comes on, selling some kind of car wax especially made for rainy weather, and Teddy watches it with interest. —I need that, he says, though we do not have a car.

—Anyways, he says, —then this big chain comes down and hoists them up.

He is quiet, watching the rest of the commercials until the weather report comes back on. —Then they cut their throats, he says. —And they bleed to death.

He switches the channel and stops at a cartoon. —Look, he says. —Cartoons.

He sits back and watches two little men work frantically to stop a leaky pipe; predictably the pipe explodes, and Teddy laughs. I look back at my article. In the picture that accompanies it, a beautiful woman is staring at a photograph of a man, touching his paper cheek with her long paper fingers.

—It's incredible, Teddy says, and I look up. He has switched back to the horse race; all the horses are clumped up coming around a curve, their sharp fragile hooves beating into the dirt.

—You should see their eyes, Teddy says. —And they make the weirdest noises. Especially when they get closer and they see what's going to happen. I guess they can smell it, too. It's like, and he pauses. —I don't know what it's like. It's like a dream. They just keep on coming.

I turn the page of my magazine; the woman in the picture is now in the arms of a different man; the photograph of the first man is on the ground at her feet. Abattoir, she whispers in her new lover's ear.

—There's blood everywhere, Teddy says. —You wouldn't believe the blood. It's up to your ankles. I don't know how those guys stand it. They have to wear rubber boots.

He sits back on his heels and watches the announcers discuss the horse race.

—I don't know, he says thoughtfully, as though he is responding to a question I've asked him. —I guess the worst thing is the smell.

He finally turns to me, his blue eyes gone white and empty. —But you don't want to hear this, he says. —No one should have to hear this.

He turns back and switches to the Yankees station, where the game is already under way. It is a slow, late game, and I go to bed before it's half over. Just as I am falling asleep, I hear Teddy turn it off. He moves slowly across the floor to my door, and I lie still until he walks away. The door to our apartment opens, closes; the lock turns. There is no window in my bedroom, so I try to hear him through the walls, but I lose the sound of his footsteps in the general shuffle of men downstairs and outside on the street. When I fall asleep, I dream of a room full of animals, with white simple eyes; they are all circled around my bed, and each holds up a paw, a leg, a piece of flesh for me to cook.

I wake when Teddy comes home and I listen to him move through the tiny rooms of our apartment. Finally he goes to bed, but in the dark I can feel him start at each noise; he sits up and stares into the corners of his room, but there is nothing there except the simple empty eyes of animals.

*   *   *

Teddy has decided to stay at the meat department in the Safeway, despite the raise he's offered to go to the abattoir. Every night he brings home meat instead of discarded fruits and vegetables; the meat seems to breed roaches, or at least attract them, and because I cannot seem to learn to cook it well, we end up throwing most of it away. It smells like something rotting in the heat, and I would like to take the garbage out after every meal, but Teddy says it would be a waste of plastic bags, so I just add whatever we don't eat to the garbage, sliding it on top of what we didn't eat the night before, and the night before that; sometimes I think I see little dark things moving around under all the big chunks of brown and gray, although it could be a trick of the light. Along with the meat, Teddy brings home odd things, like hearts of palm and pomegranates, foods we never eat. I put them in little bowls that sit on the table between us as we chew at our steak.

Tonight, Teddy has brought home a coconut, which he rolls toward me on the table. —You have to poke it in one of these holes before you can crack it, he says. —Those are the eyes. He stares at the television set; the VCR is recording a Yankees game right now; he has missed the first few innings, but, as usual, he wants to see the whole game all at once, so he watches the little red arrows run forward, and wonders when it will be safe to turn on the TV. I put the coconut in the icebox.

—So, I say. —Maybe I can come to see the store tomorrow. He looks up at me. —The store? he says. —No, I don't think so. He looks back at the television. —I don't think you'd like it. It's not very clean.

He rubs at an oily spot on his pants. —It's really not very clean at all.

*   *   *

From the outside the store looks clean and pleasant. I go first to the produce section, to see if it has changed in Teddy's absence. It looks different somehow, although the bananas seem to be where they were before, next to the apples. Donny stands in a corner and watches a woman as she looks quickly around and breaks two bananas off a bunch. Just as he is about to approach her, his yellow eyes fall on me. He smiles a kind of smile and wipes his hands on his apron, but before he reaches me, I turn and walk toward the back of the store.

I stand in the middle of the cookie aisle, where I can watch the meat department. From here the meat case looks clean and orderly: shiny rows of red steak, white pork, yellowish halves of chicken; behind it, through the window, the butcher's area looks almost surgical, all white walls and polished metal. There are no people back there, no one anywhere, until Teddy comes through the steel doors, carrying several packages of meat. He arranges them all carefully in the meat case, and turns, wiping his hands on his apron, which has become bright pink in front. He looks around, and his eyes meet mine; even at this distance I can see that he has not shaved today. He looks away immediately, and goes back through the steel doors. I turn and there is Donny, watching me with yellow eyes, smiling his yellow smile.

—Yo, a voice calls from the street. —Yo, Ted.
Teddy looks up from his steak and glances at the television. A game is starting soon, in just a few minutes.
—Don't let him in, Teddy says. —He'll talk all the way through the game.
I go to the window and look down onto the sidewalk; Donny smiles up at me.
—Yo, he says. He holds up a six-pack in one hand and in

the other a bunch of flowers. I go to the door to let him in, and Teddy slips his steak into the garbage. By the time Donny reaches the top of the stairs, Teddy is on his knees in front of the television. Donny smiles at me over the flowers, the kind they keep cold in a huge bin of ice at the Safeway. He pushes them at me as he comes in, and I bring them to my face, but they have no smell, only a kind of cold supermarket chill.

—Teddy, he says. —How's it going? He sniffs the air. —Smells like steak in here.

He winks at me. —Coming up in the world? he says, and pulls a beer from the six-pack. —Teddy, how about a beer? Teddy shakes his head, not looking away from the television, though it's only showing a car commercial.

—Okay, Donny says. —Just thought I'd stop by and say hello, see if you were watching the game. Just like old times, he says, and winks again. —Huh?

He pops his beer open and sits on the couch. I sit beside him and the three of us stare at the television, but none of us is really watching the game. Donny drapes his arm like a wet towel across the back of the couch, and Teddy draws figure eights with his finger in the carpet beside his knees.

—So, Ted, Donny says, —how's the butcher business? Teddy turns. —Did you come to watch the game, he says, —or to talk?

—Hey, Donny says. —Hey. Just trying to make conversation. He smiles, and Teddy turns back to the game just as the batter pops out to end the inning.

—Hey, Ted, Donny says, —haven't you heard about how you can get cancer if you sit too close to the TV? Some kind of X-ray poisoning or something.

Teddy gets up and takes a beer from the six-pack Donny has brought. —No, he says. —I hadn't heard that.

—Like the gas from bananas, I say, and they both look at me as if I have said something in a foreign language.

—Oh, Donny finally says. —Yeah. He nods. —You know, Ted, he says seriously, —that can really be a problem.

Teddy stands in the middle of the floor running his finger around the top of his can of beer. He stares at a spot in the middle of the rug, and Donny and I wait for him to say something, but then the game comes on and he sits back down.

—So, Donny says, looking at the back of Teddy's head, moving his arm along the couch toward me. —So, he says again, and rests his hand beside my head, then drops it down to my shoulder, where it rests a moment. I can smell the faint rotten smell of apples just turning. Donny smiles at Teddy's back and moves his hand to my neck; each cold finger feels like a spider creeping across my skin. Teddy stares straight ahead as Mookie Wilson fades back into the outfield after a fly ball; he hits the fence hard, but comes up with the catch. Now that he is no longer a Met, he is one of Teddy's favorite players, even though he's not a Yankee. Donny laughs.

—Look at that dumb spade, he says. —Mookie. What the hell kind of a name is Mookie?

He flips my hair back, over the couch. —Baseball used to be a different kind of game, he says to me. —*You* know what I mean.

I pick up my magazine as the play is shown again, in slow motion. Teddy watches it closely, nodding, and I turn to an article about recapturing the magic in a lifeless relationship.

—Hey, Donny says, —whatcha reading?

—Nothing, I say, but I show him the magazine. He reads the title, then makes a little snorting sound through his nose.

—Magic, he says. —Shit.

I go back to the article and try to pick up the thread. But

after a moment Donny reaches over and closes the magazine.

—So, he says. He leaves his hand in my lap, on top of the
magazine, and I am surprised at the way it looks, long and
thin, almost delicate.

I close my eyes and tell myself that he has the clean handsome features of one of the men in the pictures in my magazine, but when I look up at him, it is his same face, his
same greasy smile.

—What? I say, but he says nothing, only nods toward the
closed bedroom doors. I look at Teddy, stiffly alert in front
of the ball game.

—Teddy won't mind, Donny says. —Will you, Ted?

—Do you mind? Teddy says, not turning. —I'm trying to
watch the game.

Donny looks around at the things in my room. He picks up
a picture of Teddy and my mother and me. My mother is
looking distantly out at whoever is taking the picture, and
even then it is clear that her mind was on something else.

—This your mom? Donny says. —She looks zonked.

He puts the picture down and smiles. —Well, kiddo, he
says, and his eyes turn green with excitement. His hands on
my shoulders aren't rough, but they are firm, and I imagine
these same hands moving over bananas, onions, yams.
When he touches me, I can tell that he has done this a
thousand times before, and that not one of these times has
been different from any other. He closes his eyes to kiss me,
but I know he is thinking of his mother, and as his hand
crosses my skin, what it touches disappears: my mouth, my
eyes, my bones, they all disappear, and what he says to me
—honey, baby, sweetheart—these words are what I become.
His skin grates against mine until I cannot differentiate between skin and the fragile flesh beneath. After what seems

like only a moment, he pulls away, and when he stands, he
looks down to see that the sheets are stained with little
splashes of blood. His face changes, but just for a second;
then he grins.

—Well, well is all he says, and he bends to put on his shoes.
As he leaves the room, a thin trail of blood follows him,
trickling across the floor behind Teddy, who is watching the
slow-motion replay of a perfect bunt and so does not notice.
Blood trails Donny out the door and falls through the thin
cracks of the ceiling. A drop falls on the face of a man
downstairs; he looks up and then at the woman in front of
him, who smiles and wipes it away; he closes his eyes and
feels nothing but the soft touch of her hand upon his skin.

Teddy tightens his tie in front of the mirror.

—You know, he says to me,—I might like a lover. His eyes
meet mine in the mirror. —I might like a lover too. Did you
ever think about that?

I say nothing and go back to watching the morning news.

—But, he says, —I have my responsibilities. He runs his
fingers gently over his cheeks.

—You know, I say, —I could leave here. I could leave here
anytime.

He puts his face close to the mirror and turns it from side to
side. —You're only seventeen, he says. —And you can't *do*
anything.

—I could learn, I say. —I could learn lots of things. You
never know. I could do anything.

He laughs. —You could, he says. —But why would you?

He clenches and unclenches his jaw, holding his fingertips
against his cheek to feel the muscles pop in and out. He
nods at himself and turns. When he walks by the kitchen
table, he stops and looks down at the flowers Donny
brought.

—You know, he says, —these are just supermarket flowers. They're not from a flower shop or anything. We sell them in the store. He bends and sniffs them, then straightens and laughs. —They don't even smell, he says.

When he passes me, he smiles pleasantly, and closes the door gently behind him.

At this moment, Donny must be waking up, putting on his shirt, brushing his teeth. He may cut himself shaving, and as he blots away the blood, he may think for a moment of me, but my face is lost in a wash of women's faces, and he smiles at himself in the mirror. It is already clear to me that he will not return. And so, I tell myself, I will find another lover. I will find another. As I scrape the bacon left from Teddy's breakfast into the garbage, I can already feel the touch of my new lover, tracing the pattern left by Donny's hand against my skin.

When I call my mother, Stan answers the phone.

—Well, he says. —Well, hello. How are you, honey? And Teddy? How's Teddy?

—Fine, I say. —We're both fine.

—Good, he says. —That's really good. He pauses for a moment. —I guess you called to talk to your mother, he says.

—Yes, I say. —I guess so.

He is quiet for a moment. —She's a little tired, he says. —She's not really herself today, so maybe just a short talk. I can hear the soft brush of skin against the phone as Stan puts his hand over the receiver, then my mother's voice.

—Hello? she says. —Hello?

—Mother, I say. —It's me.

There is another sound, a squeak or a little murmur, a cat sound, and I know I have lost her for the moment.

—Smokey? she says.

—It's me, Mother, I say again, but she is looking down at
Smokey, at the blue marks running up and down her arms.
From the shadows of her room, the faces of her children
smile dimly out at her, but she cannot feel her arms.
—Mother, I say again. I know there must be something else
to say, but when I look around me at the walls, the tables,
the television, I can't imagine what it could be.
—Honey? my mother says. She strokes Smokey's pale fur,
and together they stare at the fish. Smokey stretches, and
she smiles down at him. —Who's my cat? she says.
—Who's my baby? And then there is silence again until
Stan takes the phone from her hand.

Teddy comes home from work while I am watching a base-
ball game, the Mets and some team from California.
—Hey, he says, glancing briefly at the game. —Look. He
pulls me to the window and points out at a shiny blue car
parked by the curb. —Look, he says again. —I rented a car.
We're going on a vacation.
—A vacation? I look back at the game. Teddy smells of
blood and there are red rings around his fingernails.
—Yeah, he says. —To the Poconos.
—The Poconos?
—Yeah, he says. —They're mountains. Upstate. Everybody
at work always goes there.
—We don't have enough money for a vacation, I say.
—Vacations are expensive.
—Hey, he says, patting his pocket. —I got a bonus. A big
one. He turns off the game and looks at me, his eyes glow-
ing. —Let's go, he says. —Let's go right now.

—Isn't it beautiful? Teddy says when we get to the car.
—This is just like the car I'm going to buy.
He opens the door eagerly; there is a grocery bag on the

front seat, a long bottle of wine resting on top. He moves the
bag to the back seat and I get in and roll down the window.
From behind her door, Madame Renalda watches us in our
new rented car. She could save us, but she watches us
through a tiny hole in her door as we pull away from the
curb into traffic; then she turns away to look into the eyes of
another man. —Don't travel, she says. —Not today.
Teddy switches the radio on and pushes buttons until he
finds a ball game. We drive straight north up Broadway, and
as we leave New York, children lean against fences and
watch us, until their mothers call them in; they turn back to
the high walls of the city, but we drive ahead into green
mountains.
It's just dusk, and the lights on the bridge glitter against the
cold water of the river. Teddy whistles quietly as he listens
to the game, and when it ends, he turns to another station,
listening to that until static erupts and he finds another. As
it grows dark, we move away from the city, and from time
to time our lights sweep over animals who sit hunched by
the side of the road, waiting to cross.
The highway is crowded with trucks, and Teddy passes
them all. He rushes up behind an animal carrier, the back
of it stuffed with pigs or cows; they are pressed so tight
against the metal slats of the truck I can hardly tell what
they are, but in the glare of our headlights I see white faces
and tiny dark eyes.
—Look, Teddy says. —Steak. Burgers. He glances at
me. —I could have been cutting up those very cows next
week. Those very cows. He smiles. —Say goodbye to all
that.
He turns the radio off, and hums to himself, while I watch
his reflection in my window. Every now and then we pass
over a bright burst of red on the road, gone so quickly it
might be my imagination. I lean my head against the window

and drift in and out of sleep; after a while, Teddy points
ahead at a ragged array of lights.
—Look, he says. —That looks like a good place to stop.
He turns to me, his eyes bright red. —I could use some
sleep, he says. —How about you?

The motel parking lot is crowded, but Teddy comes back
smiling. —We're in luck, he says. —We got the last room.
But they only had a single.
Our room is right next to the motel lounge; the metal plate
around the doorknob is dented, but inside the room is cool
and there is a large television. Teddy carries in the grocery
bag, and sets it on the bureau in front of the mirror. He lifts
the bottle of wine out carefully, then begins to pull out food:
a box of chocolates, a pineapple, two jars of macadamia
nuts. He holds one jar of nuts out to me.
—They were on sale, he says. —All this stuff was on sale.
He stares down into the bag. —Everything was on sale.
—Teddy, look, I say, —cable.
He glances at the television. —Oh, he says. —Yeah.
He looks around the room, at the orange curtains, the
orange-and-green bed, all the things he's pulled from the
grocery bag. Through the thin wall I can hear the thump of
music and the sound of men and women laughing.
—Maybe we could go to that bar, I say.
He shakes his head. —You're not old enough, he says.
—You have to be twenty-one.
He pulls the drapes open just as a woman is walking past;
she glances in at us without interest; we probably look to
her like any other young married couple. As she opens the
door to the bar, a surge of noise is let out; it fades as the
door closes behind her.
—I don't know, Teddy says, pulling the drapes closed. —I

don't know. I'm kind of tired, and I think we have a long
way to go.

He lies down on top of the bed, without even removing his
shoes; I want to turn on the television and open the box of
chocolates Teddy's brought; I want to go into the lounge and
order the kind of drink the women in my magazine would
order—a daiquiri or a margarita—and sit at the bar until a
handsome man sits beside me; I want to call my mother and
Stan. I want to do all of these things, but finally I take off
my shoes and lie down on the bed next to Teddy.

He reaches out to turn off the lamp. In the sudden darkness,
I can just make out his face in what little light filters in
through the drapes.

—Did I tell you about the one with the broken leg? he asks,
and closes his eyes.

I can feel music beat against our wall; a few feet away from
us, men and women are laughing and dancing and having
fun, but while we lie here in the darkness, terrible things
are happening everywhere, things we can do nothing about.
At this very moment, men without eyes stare at women without faces, and at this very moment, a thousand cows are
stumbling toward a thousand men, who lift a thousand ham-
mers. We cannot stop any of it, not even for a moment, and
as I listen to Teddy's sad, shallow breath, I close my eyes
and wait once again to be born.

EVENING SUN

Florence is dreaming she is in the mouth of a shark, caught at her waist; she cannot feel her feet or her legs, only the cold rush of the ocean as the shark pushes her through the glittering water. She can see herself reflected in its flat black eyes as her body comes gently apart.

—Jesus, Louis says, and Florence opens her eyes just as the air conditioner clatters to a stop. Louis is sitting on the end of the bed, in front of the air conditioner; the sheets are pulled down around Florence's waist and she can feel the last drifts of cool air on her arms and shoulders.

Louis turns toward her and she closes her eyes, waits a moment, then opens them just slightly; through the blur of lashes she can see that he is still turned toward her, watching her closely, but she does not move, and he bends back toward the air conditioner, then rises and goes into the bathroom. She closes her eyes and tries to remember her dream, but she can only see Louis, his large head propped at the end of his long delicate neck, and the lumpy ridges of his spine. When she opens her eyes again, she is startled to see his face a few inches from her own; he smells of soap and toothpaste, and stares at her patiently, waiting for her to wake.

—Florence, he says. —The air conditioner is out. She pulls the sheets up to her neck and closes her eyes.

—Call the guy, okay? he says.

She nods, and he bends to kiss her on the forehead. His dry lips feel papery and hot. Already the heat is rising in him; already his face is covered with a slick skin of sweat.

As he walks through the house, she can hear sand grating under his feet. With the air conditioner off, he has opened the bedroom windows, and the room is beginning to fill with the smell of sulphur from the sprinklers that run all night. All the water here is full of sulphur: ground water, bath water, tap water. Even after it's boiled, it has a burnt, eggy taste, and it seems impossible to Florence that anything at all could grow in water like that, but what grass there is here is bright green and the flowers are as sturdy as trees. She listens for the sound of Louis's car over the gravel, and when he is gone, she gets up and closes the windows. She tries again to remember her dream, but all she can see is Louis, his heavy head and the long bumpy bend of his back.

He has left almost no sign of himself in the kitchen, only lukewarm coffee in the pot. Steam is rising from the coffee, but when she pours herself a cup, it is tepid. She tries to remember why this happens; it's something Louis explained to her once, —"ambient pressure," he told her, but even saying the words out loud doesn't recall to her what they mean. All she can see is the earnest look on his face as he began to explain it. At that moment she had known, somehow, that she would marry him, and the sudden surprising certainty of this forced her to look away. She would be seeing enough of him from then on, she realized, and now, thinking of that moment, she can see perfectly the details of their surroundings–the stained lip of the cream pitcher on their table, the waitress leaning against the counter watching them talk, the crumpled wad of Louis's napkin–but still she cannot remember why coffee looks hot when it is not.
She empties her cup back into the pot and slits open the blinds over the sink; outside it is another sunny day. She is close enough to Mrs. Walker's house to see clearly into her kitchen–the bright plastic wrap of a loaf of bread on the counter, a cup and saucer drying in the dish drainer–and when Mrs. Walker comes outside, Florence quickly pulls the blind almost closed. Mrs. Walker turns her head at the motion and stares directly at Florence, but Florence stands still, so that she will seem nothing more than a shadow cast against the window. Mrs. Walker watches a moment, then raises and drops her hand.
She turns, takes the long rake that leans against the wall beside her door, and begins to drag it across the gravel that surrounds her house. Hers is the only house here without any grass at all, only a thin band of dirt that runs right into

the gravel; the other houses have tiny green strips of yard, but all of them float in a sea of white rocks, part of a small group of houses set between a line of shops on one side and a row of hotels right on the ocean. The houses were built before Florida land became so valuable, and they are small and uniformly ugly, little pastel boxes.

Except for Florence and Louis, the people who live here are old, and though they have all been offered plenty of money for their houses, most of them have lived here too long to imagine life under any other circumstances; they will live here until they die, and then their children will sell the small plots of land to developers, who will periodically cruise by in their black cars, waiting impatiently for the rest of the land to become available. One by one the tiny pink-and-white houses will turn up empty, and those who still live there watch the other houses anxiously for signs of vacancy; the smallest of things—a shade not drawn at night, a morning paper not collected—drive them deeper into their walls, the borders of their world shrinking daily.

Although Florence has seen the other residents shuffling across the gravel between their houses and the street, Mrs. Walker is the only person she has met in her few months here. Every morning Mrs. Walker rakes her gravel, which is always smooth and white and even; then she sits all day in a rocking chair in the sun, her chair driving deep ruts into the gravel she has raked, her skin as dark as the strip of dirt around her house.

After she has breakfast, Florence does what she does every day: she listens to the radio, then washes the clothes Louis wore the day before; he sweats so much here, he says, that if his clothes aren't washed right away, they'll be stained and ruined. The radio station she tunes in is all news, all day, and offers, as part of its programming, weather reports

every fifteen minutes. It is always warm and sunny. She
listens now to a story about a lost child who wandered off
near the Everglades and is feared dead, killed perhaps by
alligators. There was something, she remembers vaguely,
that she was supposed to do today, something Louis wanted,
but as she pours bright blue laundry soap over his yellow
shirt, all she can think of is the child wandering around and
around in the gloomy jungle.

By the time she comes outside, the sun has passed over her
house, and Mrs. Walker patiently watches her hang up her
laundry. Their gravel lawns run right into each other, but
Mrs. Walker seems to have a clear idea of the line of demar-
cation, and she observes it carefully, raking right up to it,
then situating her chair just on the border, across from the
small clothesline Louis has strung up. When Florence finishes, she will sit down, and Mrs. Walker will begin to com-
plain about her dead husband's children, who, she tells
Florence, are only waiting for her to die, so that they can
sell her house.

—They're monsters, she says, crossing herself, —evil monsters. This always brings a smile to her face. —They'll pay,
she says, nodding. —You just wait.

What *she* is waiting for, she has explained to Florence, is
the Rapture, which, as Florence understands it, is a kind of
final judgment, a day on which, according to Mrs. Walker,
the true faces of all the believers will be revealed, and all
the sinners cast into eternal torment. Mrs. Walker was
raised a Catholic, but she has incorporated the Rapture into
her own personal cosmology because, she says, it makes
more sense; this is consistent with what Florence understands about Mrs. Walker, since the Rapture seems to be a
faith based wholly on the concept of revenge: not an insult,
not a slight, not a single moment of the pain that has been
dealt her will go unanswered, and it is clear to Florence that

Mrs. Walker can hardly wait for it to happen. Florence supposes that part of the reward for the believers will be to hang
around on earth long enough to actually see the misery in-
flicted upon their enemies–that seems to be in large part the
source of Mrs. Walker's enthusiasm, and Florence knows
she keeps a list of transgressions in her head. Florence wonders if she herself has yet committed any.
When Florence finishes hanging her laundry, she sits down
in her plastic lawn chair, next to Mrs. Walker but securely
set in the gravel that belongs to Louis and Florence. Mrs.
Walker leans forward across the boundary line and removes
her hat.
—Did I tell you? she says. —They bought me a coffin.
She bends to flick a bug from her leg. —A cheap one, she
says with satisfaction. —The cheapest.
Florence wonders how she learned this, but she shakes her
head and looks out past Mrs. Walker. From here, she can
see the main street that runs past their development, just on
the other side of Mrs. Walker's house, to the beach. Her
own house is set farther back from the street, and from her
windows all she can see are the backs and sides of houses,
and from the front, a few ratty palms that grow up along the
alley. Right now she watches a small family on their way to
the beach. A woman is struggling to keep up with one child,
who runs ahead of her, without losing the other, who lags
behind. Later, they will all drag themselves back to their
hotel, trailing towels and buckets and toys, exhausted from
their day in the sun. Florence sees the woman gazing in at
them between the houses; and Florence knows she must
envy them their lives, sitting out here in the sun all day, all
year, with nothing to do but let their skin turn dark. —Oh,
her mother had said when Florence was packing to move,
—you'll have the most beautiful tan.
And it's true–everyone here is the color of copper, but when

they come close, the skin on their faces is thick and ropy;
Florence's own skin remains puffy and pale—when she goes
out, she wears a hat and long sleeves to protect herself from
the sun. She has yet to adjust to the climate here; the heat
and sun seem to have stunned both her and Louis into a
daze, and they spend most of their time inside; during the
day, they watch the sun beat through the windows, and at
night they close their door against the steamy hiss of the
sprinklers.

This is not the life Florence imagined for herself as she sat
at the window of her parents' house in Indiana, looking all
around her at the wide brown landscape. What she had
planned to live like and look like and be like had nothing
to do with that world, and when, one night, Louis's aunt
awoke and died, leaving her house and everything in it to
Louis, Florence saw it as a kind of deliverance. Louis's
aunt had been old; she was ready to die, Florence was sure.
When she had met her, several years before, her skin was
transparent with age, and she was interested in nothing
except Louis, who, she told Florence, had always been
her favorite.

Louis wanted to sell the house, and when Florence talked
about moving to Florida to live in it, he turned his face
toward the flat fields and said nothing, but only a few months
later they were leaving Indiana to drive south to their new
home. When Florence waved to her parents from the window of the car, she could hardly distinguish them from the
background; the whole scene looked as stiff and flat as cardboard: the house, the car parked in the driveway, the dog,
and behind them a cardboard sun pasted to a cardboard sky.
It was the last she saw of Indiana, and it wasn't until they
reached Georgia that she realized she would soon be in a
place where Louis would be the only person she knew. The
thought made her long for something familiar, but as they

got closer to Florida, it all became stranger, the familiar dirt and grass of home giving way to a world of alligators, palm trees, huge flapping birds. She could tell Louis was apprehensive, too. He talked the whole drive down of Buzz, his best friend in Indiana.

—Oh, he said whenever they saw anything strange, —Buzz would love that. Every time he said "Buzz," he looked in the rearview mirror, as if he expected Buzz to be following them down the highway in his little blue car.

—Jesus, Louis said the first time they saw a dead alligator by the side of the road. —Buzz would get a kick out of that. He shook his head. —Boy, he said. —I wish Buzz was here. He caught himself and glanced quickly at Florence, but she herself almost wished Buzz was there, too, to take up some of the expanding space between them. She looked away from Louis and wondered what could possess an alligator to try to cross a busy highway; even to a prehistoric brain, the odds must have been obvious, but the farther south they traveled, the more alligators they passed, tangled up in big heaps by the side of the road.

According to what she has read and heard on the radio, there are simply too many alligators to be contained in the rapidly shrinking jungles here, and almost weekly there seems to be another story about an alligator dragging itself up into a yard to snatch a dog or a cat, then sinking back down into a swamp somewhere. Florence can imagine the noise in its brain as it lurches out into the bright sunny glare, surrounded by rushing cars: they make such huge confused targets, she thinks, it's no wonder they're hit so often. Their bodies are everywhere, turning yellow in the sun, the enormous heads turned away from the traffic.

This is not the Florida that Florence imagined, not what she feels she has somehow been promised by television and magazines and posters in the windows of travel agencies.

She expected a bright world of flowers and light and pure white sand, but the sun here is so close and hot and bright that it fades everything beneath it; and though flowers grow all over, springing up almost out of nothing, they are strange impossible colors, with unpleasant rotting scents. And the sand—the sand is as white and fine as powder, but it is everywhere, in everything, creeping under her sheets, into the hot creases of her skin, between her teeth when she eats, and when she tries to sleep at night, she can feel it, a grainy sifting in her lungs.

These are all things, she thinks, to which she could, in time, become accustomed, perhaps even to like, but what she can't imagine ever getting used to is the constant, unnerving motion here, the life that springs up wherever she turns: spongy brown spiders creeping across the bathroom walls, tiny gray lizards zipping across the porch screen, big flying bugs that Mrs. Walker calls "palmettos" but that look to Florence like nothing more than giant cockroaches. The ground is covered with reptiles and the sky is full of bugs and birds—screeching gulls; clumsy pelicans as big as dogs; stiff, fragile egrets and flamingos. One of the hotels across the street keeps a few bright pink flamingos penned up in front, and all day long they stalk around, stabbing into the grass, chasing after some doomed skittering life. The surface of the ground itself seems alive, and once or twice Florence has found herself staring at some lump of vegetation that suddenly stirred to reveal itself as the slick clotted skin of a frog or a lizard. It is completely different from Indiana, where the people and the animals seemed waxy and inert, where even the leaves of the trees seemed somehow locked into place. Here she finds herself more and more having to shake herself awake, sunk in a haze of physical sensation, aware of nothing more than the baking heat, a sudden flap of wings, the smell of things kept too long in the

wet air—flowers and wood and skin rotting. She feels surrounded by this world, and she and Louis, stuck in the
middle of it all, deprived of the common details of lives lived
together in the same place, seem to have run out of things
to say to each other. When he comes home from work, his
shirt is stuck to his skin and his hair lies in thin strips across
his head. Each day he comes in and sits directly in front of
the air conditioner, leaning his head all the way back, his
mouth open to the ceiling, as the cool air beats against his
neck. It's the only way he can ever breathe down here, he
tells Florence, but he looks so uncomfortable she wants to
bend his head off and set it gently back upright on his neck.
After he is cool, he turns on the television, which is always
on when he is home. He watches sports, any sport, and
Florence can tell that as he watches he is wondering what
Buzz would say of this play, or that catch, and no matter
what Louis is ever doing or saying, she can see that his mind
is still moving across the bumpy Indiana plain a thousand
miles away. They seldom talk about Indiana, but when it
comes up, he speaks of things she does not remember: the
changing smell of the air with the shifting of seasons, clear
summer evenings full of bright stars. All she can remember
of Indiana is the flat, dry dirt, the stiff sting of weeds against
her ankles, and when she talks to her mother on the phone,
she is sure she can hear, in their big silent pauses, the noise
of machinery churning heavily somewhere in the distance.
Whenever she talks to her mother, Florence tells her that
she and Louis are both fine, they like it down here, everything is just as they'd hoped; it is clear to Florence, how-
ever, that they are both changing, especially Louis. In their
first few weeks here, he took Polaroid pictures of everything
—the house, the ocean, the pelicans and flamingos—and sent
them back to Indiana. Even then, when she looked at
herself in the pictures, she looked odd, bleached out—she

could hardly tell the difference between her dress and her skin in the bright light. When Louis grew bored with the camera, Florence finished out the film he'd bought, taking a picture of him every few days. She lined them all up along the keys of the small piano, which Louis's aunt too had used to display photographs—the top was kept down, and covered with family pictures, many of Louis, taken from grade school right up through the year or so before she died. When Florence compares the pictures she has taken of Louis—one from the lower end of the keyboard, taken in their first few weeks here, with a more recent photo—she is shocked to see the changes in him. He looks tired and washed-out, but mostly he has grown alarmingly thin. Little pockets of shadows have appeared in his cheeks and eye sockets, and his legs poking out from his shorts look sticky and useless. Cancer, she thought immediately; she had heard of such things happening after sudden changes, but even while she let her mind wander over the possibilities of such a future—chemotherapy, radiation, hospitals, doctors—she knew he was growing thin simply because he ate less and less, lately refusing even foods she was sure he liked. It started with pork chops, she can't remember now how long ago—weeks, months? She put his plate in front of him, and he glanced at the pork chop on it, looked out the window a moment, then back at his plate.

—I don't really like pork chops, he said, and she stopped chewing to consider how many times she'd served him pork chops, and if he'd eaten them. She was sure he had.

—No, he said. —I've always hated pork chops. I hate the color. And the consistency. And the way they taste. He paused, then added, —I always have.

And like this, more and more foods have been eliminated from their diet: peas, rye bread, Swiss cheese. At every meal, Florence waits, a little hum of tension in her stomach, to see if he will eat. She feels guilty if she likes what she has prepared, and as she watches him segregate the food on his plate into neat little untouchable piles, her own food turns bitter in her mouth as she chews. At such moments, she considers how time is passing for her, how her life is unfolding, and a thin wire of panic runs through her.

—Oh, her mother always said to her when she was growing up, —you'll be a late bloomer. But now that she has left her parents and come to Florida, no life has sprung up yet to bloom around her. Every day she moves cautiously around furniture she does not like, eats from dishes it would never occur to her to buy, and sleeps in a bed in which, she is sure, Louis's aunt died. In their first few weeks here, she was sure that Louis was biding his time, waiting for her to change her mind, to tell him it was all a mistake and they could move back to Indiana, but now Indiana seems impossibly far away, and every day while she waits for something to happen, someone to talk to, something to change her, she covers her face and arms and goes outside to sit under the hot bright sun and listen to the catalogue of misery that is Mrs. Walker's life.

Mrs. Walker leans forward and rubs her hands along the wooden arms of her chair. —I'm not going to let them bury me in some cheap coffin, she says. —God won't let them. He can't. She looks at Florence narrowly. —Your aunt died, she says. —But I'm not going to.

—It was Louis's aunt, Florence says. —She had a heart attack.

—Jesus Christ, Mrs. Walker says. —You'd think they could wait a couple of years. How could God do this to me? That cheap coffin. They'll try to bury me in some swamp somewhere, you wait.

Florence watches the little groups of tourists wander by on

the street, and reaches down to run her hands through the warm gravel. She scatters a handful over her feet, and Mrs. Walker shakes her head.

—If you'd rake that, she says, —it would be a lot neater.

—How could they bury you in a swamp? Florence asks. —Isn't that illegal?

—Oh, I suppose they'd find a way, Mrs. Walker says. —Or they'll try to cremate me. That's what I did with Richard. It's what he wanted, she adds quickly, as though Florence has accused her of something. She closes her eyes. —They made me take the ashes back with me.

She opens her eyes and looks at Florence. —What do you do with a bunch of ashes? People around here, they want to be tossed in the ocean, but he hated the ocean. She shakes her head. —I just dumped them out here. This house was the only thing he loved.

Florence drops the gravel she's holding. —I didn't know that, she says.

—Well, says Mrs. Walker. —Now you do.

Florence looks around at Mrs. Walker's neat gravel lawn; she wonders if any of Mr. Walker's ashes were scattered onto her own gravel, and she wonders what Mrs. Walker thinks will happen to Mr. Walker at the Rapture—if he will somehow reassemble into human form, or if he will just appear as a clump of gravel, or a puffy haze of smoke. Before she can figure out a polite way to ask about this, Mrs. Walker laughs.

—That bastard, she says. —He's where he belongs.

She turns her head. —Look, she says and Florence looks around to see Louis pull into their driveway. Someone is in the car with him, and as Louis gets out and bends down to talk to the passenger, Florence can see that it is a girl. Louis doesn't notice Florence or Mrs. Walker in the yard, and as he walks to the house, the girl in the car watches him; when she moves her head, something around her neck gleams gold, but the rest of her is in shadow.

—Who's that? Mrs. Walker asks, looking at the car.

—Louis, Florence says. —He's home a little early.

—I mean in the car. There's a girl in the car.

Through the windows Florence watches Louis's progress through the house. He stops in the kitchen, his mouth opening and closing as he looks around. She can see the spreading wet blots under the arms of his shirt, and she wonders if any of her neighbors ever look in and notice such things about her—that her hair is messy, or that she is still wearing her bathrobe past noon some days.

—I guess I'd better go in now, she says, and Mrs. Walker looks past her to the girl in the car. Gravel crackles under her chair as she rocks, sending up a fine white dust that Florence can feel settle in her lungs.

—Oh, Louis says when Florence comes into the kitchen. —I was looking for you.

He smiles uncertainly and Florence can see that he doesn't know exactly how to broach the subject of the girl in the car; he looks all around the room, then back at Florence. The skin of his face seems darker than it was this morning, and a thin band of white runs around the edge of his hairline.

—Did you call the guy? he finally asks. —About the air conditioner?

She had forgotten until now that he asked her to do this. The memory of their conversation surfaces and she thinks vaguely that it had something to do with a shark.

—He couldn't come, she says. —Maybe tomorrow.

—Oh, Louis says. He looks around again, nodding, as if he is taking stock of the room. Florence wonders if, for a moment, he is considering saying nothing at all about the girl in the car; perhaps he hopes she will grow tired of waiting and wander away. The sun has left white circles around his eyes, and at the center of each is a little burst of blue, blossoming like a flower. He sighs unhappily.

—Because, he says. —Because there's this girl. In the car. He stops and looks out the window at Mrs. Walker, who is still peering in the direction of the driveway. —A hitchhiker. She was hitchhiking.

He takes a breath and Florence notices that his pants are stained at the knee. It is possible, she thinks, that she has washed this pair of pants a dozen times without seeing that stain.

—I figured, Louis goes on, —that something could happen to her. You know. She's just a kid. She's in the car, he says again, but behind him the door opens and the girl pokes her head in.

—Hi, she says. —I was getting hot.

She is perhaps seventeen, in cutoff jeans and a faded Hawaiian shirt, and she is carrying a bright green knapsack, which she drops on the floor. She smiles brightly at Florence.

—Nice place, she says. —I love your flowers. She looks expectantly at Florence and Louis, but Louis has bent to rub at the spot on his knee.

—Thank you, Florence says, and they all wait quietly for someone to speak.

—Well, the girl says, —do you mind if I use your bathroom?

—Of course, Florence says. She points the way to the bathroom, and as the girl passes him, Louis steps back quickly, then stares at the doorknob as the lock clicks home.

—It's just, you know, he says, —all the things you read about. All the crazy people who could pick her up.

Florence tries to imagine the girl standing by the side of the road with her green knapsack, and she tries to picture Louis as he passes her, wondering if he should stop. Florence can't quite put an expression on his face as his eyes shift

between the road ahead and the rearview mirror, or as he
slows, or as he finally stops, and when she watches him now,
staring miserably at the bathroom door, she can't think of
him any way other than this. She wants suddenly to look
around at the pictures on the piano, but the toilet flushes
and the girl comes out of the bathroom smiling.

—I really appreciate this, she says to Florence. —It will
only be a couple of days.

Florence glances at Louis, but he is looking out at something
green crawling up the trunk of a palm tree.

—I just love all your things, the girl says, and picks up a
picture of Louis, taken when he was in high school. —Hey,
she says after a moment. —This is you.

She picks up another, from grade school, and holds it next
to the first. —Hey, she says again, looking up at Louis, who
is just starting to inch toward his chair in front of the television.

—Well, the girl says, and her eyes run up and down the line
of pictures on the piano, —it must be kind of hard to play
the piano.

She puts the pictures down and looks around. —Where can
I put my things? she asks Louis, but he has already found a
ball game on the television. He stares at the game intently
as he twists the color knob, turning the faces of the players
bright red, then down to shades of black and white.

The girl's name is Marybeth, and she is from New York,
which she explains as she watches Florence slice tomatoes
for dinner.

—You know, Marybeth says, —this is really nice of you. A
lot of people wouldn't do this.

Florence stops slicing, her hand on the tomato; she remembers that Louis no longer eats tomatoes, and she carries the
plate to the garbage and scrapes it clean. She can feel Mary-

beth watching her as she goes to the icebox and bends, searching through the drawers for another vegetable.

—This is really nice of you, Marybeth says again, at dinner. —Both of you. She reaches for another roll. —Really, she says. —I mean it.
Louis gently removes slices of cucumber from his salad, propping them up against the sides of his bowl.
—What? Marybeth says. —You don't like cucumbers?
—No, Louis says, —I've never really liked them.
Marybeth nods, but Florence could swear he'd asked her to buy them; perhaps he even bought them himself. She tries to remember being with him in the store; she can almost see his hand reaching out over the cucumbers.
—I know just what you mean, Marybeth says. She picks a slice of cucumber from her salad and leans it against the inside of her bowl. —They give me gas. She smiles at Florence. —They're good for you, though, she says. —Lots of vitamin C.
Louis puts down his fork and stares at the ring of pale green circles in his bowl. Though only Louis has finished eating, Marybeth stands with her plate.
—I'll clean up, she says to Florence. —You relax.
As she carries the dishes to the sink, Louis lists gently in the direction of the television, until finally he leaves the table and turns it on, switching channels until he finds a sporting event. Florence sits at the table watching Marybeth clear things away; when Marybeth has got all the dishes piled on the counter, she turns on the water and the smell of sulphur fills the room. She turns off the tap and steps back, looking at the sink.
—Jesus, she says to Florence, —what's wrong with your water?

—It's sulphur, Florence says. —It's like that everywhere here. It's in the water.

—Jesus, Marybeth says again. She turns the water on and leans back from the sink to wash the dishes with her arms stretched away from her body. It's an awkward process, and Florence can see even from the table that the dishes aren't getting very clean.

Outside, as it grows dark, Mrs. Walker emerges from her house to feed the pigeons. She feeds them regularly, always waiting until evening, when the sea gulls are sweeping the beaches for food and don't come around to the houses. She hates sea gulls, which, she tells Florence, would as soon kill each other over a piece of bread. They remind her of her husband's children, she tells Florence, and Florence suspects that Mrs. Walker feeds the pigeons primarily to deprive the sea gulls. She scatters seed and kitchen scraps in a wide arc over the gravel, and the pigeons move in clumsily, kicking up stones to get at the seed. Most of it falls between the rocks, to sprout or rot, Florence supposes; there must be a lot of it down there by now, a layer of rotting food right under the gravel, all mixed up with the dirt and Mr. Walker's ashes. When Mrs. Walker has finished, she stands in the yard with her arms crossed, staring up into the sky. Marybeth turns the water off and leans against the sink to watch her.

—What's her problem? she says. She laughs and whips the dishrag at the window.

—Knock knock, she says, and Florence thinks for a moment she is talking to Mrs. Walker.

—Knock, knock, Marybeth repeats. —It's a joke.

—Oh. Who's there?

—Orange, Marybeth says, and laughs wildly, then stops abruptly. —Wait a minute, she says. —Shit. I forgot it. She

shakes her head. —I always screw up jokes. Although she
is not done with the dishes, she hangs the dish towel over
the edge of the sink. —Oh well, she says. —It's just a joke.
She walks into the living room, where she stands next to
Louis and stares down at the television. —So, she says.
—What's on?
Louis looks up suddenly, startled, then looks at Florence,
as if she is somehow responsible for Marybeth's presence.
—Football, he says. —Pre-season.
—Football, Marybeth says. —I love football. It's so— She
closes her eyes, then opens them. —I don't know, she
says. —But I love it. Now what's happening here?
Outside, pigeons flutter off one by one, and Florence reads
a magazine as she listens to Louis patiently explain what a
first down is. His voice drones over the spray of the sprinklers as they come on, interrupted only by the occasional
thud of a moth against a screen. When Mrs. Walker goes
inside, lights go off in all but the tiny window in the corner
of her house. Florence wonders what Mrs. Walker thinks
about at night, if she stands at the window and stares out at
her neatly raked lawn, thinking about all that she owns, and
all that she must endure before the Rapture comes to
change her world. The game is still playing when Florence
goes to bed, and as she falls asleep, she can hear Marybeth's
voice.
—Knock knock, she is saying. —Come on, knock knock.

When Florence comes into the kitchen in the morning, Marybeth is already awake; she is wearing her cutoffs again, and
a Hawaiian shirt, but this one is different, blue with tiny
orange pineapples. The window blinds are pulled wide and
sunlight gleams against her skin as she opens and closes
cabinets.
—Oh, she says to Florence. —Hi. I was just looking to see

what there was to eat. She smiles and closes the drawer she
has just opened. —You seem to eat a lot of canned food.

—Louis likes it, Florence says, and draws the blinds half
closed.

—Hey, Marybeth says, —you don't like sunshine?

—I like it. It's just a little bright this early.

—Well, Marybeth says, —I love sunshine. It's why I came
here. She stops, her hand on a cabinet, and looks at Florence. —I don't see how anyone could not love sunshine, she
says.

—I like it, Florence says again. —I just like it better in the
evening.

Marybeth opens a cupboard, looks briefly at the cups and
saucers inside, then closes it. —Why?

—Oh, Florence says, and shrugs, trying to think of a reason.
She remembers a phrase she read recently, or heard on the
radio, something about the quality of light. —It's the quality
of the light, she says. —It's different then.

—Different how? Marybeth asks, and Florence waves her
hand.

—Oh, she says. —Just different.

Marybeth pulls out a cereal box, reads the label, then puts
it back. —Well, she says, —I like it all day long.

She opens a drawer that holds potholders and dish towels,
and flips through them, then closes it. She smiles at Florence. —I guess I'm just nosy, she says. —I'm not looking
for anything. Really.

She looks up as Louis walks into the room in his bathrobe,
his hair wet from the shower. —Louis, Marybeth says, —I
had the best sleep.

Louis pulls his robe tightly around him and smiles at the
window. In his bright green robe and the flat morning light,
he looks like a paper cutout.

—How about some coffee? Marybeth says. Florence can't

tell from her voice if she is offering or asking, and she goes into the bathroom, which is still steamy from Louis's shower. Things that belong to Marybeth—a few small bottles, little jars of lotion, a red plastic comb and brush—are scattered across the counter, and several long blond hairs cling to the side of the sink.

When she comes back to the kitchen, coffee has been made. Marybeth is standing at the sink, watching Mrs. Walker rake her gravel.

—What *is* her story? she says. —She's out there raking gravel.

—She always does that, Louis says. —She's crazy.

This is the first time Florence has heard Louis express an opinion on Mrs. Walker. She joins Marybeth at the window.

—She's not really crazy, Florence says. —Just kind of odd.

—Now look at her, Marybeth says as Mrs. Walker sits in her chair. —She's going to rock. In gravel.

—She's crazy, Louis says bitterly.

Mrs. Walker looks over at their window and stares at Marybeth and Florence a moment, then pulls her hat down over her eyes. Marybeth shakes her head.

—Boy, she says. —What a place. Oh well. She turns to Florence. —Are you ready for the beach? We are.

Florence has not been to the ocean since their first weeks here, when she and Louis took a few experimental trips to the public beach just down the street. It was August, a bad time to be here, everyone told them; it was blinding hot and the sand and water were full of irritable tourists and anxious hot children and shrieking gulls. Florence had never swum in the ocean before, and she and Louis only waded in, waded out, then retreated home to avoid sunburn.

It all made Florence uneasy: the fish flashing around her ankles, the slimy drifting seaweed, the sand shifting under-

neath. And later, she felt right to be frightened: Within a
month of their arrival, a boy on the coast was killed by a
shark; it was nowhere near them, really, though it was,
Florence pointed out to Louis, the same ocean, the same
water that pounded up on their own beach. Since then, Florence has not gone back; the burnt unhappy faces of tourists
straggling back home in the evening are enough to keep her
inside, that and the occasional article about sunshine and
skin cancer that her mother tucks inside her letters.

—No, she says to Marybeth. —I don't really like to swim.

—You don't like swimming either? Marybeth says. —You
don't like sunshine. You don't like swimming. So why live
in Florida?

—She's afraid of sharks, Louis says abruptly, and they both
turn to look at him. He looks startled at the attention.

—Lots of people are, he says, and smiles helplessly. —But
there's really no reason to be, he says to Marybeth. —They
never come up to the beach.

—Well, Florence says, —there was that boy last year.

—That was the Gulf, Louis says. —That was a lost shark.
It was on the other side of the coast.

—Yes, Florence says, —but it was still a shark, and it still
killed that boy.

Marybeth holds her coffee cup to her lips, her eyes shifting
between Louis and Florence.

—It didn't really kill him, Louis says patiently to Marybeth. —The boy died in the hospital.

—He bled to death, Florence says. —Because of the shark.

Louis sighs. —It was a little shark, he says to Marybeth.
—It got lost and bit this kid.

—It ate him, Florence says. —It ate his leg.

—They don't know it ate the leg. They don't know that.

He and Marybeth look at Florence, waiting for her response,
but since it is true that there is no way of knowing whether

or not the shark actually ate the boy's leg, Florence says nothing and instead watches the progress of a lizard as it moves in a slanted path across the porch screen. Its tail makes a dry rustle as it flicks across the wire.

—Anyways, Louis says. He rubs his hands across his chest, smiling blankly at them, then at Mrs. Walker. He watches her rock for a moment, then rises. —Guess I'll get ready. When he has left the room, Marybeth turns to Florence. —Did the shark really eat that boy's leg? she asks.

—I don't know. He didn't have one when they found him.

—I can see why you're afraid of them, Marybeth says.

—I'm not really afraid. I just think it's best to be safe, Florence says. But after it happened, she thought about it for days, wondering what it must have felt like: the sudden rough jolt, the thousand teeth closing over the delicate bones of the knee, and she wondered if it hurt, or if the shock stunned the boy into a loss of sense. It was possible, she considered, that he felt nothing at all as he paddled after his lost leg, searching out over the white sand for the face of his mother as she slid her hand across her magazine and drifted into a hot sunny sleep.

—Well, Marybeth says, —shark or no shark, I'm going swimming. You should see the water in New York. It makes sharks look safe. Besides, I don't like to be afraid of things.

—I'm not afraid, Florence says again, but Marybeth turns her eyes on Louis as he comes back, wearing a white terry-cloth jacket his mother gave him before they came here. Florence has only seen him wear it once or twice before. On his feet are green plastic sandals that flap against the carpet; they are the same color as the artificial grass carpet on the porch.

Marybeth pauses at the door. —Well, she says, —have a nice day.

Florence watches them from the window as they walk down

the street, until all she can see is the white sun at the end of the road. When she turns back to the familiar rooms of her house, something is different somehow, and it takes her a moment to realize that it is the smell, the heavy flowery scent of Marybeth's perfume. She closes her eyes and breathes in, wondering what it would be like to smell like that inside her own skin.

She pauses at her door a moment before going outside; Mrs. Walker is leaning back in her rocking chair, staring directly up into the sun, and when Florence sits down beside her, Mrs. Walker does not look at her.

—Well, she says, —they're coming. To put me down. Or whatever they call it.

Florence can hardly stand to look at the dark, hard skin of Mrs. Walker's face, burning in the bright light. When Mrs. Walker finally turns to her, her eyes look like shiny black rocks almost buried in mud.

—Who's that girl? she asks, and Florence looks past her, to the street.

—At your house, I mean, Mrs. Walker says. —That blond girl.

—Oh. That's Louis's cousin. Niece. From Indiana.

—She talks too damn loud, Mrs. Walker says. —Too loud for here. She reminds me of my husband's children.

She closes her eyes and leans back. —Did I tell you they were coming? she asks. She moves her lips, then opens her eyes into the sun again. —What will happen to me? she asks.

Florence stands, but Mrs. Walker doesn't shift her gaze from the sky. —What will happen to *me*? she says again.

Florence stops at her door; when she turns back to ask Mrs. Walker when her husband's children are coming, Mrs. Walker is leaning forward in her chair, gazing at the neat white gravel around her.

* * *

Florence is sitting at the kitchen table, listening to a radio call-in show about the alligator problem, the panthers in the Everglades, the trouble with wildlife in general. It is late afternoon, and she expects Louis and Marybeth back at any moment, but it is only when she hears their voices through the window that she remembers again, suddenly, that she was to call the air-conditioner repairman.

She snaps the radio off and goes to wait at the sink. When the car doors slam, she turns on the water and begins re-rinsing the dry dishes from breakfast and lunch, but she is done before they come in, so she rinses them all again, and turns when they finally enter.

—Oh boy, Marybeth says to Florence. —Are you going to be surprised. Her hair is streaked yellow from the sun. Louis follows her in, holding two small lobsters aloft.

—Look, he says. —Lobsters.

The lobsters wave their pinned claws sluggishly through the air at each side of Louis's head. Marybeth watches them without expression.

—They *were* in a box, she says to Florence, —when we bought them. They all stare blankly at the lobsters until Marybeth says brightly, —Don't you just love lobster?

Florence has had lobster here in Florida only once, shortly after their arrival; she and Louis went to a restaurant where they had to wait in line almost forty minutes for a table, and while they waited they were told to pick their own lobster from one of several that crept darkly around the bottom of a grimy tank. Florence said that any one would be fine, but Louis crouched in front of the tank and watched each carefully before choosing his. Florence never saw any of them actually removed from the tank, and she wondered if the lobster Louis was served was actually the lobster he had chosen. As they ate, she tried not to think of the ones they had pointed at being lifted from the tank and dropped into boiling water.

—I don't know, she says. —I read somewhere that lobsters scream when you cook them.

Louis looks from one lobster to the other, and slowly lowers his hands. —No, he says. —It's painless. They wouldn't do it that way if it wasn't.

—That's right, Florence, Marybeth says. —I think that's right. The shock of the boiling water kills them instantly. Instantaneously.

The lobsters dangle listlessly from Louis's hands, hardly bothering to move at all. Florence wonders if they can breathe, so long out of the water.

—Well, Marybeth says, —let's get that water boiling. She begins to clatter through the cabinets, looking for a pot big enough to cook both lobsters, while Louis stands behind her, holding the lobsters at his side.

Florence waits in the bathroom while they cook the lobsters; she is sure she's right about the scream, though she knows she would be more persuasive if she could remember where she read it, or some of the exact details. She stands at the sink and tries to recall. In the mirror, her hair looks dry and twiggy, and her face seems somehow waterblown, as if it has been left out in the rain. She turns on the taps in both the shower and the sink, to cover any sound the lobsters might make, and watches as steam rises against the mirror, slowly covering her face, from the bottom up.

When she comes back to the kitchen, the lobsters are cooked; their shells are bright red and the little wooden pegs in their claws are dark, soaked through with water.

—See? Marybeth says. —No scream. I really don't think they feel it at all. It happens so fast.

The lobster tastes odd to Florence, fishy, but in a rotted way, and she believes it tastes the same to Louis because he eats cautiously, examining it closely, not looking at Florence as he dips each bite into the little bowl of butter in the middle of the table. Only Marybeth seems to enjoy the lobster, and when they are done, Louis wraps the shells in newspaper and folds it all carefully into the garbage can, but the odor lingers. Florence can smell it on her hands and in her hair.

—Well, Marybeth says, looking around expectantly, —now what?

Soon it will grow dark; the sprinklers will come on, Mrs. Walker will wander out to feed the birds, Louis will find a game on television, and Florence will sit on the couch behind him, reading a magazine or perhaps writing her mother.

—There's a game on, Louis says. —The Colts.

—Oh, Marybeth says. —The Colts.

She stares out the window and taps her nails against the table. They look freshly painted, unchipped, and Florence wonders when she had a chance to paint her nails, hitchhiking down from New York.

—I know, Marybeth says. —Let's play cards.

Louis looks at the television. —Cards? he echoes unenthusiastically.

—Sure, she says. —I always carry a deck of cards. It helps pass the time. You know what I mean, she says, nodding at Florence.

—You two play, Florence says. —I have to write some letters.

A look of mild disappointment crosses Louis's face, like a shadow moving over a wide field, leaving behind as it passes only the same regular landscape, unaffected by the changing weather above.

* * *

Florence listens to them play cards as she writes her
mother. *Dear Mother,* she has down so far. *Louis is fine. We
are both fine. The weather is beautiful, bright and sunny.
Tonight we had fresh lobster.* She tries to think of some way
to mention Marybeth: a friend of Louis's, she considers, or,
simply, a houseguest. She imagines her mother reading the
letter, and putting it down on a table somewhere, half finished, then forgetting where she left it as she tries to tell
Florence's father what it said: Oh, something about a houseguest, she would say, some sort of friend of Louis's.

Florence finishes the letter without mentioning Marybeth,
then writes two more, almost exactly like it, one to her aunt,
the other to a woman she worked with briefly. She wonders
what they will all think her life is like when they read the
letters–if they will imagine her at the beach, diving in and
out of brilliant water, tan and lively, as she herself once
imagined it would be.

When she is done with the letters, she looks carefully
through the newspaper for any articles that might interest
her mother; she is searching especially for any stories about
alligators, with pictures of them resting innocently on neat
suburban lawns. She takes her time with the paper, reading
every editorial, every letter, every comic strip, but even so,
when she finally rises to go to bed, Louis and Marybeth are
still at their game of cards, their heads bent over the table;
the light above them picks out the shiny blond streaks in
Marybeth's hair.

Florence lies awake until Louis comes to bed; she stays still
while he settles down onto his elbow beside her and she can
hear a slight wheeze as he breathes; it occurs to her that it
is, after all, possible that he does have some trouble breathing here, something more than the discomfort everyone has

with the hot, damp air. She can tell by his stillness that he
wants to say something to her, and he reaches his hand out,
his fingers coming to rest in the hollow at the base of her
neck.

—I just wondered if you were awake, he says.

She pulls her neck away from his hand. —I was sleeping,
she says, and turns her face to the wall. The bathroom door
opens and closes, but nothing follows, no flush, no running
water; she is sure that Marybeth is listening to them, leaning
her head against the mirror and listening as she smiles and
admires the bright pink gleam of her fingernails.

By the time Florence gets up in the morning, Louis has
already risen and showered; he sits at the table, reading the
paper as Marybeth shakes coffee from the can into the cof-
feepot.

—Florence, she says. —How did you sleep? Louis looks up
at her, and when she says fine, he looks back to the paper.

—Me, too, Marybeth says. —This is the best sleep I've had
since I left New York. She smiles, and waves the coffee
can, scattering coffee across the counter. —The air is so
clean, she says. —I feel like I can breathe again.

Florence turns on the water in the sink, to run the sulphur
off. Mrs. Walker is already in her chair, rocking gently into
the gravel. She holds her hands up in front of her, her palms
to the sun, and stares at them, then drops them and looks
down at the ground.

—You know, Marybeth says, —you waste a lot of water like
that. Water is not, she says, turning to Louis, —a renewable
resource.

—You have to, Florence says, but she turns the water off
and watches it drain from the sink.

—Look, Louis says. —The Mets lost.

Marybeth joins him at the table, and together they read

through the box scores. Florence turns the water back on
and lets it run over her hands until they feel numb. When
she shuts the water off, she can't feel them; they are like
empty spaces at the end of her arms. Behind her, Marybeth
offers Louis another cup of coffee.

—Okay, Marybeth says. —Let's get moving. She walks to
the sink, holding her cup out in front of her, balanced flat
on the palm of her hand.
—Florence, she says, —you really should come with us. The
sunshine would do you good. She drops her cup in the sink
and turns. —You can think about it while we get ready.
Florence sits at the table, listening to the sounds Marybeth
makes in the bathroom: the water running, the slap of lotion
against her delicate skin. Louis comes in dressed for the
beach, in his green shoes and terry-cloth jacket. A pair of
sunglasses hangs around his neck, suspended from a bright
new blue cord, which he runs his fingers up and down self-
consciously. Marybeth comes back into the room smiling.
—Are you sure you don't want to come? she asks, and Louis
puts his hand on the doorknob. —It will be fun.
Florence stands in the middle of the room, looking around
her. —Well, she says, —if you really want me.
Louis takes his hand from the doorknob and carefully arranges his sunglasses in the exact center of his chest.

The beach is noisy and crowded, and they stand at the edge
of the parking lot, looking out over the sand. A baby totters
by in front of them, and behind it a young woman follows.
—Janette, she calls as the baby lurches toward the road.
—Janette, you wait, but she seems uninterested in catching
up with the baby, lounging slowly after it even as she calls
its name.
—Oh, Marybeth says, —there's a perfect spot.

They follow her out across the sand until she stops abruptly
and drops her knapsack. —Is this perfect? she says. She
unbuttons her shirt and watches as Florence takes off her
blouse.

—Boy, Marybeth says. —You must have the whitest skin in
Florida. Look, and she pulls the strap of her bathing suit
away from her shoulder to show a thin pale strip of skin.

—Even where I'm not tanned, she says, —I'm darker than
you. You'd better be careful. You could get a bad burn.

She nods and stares out at the water. —You need to tan
gradually. Otherwise you'll burn and peel and that's bad for
your skin. It will make you old before your time. She nods
seriously, and Florence can tell she likes the sound of the
words. —Yep, she says, —old before your time. You'll look
like that old woman in that rocking chair.

Louis places his hands flat against the sand and moves them
in small circles, widening outward; then he lifts his hands
and looks down at the designs he's made, smiling, pleased
with what he's done.

It makes Florence wonder a moment, at the touch of his
hand, the whisper of his breath on her neck in the morning.
She stands.

—I think I'll get a drink, she says, and leaves them in the
sand, Louis still looking down at his circles. She is conscious
of Marybeth watching her walk away, and she tries to move
gracefully, but her heels sink into the sand, and she feels
like an animal lumbering up a hill.

The concession stand sits on a concrete slab under a flat
roof; there are several picnic tables, full of people with
bright red unhappy faces; they look dazed, and they eat and
drink mechanically. Just at the edge of the concrete, sea
gulls flap and pace, giving out coarse, starving shrieks, but
signs everywhere forbid the feeding of them, and the few
that venture onto the patio are ignored or kicked aside.

Florence buys a box of popcorn and carries it across the
sand to a stunted palm that offers a few feet of shade; she
crouches at its base and experimentally throws out a few
pieces of popcorn. Almost immediately a sea gull dives into
the sand and pecks it up; another follows, then another, and
in only a few moments she is backed against the rough trunk
of the tree, surrounded by a chaos of flapping wings. Gulls
peck roughly at the sand, and at each other, every now and
then sending up a harsh chorus of cries.

Florence realizes that there are far too many gulls for the
small amount of popcorn in the box, and a faint wind of fear
rises in her throat. She tosses handfuls out away from her,
into the heap of birds, and as they peck and quarrel, she
empties the box and walks quickly away. She stops to drop
the empty box into a garbage can, and looks behind her;
some of the gulls on the edge of the circle have flown off,
but the rest have stayed, in a little bunch that's moved to
cover the ground where she was standing. She is surprised
to realize her heart is pounding, and as she walks back over
the sand, she tries to think of an amusing way to describe
the gulls to Marybeth and Louis, but when she arrives, they
are standing, waiting for her.

—We've been waiting for you, Marybeth says. —We didn't
want to go in without telling you.

—You don't mind? Louis says. —Being left alone?

They walk to the water side by side–Louis plodding carefully, Marybeth gliding lightly over the sand–and stop at the
water's edge.

Louis enters first, walking in up to his knees, then looks
back at Marybeth, who splashes in and falls over sideways
next to him. Florence watches them swim out until they are
nothing more than tiny heads, round dark things carried
over the surface of the waves.

She lies back on her towel and tries to pick out Louis's voice in the rush of sound, and for a sudden shocking moment she can't remember what his voice is like, if it is deep, or high and reedy. She sits up to look for him. Far out on the water are two little figures, but waves climb and fall stiffly in front of them just before she can make out their features. She closes her eyes and imagines Louis and Marybeth underwater, their faces meeting in a kiss. When she looks out again over the water, she can see no one who looks like Louis. She concentrates on each drifting head until something–the length of the hair, the shape of a jaw, an unfamiliar gesture –reveals it to be someone else, and she gazes out at the sea until all she can see is light; she is sure not one of the heads belongs to Louis. Up and down the beach, people walk or sit or lie, but none of them is Louis, and when Florence looks closely at the waves, she is certain she sees a shadow, something large and dark moving to the surface, gliding back under. She has a sudden image of Louis's head caught in the jaws of a shark, and she looks around for the lifeguard, who is smiling down at three women who stand around his chair; he laughs as he looks from one to the other, his nose gleaming bright white. Florence wills him to look out at the swimmers; it is possible that Louis and Marybeth have drowned while he has been talking to the women; it is possible that a shark is moving at this moment, unnoticed, just beneath the surface of the water. Florence cannot imagine moving the women aside to talk to the guard, or his face as he looks down at her, and she tries to picture Louis swimming confidently up and down the coast, but all she can see is his fragile head pressed against the floor of the ocean, his skin the color of sand, sand in his eyes, and sand stopping up the back of his throat. As people move in and out of the water, light flashes against their wet skin, so that they look hardly human, glittering in the bright air. The sun blinds her eyes, and she closes them, lying back against the bumpy sand.

She is aware of something strange and stiff about her skin as she lets herself drift toward sleep. Somewhere, she thinks, a shark is gazing hopefully up through blue water at a green sun; somewhere an alligator lifts its stony head and heaves toward the legs of a child; everywhere there are animals lying in earth and sand and water, dreaming of closing their jaws on something human.

When Florence opens her eyes, Louis and Marybeth are standing above her, two black shadows against the sun. She cannot see their faces, or make out any features at all, but they speak to her as though nothing has happened, and she realizes she has been asleep.

—The water's great, Louis says. He pats his stomach. —We didn't see any sharks. Or even any fish.

—I saw plenty of fish, Marybeth says. —Did you see that skate? Jesus. She sits down beside Florence and holds her hands a foot apart. —That sucker was huge. Florence puts her hand up to block the sun.

—I thought you had drowned, she says. —I couldn't see you anywhere.

—Why would we have drowned? Louis asks.

—You thought we had drowned and you were taking a nap? Marybeth says. She laughs. —Counting up your pennies?

—I couldn't see you at all, Florence says. —Anywhere on the beach.

—Well, we were there, Louis says. —Swimming.

As Florence sits up, she feels a rubbery tug at her face; it is her own skin, she realizes, and when she looks down at herself, her arms and legs look like parts of someone else's body.

—Oh my, Marybeth says, —look at that.

She lays her hand flat across Florence's thigh, and Florence stares down at it. Marybeth's fingers are long and narrow, her nails perfectly shaped, and when she lifts her hand, there it is, a long white outline on Florence's red skin.

—You're going to pay for that, Marybeth says. —Big time. She shakes her head. —That skin's going to come off in sheets if you don't put something on it. Maybe even if you do.

Louis nods. —You'd better get out of the sun, he says. —That's going to be a bad burn. Do you want me to walk you home?

Tiny spots float in front of his face, and even though Florence knows it's an effect of the sun, it is distracting nonetheless. He rubs sand from his mouth, and she tries to imagine the feel of his sandy face against hers. She closes her eyes, but all she can feel is heat rising in her bones, firing her skin into a fine powder that will be swept across the wide stretch of white sand.

—Florence? Louis says.

—No, she says, —I'll just go by myself.

As she stands, she feels nothing, just the stiff mechanical workings of her bones and muscles. She knows this will hurt later, but for now she feels nothing, not the sand beneath her feet, nor the hot pavement, nor the sun beating down on her as she walks home, half in a dream.

She stops to look at the flamingos in front of the hotel; if they didn't move, they could pass for plastic, as stiff and as pink as those she saw occasionally on some of the more adventurous lawns back in Indiana. She waits now until she's seen each bird move before she turns toward her house.

Before she can get inside, Mrs. Walker calls out to her, and

as Florence walks across the yard, she feels as though she
is skimming lightly over the surface of the gravel, though
she knows it must be sharp and hard.
—Look, Mrs. Walker says. She holds her palms up to Florence. —It's a sign. God sent me a sign. After all these years.
She looks up into the blazing sky, then at Florence. —What
does it mean? she says. —Who do I call?
Florence looks at her hands; they are covered by deep spi-
dery creases and dry age.
—There's nothing there, Florence says, and Mrs. Walker
looks down at her palms, then leans forward in her chair
and rubs them in the gravel.
—Look, she says. —Look again. It's a miracle.
When she lifts her hands, blood stains the white rocks, and
Florence can feel something rising inside her. Across the
ocean, saints are stirring, and the Pope gazes idly at the feet
of his prelate, noticing for the first time how soft they are,
how white the skin; his mind moves against the thought and
blood stains the delicate white toes. A miracle. Florence
closes her eyes.
—There's nothing there, she says, and turns toward her
house.
—Wait, Mrs. Walker says. —Wait. Florence looks back at
her; she is gazing down at her hands, but the rocks around
her are perfectly white, perfectly raked but for the deep
furrows of the rocker.

Florence wakes to what she is sure are the sounds of Marybeth and Louis making love. She can hear his hand stroke
Marybeth's skin, the soft whisper of her hair. She feels as if
she is lying in flames, except for a cold weight on her stomach, and she is surprised to find that it is her own hand. She
moves it to her face, to touch the dry burning skin, and
imagines Marybeth holding her arms out to Louis, the

scrape of her thin fingers along his back; she can see the pulse beat in his neck as he bends to kiss her, and he is thinking about nothing at all, nothing but a wide stretch of sand, and beyond that the glittering sea.

She rises and stands at the door, listening for their voices, but when she walks into the kitchen, their heads are bent over a game of cards; Louis is staring at Marybeth as he slaps down a card, and she snatches it up.

—Ha, she says. —I knew you were going to do that.

She spreads her cards out across the table. —Gin, she says, and begins to count up her points. Florence rustles forward, and they turn to look at her with big empty eyes.

—You look terrible, Marybeth says. —You must be burning up. You should draw her a cold bath, she says to Louis.

—With vinegar. She closes her eyes a moment. —Or maybe it's tomato juice. I don't know. She goes back to her cards, then looks up at Louis. —You really should, she says, and he pushes his chair back.

—I think I just need some air, Florence says, and walks past them.

Louis looks up at her helplessly, and Marybeth adds her points to the total score on a piece of paper. Louis's cards are all low, threes and fives and sixes, while Marybeth's hand is full of jacks and queens.

Outside, it has grown almost dark; the little houses cast shadows that turn the gravel gray and dirty. Florence tries again to remember what it was she read about the evening sun, the quality of the light; but except for the shadows, it seems no different from the light at any other time of day. Inside, Marybeth and Louis lay out cards, pick them up, lay them out again, and do not think of her. All the lights are lit in Mrs. Walker's house. Soon, perhaps tomorrow, her husband's children will come for her, but for now she moves from room to room in a frenzy of faith, her face changing and changing back again. Florence sits in Mrs. Walker's chair and rocks gently; underneath the crackling gravel, earth and ashes stir, and she closes her eyes to wait, breathing in the dark sulphur of the air.

Going

Anne leans her head out the car window into the rush of hot air and tries to remember just exactly where it was that she decided to leave David. Cincinnati, she thinks it was, or perhaps Cleveland. It was on the edge of some large Ohio city beginning with C, and she wants to be sure which one;

she wants to be able always to think back on this decision
and remember it exactly, to have a place and a name to
attach to it. Oh that's right, she will be able to say, it was in
Cincinnati that I finally decided to end it; then, for the rest
of her life, Cincinnati will have gained this relevance, and
every time she hears the name or sees it, she will be re-
minded of David, and it will keep her from going back to
him, or to someone like him. It will be like a charm whose
magic is clear only to her, and now she can't remember
where it was.

She closes her eyes and tries to recall a landmark of some
kind, a sign or a water tower. There are so many cities in
Ohio and so many of them begin with *C*. All she can really
remember is that they had just left the rest stop where David
bought the peanuts, but that's of little help, since that stop
was like every other rest stop on the highway, each of them
laid out in the same configuration of snack bar, bathroom,
and gift shop, all selling the same newspapers, gifts, and
food. Even the people who work in them resemble each
other slightly, like distant relations.

Anne and David have stopped at every rest stop they've
come to. David takes great pleasure, Anne can tell, in the
sameness of the places; he walks right in and heads, without
even a moment's orientation, toward the bathroom, or when
he gets coffee, he reaches around behind him, without looking, to the little islands that hold cream and sugar. Anne
always goes to the bathroom, whether she needs to or not.

—You'd better go now, David says at each stop, —you never
know when you'll get another chance, though she knows
they'll pull in to the next one down the road. In every bathroom she splashes water on her face, blots it off with toilet
paper, and leans for a few moments against the cool tile
walls, then goes to wait for David by the glass entryway to
the rest stop, where she watches the steady flow of families.

It is late August, and the families are rushing to accomplish their vacations before the summer ends; their faces show the strain of driving relentlessly across the country, only to return home by the same road, dazed and drained, a week later. They all look so familiar that Anne wonders if maybe some of them *are* the same, if some of these families might be following David's pattern of stopping at every opportunity, regardless of need.

It was at the last stop, or the one before, that David bought the peanuts; Anne looked up from the newspaper box by the doors, in the middle of an article she had started reading three or four stops earlier, and was surprised to see David actually buying something in the gift shop. Usually he only browsed, but this time he was handing the clerk money, and through the glass wall of the store his plain pleasant face was happy and a little flushed as he chatted with her.

—Look, David said when he joined Anne. He held out a can with a bright yellow label and an inartistic drawing of something that looked both foreign and oddly familiar. Only after a moment did she realize it was a picture of a bowl of peanuts, heaped up in their shells; they were boiled, the label said, and preserved in brine. It was cracker food, food eaten by Kentuckians and Southerners. She looked up at David's pleased, expectant face.

—Boiled peanuts? she said.

—I thought it would make a nice housewarming gift.

—It's not a new house, she said, handing the can back.

—You know what I mean. A guest gift. Whatever they call it.

—A hostess gift. She's my sister. You don't have to bring a gift.

—Well, I've never met her. I should bring something.

Anne could see that David was disappointed in her reaction, but she felt suddenly annoyed by it all—the picture, the peanuts, the kind of cheap little store that would sell such things.

—Who would eat them? she said. —Who would eat boiled peanuts?

—They're not to *eat*, he said. —That's not the point. He held up the can. —Look at them. He glanced unhappily at the picture on the label, then gazed around at the rest stop. After a moment he seemed to draw enthusiasm from the familiar glazed faces of children, the grim tight men. —It's a gag, he said. —It's like a gag gift.

—Well, she said, turning away, —let's go.

She still doesn't know what bothered her about the peanuts; it was just a small joke, but now the can sits on the seat between them, a bright reminder of this most recent failure. There is something pathetic about the jauntiness of the label, and the can rolls with the pitch of the car whenever David takes a sudden swerve to pass another station wagon full of tired parents and unhappy children.

Anne wants to be sure to get her sister alone later and explain that she had nothing to do with the peanuts, that they were David's idea. You know how men are, she'll say, waving her hand, and Nancy will nod distractedly, leaving the peanuts on the counter until David and Anne are gone; then she will put them in a cabinet, where, over the years, they will gradually be pushed to the back, making way for cans and boxes of real food, until one day Nancy will come upon them as she cleans her cupboards and wonder what on earth possessed her to buy a can of boiled peanuts. She'll blame it on her husband or decide one of her children must have begged her for them; by then she will have forgotten all about David, but Anne is determined to remember every detail. She wishes she could keep the peanuts, take them back home with her, carry them around. Cincinnati, she thinks, Cleveland, Columbus.

The car jerks suddenly, and Anne opens her eyes to see David gazing anxiously at an exit ahead, but when he discerns that there is no rest area off the highway, he picks up speed again. Anne leans her head on her elbow and lets the wind whip her hair across her face. It's been in the nineties all day, and even the wind that passes through the car is breathless and heavy. Her skin feels like a layer of plastic wrapped around her body, but David refuses to run his air conditioner; there's something wrong with it, he says, and he doesn't want to take the chance of overheating the car in this weather, but she suspects him of trying to cut costs, since this trip is, after all, for her, with nothing much in it for him other than the ride, something he calls her attention to every now and then.

—You know, he'll say, —this isn't exactly how *I* would choose to spend this weekend. But then, after his point has been made, he looks happily back at the road ahead or the greenish fields to either side, pleased with what a good sport he is, how helpful he has been. The purpose of their trip is to pick up several pieces of furniture–a table, some chairs, a secretary–that Nancy has been keeping since their parents moved to a retirement center in Florida. Anne has no real need for the furniture–she already has too many things in her small apartment–but lately Nancy has referred to it more frequently in her letters, finally almost insisting that Anne come and retrieve it. The furniture has become a kind of theme in letters that have grown increasingly bland, empty of all but a kind of brittle newsiness, little facts about the house, her children, her husband Andy. Any break in the clutter of minutiae is bridged with cryptic remarks, oblique suggestions that things are not quite right, grim little homilies apropos of nothing.

—*Well, what goes around comes around,* Nancy will write,

but then it is back to the report cards, the lawn, a store
clerk's rudeness.

Anne hasn't seen Nancy for almost three years, and what
limited sense Anne has of her life comes from her letters
and the Christmas photographs of Andy, Nancy, and their
three children. Anne can hardly keep the names and ages of
the children straight, and they all look alike, with blond hair
and serious, composed faces. They look like no one in
Anne's family, but neither do they resemble Andy, who is
tall, with a sharp bitter face that grows more closed with
each picture. Before she and David left, Anne found the
most recent photograph in order to remember the faces and
names of the children. In this picture, Nancy's hair is tied
back sloppily and she gives the impression of gazing off into
space, though, like the others, she is looking stonily into the
camera; her arms are wrapped around her sides, and her
children squat in a little line in front of her. Nancy writes
about them often, but every sentence seems punctuated by
a heavy sigh: this one doesn't sleep well in the summer, that
one needs glasses or has to go to the doctor again, and they
all need shoes all the time. Anne memorized the children's
names and ages and put the picture back in a drawer, but
now all she can remember is that Jimmy is nine.

—Hey, David says, but she ignores him and tries to recall
the other two children's names.

—Hey, he says again, and she moves her head away from
the window. Her skin feels puffy from the heat and wind.

—What? he says. —Were you asleep? He glances at her,
then back to the road, and she shakes her head.

—You know, he says, —it's kind of boring, just driving like
this. This trip is a lot longer than I thought it would be.

He looks down at the odometer and she wonders if he is
keeping track of the mileage; she knows it would not occur

to him to ask her to pay for the miles traveled, but it bothers her that he might be keeping track—that when he thinks back on this trip, he might remember it as the number of miles he put on his car for her.

—It wouldn't seem so long if we had air conditioning, she says as a truck pulls up beside them on the left. David steps on the gas, shooting ahead, then slides into the left lane, in front of the truck. He looks in the rearview mirror and smiles; it is a minor victory, but it restores his good mood and he settles back in his seat.

This annoys Anne, this easy equanimity; she likes to think it betrays a lack of depth, and most of the time she feels secure in this perception, but sometimes, late at night when she wakes and he is sleeping, she is struck by the uneasy thought that perhaps it is she who is missing something, that her impatience with David is a failure of imagination on her part. She tries now to watch him surreptitiously, but he glances over and offers an uncomplicated smile, his mild resentment already forgotten. She looks away. His friendly mood won't stop her, she tells herself; it is over, and she is going to end it. David presses on the gas, and they surge forward into a future apart, a future she saw as far back as Columbus, perhaps even Cincinnati. In the bright light of such a future, she can see that there is something sweet about David, something nearly likeable; even the peanuts provoke a slight fondness in her, and she smiles and leans her head back to plan the end of their affair.

By the time they are approaching Marion, where Nancy lives, Anne has gone over their breakup so many times— what she will say, how she will say it, how David will look, and how she will comfort him—that she feels pleased and settled, as though something has already been agreed upon between them, and their years together, which have been unexciting and untroubled, end in a gloriously friendly burst of sympathy. Anne pulls the visor down to look in the mirror, but nothing is changed, she is still the same: her hair, which she wore up to keep neat, looks messy and dirty, and the shirt she thought would travel well is wet and rumpled. She wonders how she will look to her sister and to three children who have not seen her since they were toddlers. Oh, she will say to each of them, you've gotten so tall. She practices a smile to go along with this, the mild smile of an aunt, with her eyebrows raised, but in the mirror it looks fake and comical, so she lowers her brows, but the effect is slightly demonic.

—What are you doing? David asks. —Did you get something in your eye?

Anne pushes the visor up. —Do you think we could have some air conditioning for the rest of the drive? she says.

David takes a quick look at the dashboard panel. —I don't think so, he says. —I don't want to put too much stress on the engine. What if it overheats? We'd be stuck in the middle of nowhere. He glances in the rearview mirror. —After all, he says, and looks at her earnestly, —this isn't exactly a pleasure trip for me, you know.

She forces a smile; it is moments like these, she tells herself, that are forcing her to leave him, small moments that in themselves are only remotely irritating, but that all together add up to something large and impossible. Soon they won't be lovers anymore, she reminds herself; in fact, since Cincinnati—and she is nearly certain it was Cincinnati—it is almost as if they are already no longer lovers. She closes her eyes, and until he asks her for directions, she imagines her life without him. In a perfect quiet room, she will sit by the window, and not once will he wander by and ask her what she is doing, or sit down on the couch opposite her and smile, wondering what they will do next. These are small things, she knows that, but even so, when she thinks of a life without him, the days and weeks seem to stretch out like a big clean icy block of time, undisturbed by any sound or voice or presence other than her own.

When they arrive in Marion, David looks distastefully around at the stretch of strip malls and fast-food places on the edge of town; Anne was born here, and lived here until she left for college. She has always hated it, but it seems worse even than she remembers, a huge complicated garden of shiny glass and metal huts.
—You were born here? David asks. —No wonder you never want to come back.
He is from Oregon, and his tone, when he speaks of it to Anne, is both wistful and patronizing, as if anyone from the Midwest could never quite understand the magic of such a place. Although Anne herself feels oppressed by the dozens of unnecessary restaurants, the stacks of light-colored brick apartment buildings with tiny terraces stuck to the sides, the little square gas station/food marts evenly spaced a block apart on each corner, she feels she must defend it from him before he begins to compare it to Portland.
—It's not so bad. The people are very down-to-earth, she says, although in fact she remembers them as generally not very good-tempered. She moved away as soon as she could, and she has always been surprised at Nancy's decision to settle here.
David shakes his head. —There are a lot of fast-food places, he says. —In Portland you don't see that many fast-food places. He glances at her. —Really, he says. —It's mostly just diners and things. Real food.
A mile or so into town, they pass a small carnival set up in the scrabbly lot next to a discount store. There are only a few people wandering through the carnival, and from the car the rides look rickety and cheap.

—Look, he says. —Even the circus is tacky.

—I don't see, Anne says, —how someone who's bringing boiled peanuts as a hostess gift can call anything tacky. Though she meant to say it lightly, she can hear the reproof in her tone, and he looks at her in surprise.

—Hey, he says seriously, —it's a joke. Don't you get it?

—Oh sure, she says, and tries out the smile she practiced for the children. —Turn here.

For the rest of the way, she guides him through the flat wide streets, past houses built according to the same blueprint, all sitting nakedly in the bright centers of close-cut lawns that sprout trees still years too young to cast any shade.

When Nancy opens the door, Anne looks at her closely for some sign of the age and unhappiness that have seeped into her letters, but she looks unchanged by the years and her life, and she still possesses the kind of untouched, untroubled beauty that always impressed the men Anne introduced to her. David steps back, glancing at Anne, and looks down at the can of peanuts, then slides it down his thigh, almost out of sight.

His face changes when they step inside the house. There seems not to be a single uncovered surface in the room: piles of folded clothes rise from chairs; records lean against the legs of furniture; books and magazines and boxes are stacked carefully on tables and against walls. David shoots Anne a look as if to ask why she didn't tell him about this, but she turns her head; she supposes she should have mentioned it, though this is how Nancy has always lived. Even as a child, rather than put her clothes into her drawers, she folded them neatly and left them in piles around her bed, as if she could not bear to lose sight of the things she owned.

The precariousness of the living room makes Anne want to stand in a corner and hold her breath, but Nancy glides through it easily. When she turns, she seems surprised to see them still standing at the doorway, and she comes back. —So you're David, she says, as though Anne has told her all about him.

David flushes at the attention, looks at Anne, and finally holds the can of peanuts out to Nancy. —Here, he says, looking down at the can. —We brought you these.

Nancy takes the peanuts, reads the label, and nods. —Boiled peanuts, she says. —I've heard of them.

She turns away. —Kids, she calls, and almost immediately the door to the kitchen is filled by three children, who stare at Anne and David without curiosity. Their faces are familiar to Anne, but oddly so, the way letters jumbled randomly together resemble words. She tries to recall names and ages; the oldest is Jimmy, and the youngest is the girl, Jenny, she thinks. She has forgotten the name of the middle one. When Nancy introduces the children to David, Anne wonders what to do; as an aunt, she supposes, she should bend down and hug them, but as a niece and nephews, it seems that they should have run happily to her in order to be hugged. They all seem like little strangers, so she smiles brightly.

—Well, you've all certainly grown, she says. Nancy looks somewhat surprised, and gazes at them as if in fact they have not grown at all, then turns back to Anne.

—Yes, she says, —I suppose they have. Their feet have, that's for sure.

The children wait patiently at the door until Nancy says, —Okay, and as a unit, they turn and leave.

—Well, Nancy says, —Andy's not here. He's going to pick up some steaks on his way home, though. For dinner. She looks down at the can of peanuts in her hand, as if she is surprised to find it still there. —Do you want a Coke? she asks David, but before he answers, she takes Anne's elbow. —Come on, she says, —we'll get you one. You sit down,

she tells David, and a kind of dismayed panic comes into his
face as he looks around for a seat secure enough not to bring
a stack of things down on his head.

Anne follows Nancy into the kitchen, which, like the living
room, is jumbled full of things that seem to have arrived
randomly at their places: empty pots and pans are spread
out across the stove, clean dishes are stacked up under the
cupboards, and boxes of food sit neatly on the counters,
lined up against the wall.

—So, Nancy says, —that's David. He's going bald.

—All men go bald, Anne says. —Or they might as well. It's
all they ever think about.

—Andy doesn't think about it, Nancy says absently, looking
down at the can of peanuts. —At least as far as I know he
never does. She turns the can around and around, reading
all the printing, and something about her lack of attention
causes Anne to lower her voice and lean forward.

—I'm breaking up with him, she says. —After the trip. I
decided in Cincinnati.

Nancy looks up from the can; there is no expression at all
on her face, but already Anne feels more certain, and becomes aware of a growing anxiousness to get home and get
on with it. She nods her head eagerly. —Really, she says.
—I am.

Nancy looks around for a place to put the peanuts. Finally
she sets it on the counter behind her. —Well, she says,
—good luck. It's not as easy as you might think. I've wanted
to leave Andy for years now, but, well, it's just not so easy.
She picks up the peanuts again. —What exactly do you *do*
with these things?

—You're married, Anne says. —You have kids. It's harder
with kids.

Nancy looks up. —What does that have to do with it? You
can always figure out what to do with kids. That's not what

I meant. She opens the icebox and puts the peanuts inside.
—It's just not that easy is all I'm saying. Listen, she says,
bending and peering into the icebox. —We don't have any
Coke. All we have is ginger ale. She holds out a big plastic
bottle with an inch or so of ginger ale sloshing around the
bottom. —Besides, he seems okay. I don't see what's so
wrong with him. Except maybe his hair. I don't really like
bald men.

—There isn't really anything *wrong* with him, Anne says,
and Nancy looks at her, waiting. —I mean, she goes on,
groping through her history with David, searching out some
transgression, something horrible and mean, but all she
comes up with is his cheerful bulky presence, shadowing
her at every turn, blocking the path between her and what
she hoped would be her life. It doesn't seem enough right
now, not even to her; she can feel her resolve slipping, and
she reaches out blindly to snatch it back.

—It's like those peanuts, she says. —I mean, he picked out
those peanuts. I didn't.

Nancy takes a glass from the top of the icebox and examines
it carefully, then turns to Anne. —I hardly think, she says,
—that buying a can of peanuts is a good reason to break up
with a man. Andy does worse things than that in his sleep.

Anne leans back against the sink and watches Nancy pour
the ginger ale; it fills the glass only halfway, so Nancy adds
tap water almost to the top. She places it on the stove, and
turns to Anne.

—But you want to know the worst thing? she asks. She
picks up the glass and calls out, —Jimmy, then opens the
freezer and dislodges from a tray a single ice cube, which
she floats on top of the ginger ale.

—The worst thing is he wants to leave me, too. He won't
say it, but I can tell. She shakes her head. —It's like we're
in a race, she says. —And I'm going to lose.

Anne turns at a noise behind her. Jimmy is standing in the doorway, and Nancy holds the glass out to him. —Here, honey, she says. —Would you take this in to David? And keep him company while we talk. I haven't talked to anyone in a long time, she says to Anne. —Maybe tomorrow we could go out to lunch or something. Just you and me. I never get away anymore.

Jimmy turns with the glass. —Mom, he says, —what about the carnival? Nancy looks at him blankly.

—By the K Mart, he says, and she nods.

—I thought your father took you, she says. —Wasn't he supposed to take you?

—No, Jimmy says mournfully. —You were. Tomorrow's the last day.

Nancy sighs dramatically. —Well, she says, —your Aunt Anne is here. I don't see how I could manage it now.

She turns back to Anne, but Jimmy waits, and Anne watches his face change as he considers and rejects arguments.

—But you said, is all he can finally come up with, and Nancy smiles patiently.

—Honey, she says sweetly, —there will be other carnivals. This just isn't a very good time for me to take you. You understand.

He nods, but lingers a moment longer, then turns and leaves the room.

—Where was I? Nancy says. She pushes a stack of dishes away from the edge of the counter with a sharp rattle of porcelain, and leans back heavily. —Sometimes I wish he'd just disappear, she says. —I wouldn't really want him dead. She shakes her head. —Sometimes he won't even look at me. She glances at the doorway. —I think he wanted to hit me last week. I really do.

A kind of crazy light comes into her face as she talks, and

Anne looks around the kitchen, then stands. —Maybe we'd better check on David, she says.

When they come into the living room, David is perched on the edge of the couch, poised between a stack of newspapers and a box full of clothing.

—Oh, Nancy says, —just move those papers. Andy was supposed to recycle them.

She bends to move the box, her face passing only a few inches in front of David's, but he stares straight down at the floor, then raises his glass to his mouth, though Anne can't tell if he actually drinks any of it. Nancy sits beside him.

—So, she says, —tell me all about yourself.

David turns carefully to her, resting his glass solidly on his knee.

When Andy comes home, David is telling Nancy how difficult the drive was, though, he says, he was very happy to come; in fact, he confides, not looking at Anne, he has always wanted to meet Anne's family. He has never told Anne this, and she wonders if it is true. He seems almost disappointed when Andy comes in, and his eyes move immediately to Andy's hair, which is full and dark.

—Anne, Andy says, clearly surprised to see her. —When did you get here?

—They got here an hour ago, Nancy says. —I told you they were coming.

Andy looks at her, considering. —No, he says. —I'm sure you didn't. When?

—For the furniture, Nancy says.

—What furniture? He looks around. —Our furniture?

Anne had forgotten about the furniture, but as she looks around the room, it is clear that nothing has been packed or prepared; the one piece she does recognize, the secretary, is open, and covered with stacks of letters and envelopes, each little cubbyhole stuffed with something. When Anne gets it home, she will put it in the corner of her apartment, with only one thing in each slot.

—Jesus, Nancy says, but in a neutral, almost conversational tone. —I suppose you forgot the steaks, too?

Andy brightens. —We're having steak?

—We were, Nancy says, —but you were supposed to get them.

—Oh, he says. —Oh well. He looks for the first time at David, who is searching around for a place to put his glass; finally he transfers it to his left hand, then stands tentatively, his eye on the stack of newspapers at his side. He wipes his hand across his thigh and holds it out to Andy.

—Listen, David says, —we can go get steaks. Anne and me.

—No, Nancy says. —You sit back down. We'll find something to eat. It just won't be steak, she adds with a look at Andy, who sways a moment, back and forth on his heels, clearly torn between conflicting desires.

—Okay, he finally says. —Whatever. He shoves the newspapers aside to make a place for himself on the couch.

—So, Dave, he says, and David looks at him attentively. Whenever Andy looks away, David's eyes move to his hair, curling down over the edge of his collar. Nancy heads to the kitchen and motions to Anne with a jerk of her head to follow.

—See? she says loudly when they are inside the kitchen.

—This is what I'm talking about. You see what I mean? He didn't get the steaks. He didn't even remember you were coming.

—It's okay about the steaks, Anne says. —I don't really like steak anyways. She tries to think of something more to say, but Nancy is not listening; she is rooting around in the jars

and boxes on the counter, finally pulling out a box of macaroni and cheese. From a drawer under the sink she takes a
few potatoes.

—There, she says. —This ought to be enough for everyone.

As Anne and Nancy prepare the dinner, the children wander
from the living room to the kitchen restlessly, like bored
guests; they are always together, in a little huddle, and their
faces show no expression, but Anne can see the tension in
their knotted knees and elbows and in the way they seem to
avoid touching even each other. Perhaps it comes from living in the presence of so many piles of things about to top-
ple; she wonders what their own rooms look like.

Nancy opens the icebox and pulls out the can of boiled peanuts. —Well, she says, —I suppose we ought to do something with these.

She opens a drawer that is crammed full of utensils, and
pulls things out, one by one, until she comes to a can
opener; then she closes the drawer, leaving its contents—an
eggbeater, the potato masher, several large spoons—in a
heap on the counter. She opens the can and stares into it,
then sighs.

—Well, she says, —it *was* a present. She takes a bowl from
the sink, and looks inside it before she empties the can into
it; they both gaze a moment at a lumpy heap of greenish
soggy things that resemble peanuts only in the shape of their
shells.

The peanuts sit in the middle of the table, and occasionally
David casts them a quick dismayed glance, then looks
around the table. Dinner is already half over, and no one has
touched the peanuts until at last Nancy takes a small spoon-
ful of them, which she sets gingerly at the edge of her plate.

—So, Dave, Andy says, —were you in Nam?

Andy's service in Vietnam seems to have been the major
event in his life, and though Anne has never been sure
whether he was in favor of or opposed to the war, her strong-
est memory of Nancy's wedding was Andy sizing up, then
approaching every male guest. —So were you in Nam? he
demanded of even those who were clearly too young or too
old to have been much concerned with a war so far away
from themselves. He nodded thoughtfully at whatever answer he received, then moved on to the next nearest man.
David looks up at the question, surprised, his mouth full.
He swallows without chewing, and assumes what Anne can
tell is his best effort at a rueful smile.
—Too young, he says, as though this has been great cause
for regret in his life. —I was in high school.
Andy nods, then narrows his eyes. —How old are you anyways? he asks, then turns to Anne. —How old is he anyways?
Anne thinks a moment. His birthday is in July; she should
know this.
—Thirty, she finally says, which is her own age.
—Thirty-two, David corrects, and Anne nods as though she
knew this; she looks uneasily around the table, but it is clear
that no one else thinks there is anything wrong in not knowing the age of one's lover.
—Yep, David says cheerfully, —I was just too young.
Andy nods. —We were all too young, he says ponderously.
Nancy rolls her eyes and sighs heavily enough to draw a look
from Andy, but she ignores him and reaches toward David's
plate with her fork. She prods at his baked potato, which is
only half eaten.
—You should eat the skin, she says. —It's good for you.
David opens his mouth, then closes it as she sticks her fork
into his potato and lifts it onto her own plate.
—But you look pretty healthy, she says, and looks at

Anne. —So how healthy is he? she asks, and for a moment everyone stops eating or chewing to stare at David, who is looking at his potato on Nancy's plate.

He looks up at them all, startled, and suddenly everyone begins again to eat. Anne could not say what had just happened, or what that moment was, only that it descended over them like a glass, then lifted just as quickly.

Nancy smiles at David as she eats the rest of his potato, and Andy watches him; Anne can tell he is trying to calculate his age, to figure if, in fact, a thirty-two-year-old would have been in high school during the whole of the war in Vietnam. The children eat like well-behaved animals, intently, but with careful, precise manners; even the youngest leans his fork neatly against his plate before he takes a drink of milk. The gesture makes Anne long to offer them something; she is their aunt, after all, and she would like them to remember her as more than a stranger who came to take away their furniture, accompanied by a cheerful, balding boyfriend.

—So, she says to the three of them at large, —school must be starting soon.

They look up, surprised to be addressed, and finally one of them says, —Two weeks.

—I suppose you must be sad to see summer end? she presses on, and they look at each other, then nod.

—Hey, David says, and everyone looks at him. —How about that circus we saw? That must have been fun. He beams at Anne, pleased with himself for having made this contribution to her conversation with the children, pleased to have remembered the carnival.

—Jesus, Nancy says. —Now you've started it. They've been bugging us to go to that carnival since it got here. Andy was supposed to take them.

Andy stops his fork an inch from his mouth, then slowly lays it on the table and leans forward on his elbows. —I work all

day, he says. —I work all goddamn day. You could have
taken them.

—I work too, she says. —I work all goddamn day too. She
folds her hands on the table in front of her plate and leans
back, gazing at him.

Anne is struck by the disparity between their words and
their tone. Their voices are quiet, almost friendly, and to
someone who didn't understand the language, they might be
discussing the weather, or planning a family vacation.

David is looking alertly out the window, and Anne glances
at the children, who have not broken the rhythm of their
eating. Indifferent to all but the outcome, they cut their food
and put it in their small strained mouths.

—Hey, Anne says, —I can take you to the carnival.

Everyone looks at her, and she smiles. —Tomorrow, she
says. —Before we go.

The children's eyes flick to Nancy, who stares at Anne a
moment, then sighs. —Whatever, she says, and the children allow themselves cautious little smiles before they go
back to their food.

Andy picks up his fork, leaving a bright orange lump of
macaroni on the table, and Anne can feel the pressure of
looks from David on one side and Nancy on the other. No
one other than the children seems very happy with this development, but they all finally begin to eat again, and Anne
keeps her eyes on the bowl of peanuts for most of the rest of
the meal.

—You know, Nancy says in the kitchen as they make coffee, —you shouldn't have said you'd take them to the carnival. Andy was supposed to do that. She turns the gas off
and picks up the kettle, then puts it back on the stove.
—He really was, she says. —I know you don't believe me,
but he really did say he'd do it.

—Well, Anne says, —it didn't look like he was going to. And tomorrow's the last day.

—I know that, Nancy says. —Jesus. Who else wants to tell me that? She rattles aside a stack of bowls and corrals four coffee cups. —But doesn't it mean anything that he said he would and didn't? she asks. —Doesn't that mean anything?

—I don't know, Anne says. —I just don't see why you couldn't have taken them before now. Those carnivals are usually around for half the summer. You could have taken them.

—Yes, Nancy says calmly. She pours water over the coffee grounds and waits while it drips through. —Yes, I could have. But I didn't.

She turns, and Anne is jarred by the sudden anger in her face. —You don't understand, do you? she hisses. —You don't understand. She shakes her head and goes back to the coffee, calm returning as suddenly as it left. —No, she says. —You don't. No one does. She lifts the plastic filter from the pot and stops on her way to the sink; blackish water still drips through the filter, splattering on her white sneakers.

—Look, Nancy says. —Taking them or not taking them is not the point. There will be other carnivals. They have a carnival every year. How many carnivals did we get to go to? We survived. That's not the point. The point, she says, waving the filter in the air, —is something else entirely.

—What? Anne says. —What *is* the point?

—That's the problem, Nancy says. —I'm not exactly sure yet. I'm just not exactly sure. But it's bigger than some carnival. She stares at the coffee filter. —I'm sure it is. I really am.

—You're dripping coffee, Anne says, and Nancy looks down at the spots on her shoes, then glances around for a place to put the filter. Finally she sets it carefully inside a pot on the stove, while Anne pours out four cups of coffee. Nancy watches Anne, then picks up the bowl of peanuts from the counter.

—No one ate these, she says. —I guess I can give them to the squirrels. She stirs a spoon through the peanuts. Light flashes off the buttons of her shirt, and Anne imagines Nancy dressing this morning, choosing this outfit, gazing at herself as she buttoned the shirt, dressing for another day with a man she already knows is going to leave her.

Nancy goes to bed early; she is tired, she says, smiling at David. She is always tired, she tells him, but with a glance at Andy, who is already in front of the television. When Anne follows David into their room, she is sure Andy is watching them; she feels an urge to cover her back, but when she turns to say good night, he is looking at the television, his head a dark blot in the middle of the glowing screen.

They are staying in one of the children's rooms, but Anne can't tell which child it belongs to, since the room is so orderly: books are lined up evenly on little shelves; the closet door is closed, with not an article of clothing in sight; even the toys are neatly arranged in a plastic basket in the corner. David leans against the pillow and watches Anne undress with a kind of clinical disinterest, as if he is curious about what color her skin might turn out to be. It makes her self-conscious, and she unbuttons her shirt slowly.

—You know, he finally says, —she treats those kids like pets.

He is right, she knows he is right, but she does not want to agree with him. She feels as if somehow he will hold her responsible for it, and she wants to tell him that she and Nancy were not, as children, treated like pets, that this is something Nancy came to all on her own, something that

Anne had nothing to do with, but she knows that whatever she says, when he looks back on this trip he will say, —Oh yeah, Anne's sister treats her kids like pets, and he will look at Anne, and somehow this will forever be a part of who he thinks she is.

She lays her shirt over the back of a chair, and reminds herself that just a few hours ago she decided to leave him and that just a few hours from now she will. Cincinnati, she says to herself, and she thinks of the peanuts, all humped up in a bowl in the icebox–but the thought offers little comfort in the face of how he must be seeing her at this moment. —Oh now, she finally says, —oh now. She turns to face him, but he is looking down at a large colorful book, one of the children's, with bright orange tigers leaping across the cover. He smiles up at her.

—But she sure is pretty, he says, and snaps the book closed.

He falls asleep quickly and, lying beside him, Anne plans her future: first she will clean out her apartment; she thinks about all the things she will discard, organizing garage sales, making donations of clothing and furniture to churches. From now on her life will be uncluttered, like a big empty house, full of room after room of nothing but space; in her mind it is all so clean and ordered and easy that when David stirs beside her she is startled; she had thought he was already gone.

When she wakes, it could be any time at all: it is dark and quiet, and the shadows cast by the children's things are sharp and clean; the only thing out of order is a lumpy shape in the corner, which she realizes, after a moment, is her shirt, draped over the chair. She turns to David, who is sleeping peacefully, with no thoughts for how many miles he has put on his car, or how much hair he has lost today. He is safe and happy; asleep, they are all safe and happy, at least for now, all of them incapable of feeling or causing hurt, responsible for nothing that happens in the world, and —as long as they sleep—nothing can happen. Anne will not have to tell David she is leaving him, Andy will not leave Nancy, the children will not have to endure whatever disappointment awaits them next.

Anne turns on her side and sees a streak of light under the door, coming from the living room just outside. Quietly she gets up and slips out the door, closing it gently behind her. Nancy is sitting, hunched over, at the secretary, writing. She hasn't heard Anne, and she writes quickly across a piece of paper; when she reaches the bottom, she turns it over and continues, not looking up, hardly breaking her stroke. Anne watches for too long to feel she can turn back, so she shuffles her feet on the carpet until Nancy looks up.

—What are you doing up? Nancy asks. —You're supposed to be asleep. She puts her pen down and looks at the page she has already half covered with writing.

—A nightmare, Anne says. —What are you writing?

—Oh, Nancy says, —nothing. She folds the paper in half, then quarters. —A letter, she says, then looks up hopefully. —Do you want to read it?

—I don't know. I guess so.

—Okay, Nancy says, and unfolds the letter. Even from several feet away, Anne can see that the page is covered, top to bottom, with a tiny crabbed script, not at all like the large looping handwriting of Nancy's letters; there is almost no white space on the page at all.

—I'll read it to you, Nancy says. —Dear Andy, she begins, then stops and looks up. —It's to Andy. She clears her throat. —Dear Andy. First of all, she reads, —no one cares about Vietnam anymore. Everyone is bored by it. I'm bored by it. The kids are bored by it. Anne and David are bored by it.

She stops again. —You *were* bored by it, weren't you? she asks. —I could tell David was just being polite.

She doesn't wait for an answer and goes back to the letter. —Vietnam was a long time ago. Second. The way your skin smells. This has always bothered me, even before you started at the plant, but it's gotten worse. I was noticing it tonight at dinner. She looks up. —Did you notice that smell? It's like some kind of food, she says. —Or animal. It's weird.

She looks back at the letter, then shrugs and puts it down. —Anyways, she says. —It's just more like that. It tells him how I feel about him. She looks at Anne calmly, as though Anne should have some particular response to this, and Anne tries to imagine what it could be.

—Why don't you just tell him? she finally asks, and Nancy shakes her head. —If I tell him, she says, —he'd know. Then he'd leave right away. She looks down at the letter. —The thing is, I'm waiting for him to actually leave. I know he will. He could be going any day. She looks around the room. —He doesn't like it here. He doesn't love me. He doesn't love the kids. You can tell, can't you?

She looks down at her lap. —So anyways, she says, —when he goes, I'm going to give him this. I want him to know I felt the same way about him. I don't want him to think I love him if he doesn't love me.

Anne wonders if anyone can hear them talking, Andy, or the children. —Why don't you tell him then? she says. —When he goes.

Nancy shakes her head. —Don't you see? If I tell him then, he won't believe me. He'll say it's just because he's leaving. But this—she taps the pages she's written—this has dates.

She pulls open the drawer of the secretary and takes out a stack of papers, then holds them up and flips through them. There are twenty or thirty pages, all covered with the same cramped writing.

—These all have dates, she says. She leafs through them, and looks up at Anne. —You probably think I'm crazy, don't you? I know it must seem that way. I just don't want to give him the satisfaction of thinking he's breaking my heart. He can leave if he wants, I can't stop him, but I don't want him to think that.

She adds the pages she's just written to the stack. —I'm right, aren't I? she asks. —Aren't I?

She gazes at Anne, her face tired and drawn in the bright light, and Anne wants to say, Yes, you are, or, No, you're not—she doesn't care which—but neither seems to be correct; she wants a third choice. The confusion makes her long for the solid wall of David's back, the warm pillows, and she stands with her hand on the doorknob behind her, turning it gently, unable either to answer or to move.

—What about the kids? she finally says, because that is all she can think to ask.

—The kids? Nancy says. —Why do you keep talking about the kids? This is not about the kids. This is between me and Andy. The kids are fine.

She reads over the page she's just written, then looks up.

—But I'm not, she says. —I'm not. What else can I do?

Anne realizes that the color of the nightgown Nancy is wearing, a bright yellow-green, is all wrong for her; it makes her skin look worn and pasty. In another color, she might look fine and happy and bright, and Anne wants to tell her this. Just change the color of your nightgown, she wants to say, and everything will be fine, but she stands at the door, twisting the knob back and forth, while Nancy gazes up at her, waiting for an answer.

* * *

When Anne wakes in the morning, David is already up,
sitting on the edge of the bed. A few soft dark hairs are
scattered across his pillow, and she looks away quickly before he turns and sees her noticing them. She can feel a
storm rising: the air is heavy and electric, and her skin feels
like a rain cloud, puffy and dense. Soon they will be going,
soon they will arrive home, soon everything will be changed.
David turns when she moves.

—Hey, he says, —it's going to storm. If we leave right away,
maybe we can beat it out.

—Okay, she says. —Let's just get some coffee first.

—You don't mind skipping that circus?

She doesn't want to tell him that she had forgotten about the
carnival, even for a moment, but the thought of it fills her
with weariness. —Oh, she says. —I can't. I promised.

She can see that he is about to object. The later they leave,
she knows he will say, the later they will arrive, and it will
be dark and stormy and they will be tired for work tomorrow, but finally he sighs.

—Whatever, he says. —Andy and I can talk about Nam
some more.

He stands and walks across the room flatfooted, without a
thought that she might be watching; there is something
touching about his lack of self-consciousness. She looks
back to the few hairs left on his pillow; each one is like a
little needle in her heart. She wishes now that she had at
least tried the boiled peanuts last night, or laughed when he
bought them, and she realizes suddenly that leaving him is
not going to be as easy as she had thought. Perhaps today is
not the best day for it, perhaps tomorrow, or the next day,
after they are safe home, out of the storm. She blows the
hairs from the pillow as he bends to put on his socks.

* * *

—Well, Nancy says when Anne comes into the kitchen,
—you're finally up. She takes an English muffin from the
toaster and adds it to a plateful already on the table, then
smears jelly across each one. The children sit at the table,
watching Nancy, their hands hidden in their laps.
—There's a storm coming in, Nancy says. —You'll probably
want to leave right away. She hands a muffin to each child,
and they begin to chew without looking at Anne.
—Oh no, Anne says. —I think we have time for the carnival. I'm sure we do.
Even the restrained flash of surprise that runs across the
children's faces doesn't restore her enthusiasm for the carnival, which seems, in the gloomy light of day, a bleak pros-
pect at best. She tries to remember what stirred her to offer
to take them; surely they'll have forgotten it in a few
months, maybe less. Nancy shrugs.
—It's your time, she says, and looks at the children. —I
suppose they'd better hurry and get ready. Shoes, she says.
—Long pants. And I guess I'll have to dig out their rain-
coats.
She takes a sip of her coffee and looks out the window at
the yard, but does not move.

The carnival is even smaller than it appeared from the road;
there are only a few unstable-looking rides, several games
of chance, and under a red-and-blue awning, a small petting
zoo, which seems to consist mostly of domestic animals—
some goats, a sheep, a few ducks, and, surprisingly, a
llama, poking its head up hopelessly over the wire of its
cage. A few fragments of families wander around aimlessly
from attraction to attraction; the air is swollen with rain
about to fall, and it is clear that the carnival is preparing to
fold up—some of the tents are already closed.
The children look around anxiously, trying to choose, and

finally settle on the petting zoo. Anne buys them little cups of brown pellets to feed the animals, and they hop quickly from cage to cage, holding out handfuls of feed, then withdrawing their hands as the animals bring their heavy noses toward them.

Anne leans against a post and watches the sky and the street for rain; a light brown station wagon, just like Nancy's, passes by slowly. It circles around, then passes again, and though the car is a fairly common color and make, Anne is sure it's Nancy. She looks closely for the dent she noticed earlier, but by the time she's spotted a shadow on the right bumper, the car is too far away to identify for certain. There was a woman driving, accompanied by a man, but Anne was so intent on finding the dent, she didn't look closely at the people inside. She is watching the street, waiting for the car to return, when rain begins at last to fall.

Men who have been standing around, leaning against poles and tossing their cigarette butts in the dirt, now jerk into motion, coiling ropes, winding up awnings. The few customers move toward their cars, and Nancy's children look up, alarmed, then come reluctantly to stand beside Anne.

—Well, she says, —it's raining. They look forlornly around at the cheap rides, then up at her, and she can see by their faces that they have forgiven her before it's even occurred to them to hold her responsible: it's not her fault the carnival is cheap and small and ugly, and it's not her fault it's raining. The ease with which they absorb this disappointment makes her walk to the nearest carnival worker, who is jerking down a tent; she stands beside him a moment, then touches him on the arm. He is like all the men she has ever seen work such carnivals: young and stringy-looking, with longish dirty hair under his cap. "Terry" is written in yellow thread across his pocket. He looks up, not interested.

—We just got here, she says. —Can they ride just one ride?

—Lady, he begins, and she says, —Please? It's really important. Just one. He looks around. Soon it will rain hard, and the dust will turn to mud, making the machinery difficult to handle, spooking the animals.

—Lady, he says, —we're folding up now.

The children come out from under the petting-zoo awning and form a little huddle around Anne; as they realize she is bargaining for them, they look at the rides, picking one out in case she wins.

—Just one? she says again, and he looks at her. His eyes are light green and mean-looking. —We came a long way for this carnival, she says. —All the way from Cincinnati.

No one could believe this, she knows, but perhaps he is not from around here, or doesn't have a good sense of geography. He looks at the rides dubiously, then twists the rope he's holding once around his hand.

—It's my daughter's birthday, she adds, and puts her hand on Jenny's head. It occurs to her that she ought to bribe him; she wonders how to do this discreetly, how much it would take, and if she has enough money, but as she calculates, he looks down at the kids and says, —Well, if it's her birthday.

He looks around at the rides. —I guess they could go around once on the cars, he says, and gestures toward the nearest ride, a set of tiny cars that goes over a mildly bumpy circular track; even Anne can tell that it is the least exciting of the rides here, but the children move automatically toward it. As Terry drops his rope and moves forward, rain splatters in the dust in front of him.

—Hey, he says, —it's getting worse.

—Please, she says, taking his arm. Machine oil coats the stiff cloth of his shirt and she can feel the hard knobby bone of his elbow. He looks at her and she almost expects him to smile and say, Hey, I have kids at home, or, Yeah, I remem-

ber what it's like to be a kid, but he looks quickly down her
body, then up to her face and grins at her; then again he
looks down, more slowly this time, bolder, realizing she has
given him permission to do this in exchange for the ride.
—Okay, he says to the kids, —but hurry, and they run to
the ride, and stand in front of it, choosing their cars. Each
is modeled after a real car; they are all convertibles, but one
or two have Cadillac fins, another is round and humped like
a Volkswagen bug, and there are several racy sports cars.
—Hey, he says, —hurry, and each child goes to the nearest
car, climbs in, and ties the seat belt. —Okay, he says, and
the children look at him as they wait, holding tight to the
wheels of their cars, wondering how long he will let them
ride.
When he pulls the lever and the cars jerk to a start, they
stare straight ahead expectantly. The rain picks up, and
Anne moves back, under the awning of the petting zoo,
where men are beginning to dismantle the pens. Terry turns
to say something to her, then looks around; when he spots
her under the awning, he looks annoyed a moment, then
grins. She smiles unwillingly, and thinks of the drive home,
of the life ahead of her. She wonders if David will want to
stop at all the rest stops again, and if he will notice anything
different when they pass through Cincinnati. She wonders
how old he will be when he finally goes bald, where he will
be living, with whom. She wonders what his life will be like
without her, if he will be lonely, if he will wonder where she
is and what she is doing.
A sudden pull at her elbow startles her, and she looks down
to see a goat nibbling on the sleeve of her shirt. She pulls
her arm away, and the goat looks mildly up at her, then
turns and shuffles back across to the corner of its cage. As
she watches it nose through the sawdust for any dropped
pellets of food, she realizes suddenly that David's life will

be just as it is now, only without her: a peaceful series of mild joys and mild disappointments, an equanimous acceptance of blows that—like the one she herself is about to deal him—will never come close enough to do much damage. Leaving him, she understands, will not matter to him in the way she had thought; he will not take it personally, and he will let her go without rancor. The thought of it leaves her unsettled, somehow slighted, and even though it is she who is leaving, she feels suddenly abandoned.

She inhales sharply, breathing in the oil and dust and rain, and knows that when she remembers this trip, it is this moment—not anything that happened in Cleveland or Columbus or Cincinnati—but this moment that she will remember: the touch of Terry's stiff oily shirt between her fingers, the animals snorting uneasily as their pens come down around them, and the children going slowly around the track while rain streams down on their small heads, their faces set in grim determined joy but their hearts already gone numb.

In 1768, two years after William Caslon died, Giambattista Bodoni (1740–1813) established his press in Parma under the patronage of the Duke of Parma. While his first specimen book appeared in 1771, it was not until 1818 that his widow completed his *Manuale Tipografico*. There were two phases in Bodoni's career: first he used old-style or transitional type, plentifully decorated; while later he employed types designed by himself and depended for his effects on pure typography without ornament of any kind.

Gradually he developed the "grand manner," producing large volumes in the most sumptuous style, with extravagant margins. His types were rather too rigidly perfect in detail, his later designs still further contrasting the thick with the thin wiry lines, and it was without doubt this feature that caused William Morris to condemn the Bodoni types as "swelteringly hideous." Even today certain typographic experts say they are "bad." But Bodoni's types are neither hideous nor bad, and the modern version, designed not as a reproduction of any one of Bodoni's fonts but as a composite conception of the Bodoni manner, if used with care can produce results at once pleasing and effective.

COMPOSED BY
DIX TYPE, INC.,
SYRACUSE, NEW YORK

Book Design by Chip Kidd

PRINTED AND BOUND BY FAIRFIELD GRAPHICS, FAIRFIELD, PENNSYLVANIA